NO SUCH THING AS MAGIC

STEVE HIGGS

BOOKS

Vinci Books

vinci-books.com

Published by Vinci Books Ltd in 2025

1

Copyright © Steve Higgs 2025

The author has asserted their moral right to be identified as the author of this work in accordance with the Copyright, Designs and Patents Act 1988. This work is a work of fiction. Names, characters, places and incidents are the product of the author's imagination or are used fictitiously. Any resemblance to actual persons, living or dead, places and incidents is entirely coincidental.

All rights reserved. No part of this publication may be copied, reproduced, distributed, stored in any retrieval system, or transmitted in any form or by any means, including photocopying, recording, or other electronic or mechanical methods, nor used as a source for any form of machine learning including AI datasets, without the prior written permission of the publisher.

The publisher and the author have made every effort to obtain permissions for any third party material used in this book and to comply with copyright law. Any queries in this respect should be brought to the attention of the publisher and any omissions will be corrected in future editions.

A CIP catalogue record for this book is available from the British Library.

Paperback ISBN: 9781036708733

The EU GPSR authorised representative is Logos Europe, 9 rue Nicolas Poussion, 17000 La Rochelle, France contact@logoseurope.eu

By Steve Higgs

Blue Moon Investigations

Paranormal Nonsense
The Phantom of Barker Mill
Amanda Harper Paranormal Detective
The Klowns of Kent
Dead Pirates of Cawsand
In the Doodoo with Voodoo
The Witches of East Malling
Crop Circles, Cows and Crazy Aliens
Whispers in the Rigging
Paws of the Yeti
Under a Blue Moon
Night Work
Lord Hale's Monster
Herne Bay Howlers
Undead Incorporated
The Ghoul of Christmas Past
The Sandman
Jailhouse Golem
Sparks in the Darkness
Shadow in the Mine
Ghost Writer
Monsters Everywhere

Modern Fairy Tale
No Such Thing as Magic

Albert Smith Culinary Capers

Pork Pie Pandemonium
Bakewell Tart Bludgeoning
Stilton Slaughter
Bedfordshire Clanger Calamity
Death of a Yorkshire Pudding
Cumberland Sausage Shocker
Arbroath Smokie Slaying
Dundee Cake Deception
Lancashire Hotpot Peril
Blackpool Rock Bloodshed
Kent Coast Oyster Obliteration
Eton Mess Massacre
Cornish Pasty Conspiracy
The Gastrothief
Lyme Regis Layover
Majestic Mystery

The Vault, Rochester

TUESDAY, JANUARY 2ND 2017HRS

No one noticed the man in the black cloak. He knew they wouldn't. In many ways getting ignored by those around him was a skill, though it took him a long time to see it that way. Throughout his youth, not being seen was a curse. Until he embraced it.

The bottom edge of the cloak touched the floor, and its hood came up and over his head, covering not only his hair but also the top half of his face. The features still exposed were hidden in shadow, so anyone looking would only see the bushy black beard that covered his chin, and his mouth, which he'd set into a firm scowl.

Why would he show the world anything else?

The bar was crowded, just as he knew it would be. It was Rochester High Street on a Friday night, and *The Vault* was one of the most popular places to be. Not that he cared about being part of 'the scene'. No, he was there only to deliver a message.

A rather final message, one might say. So far as the message's recipient was concerned, anyway.

Passing through the press of people he got a few glances. He always did. The cloak saw to that. He looked different to everyone else, but that was okay because he was different. At school they called him weird, the older kids and his classmates alike all picking on him. Even the girls.

Except one. Except Elaine.

Striding through the bar, his muscular form and height eased his passage for most people moved out of his way. Nevertheless, the crowd slowed his pace and filled the gap he left in his wake.

A man made a comment, laughing with his mates about the weirdo in the hood, but Zephyrus Frostwind, the name he'd given to this side of his personality, ignored the jibes. Their smiles would be gone soon enough.

His target was here. He knew the man's patterns and habits, but to be sure, had followed him this evening. Attacking him in public and surrounded by witnesses might seem rash or foolhardy, but what he planned required an audience. Unlike the two previous lessons, this one would be seen, and people would learn.

Specifically, they would learn to fear.

Word would spread fast, and soon it would be impossible to walk into a crowded place without being recognised. Tonight, though, tonight the drunken fools had no clue of the danger passing through their midst.

Lifting his head slightly to peer under the lip of his cowl, he searched the crowd, rotating slowly on the spot until he found the person he sought.

Gill Carlson had his back to the room, his eyes focused on the bartender a few feet away. Waiting to be served, he'd been trying to attract the man's attention for more than a minute. The bartender was far too busy serving a trio of pretty, flirty girls in low-cut tops.

Lifting his arms up and out with a flourish that sent his black cloak billowing, he wove patterns in the air at chest height. Purple sparks flashed into existence, trailing where his fingers led and swirling through the air.

Eyes flared and those who spotted the display nudged their friends. Fingers pointed and murmurs replaced the background din of conversation, loud as it was to be heard above the thumping bass from the DJ booth. Unworried, the onlookers assumed they were seeing some kind of show put on by the bar's management.

Despite the music, a hush fell, and the cloaked figure drew a deep breath to fill his lungs.

"Gill Carlson!" he bellowed, the glowing sparkles between his hands coalescing into an orb of light.

Gill twisted his body, surprised to hear his name called out loud. He was one of very few not already looking at the magic being conjured in the centre of the crowded bar. No one was trying to walk past the figure in the black cloak anymore and those nearest had moved away, distancing themselves from the strange display.

Suddenly alone at the bar as the punters to Gill's left and right chose to be somewhere else, he froze. Gill couldn't see the eyes of the man inside the hooded cloak, nor could he guess his identity or understand how he knew his name, but when it finally occurred to him that now might be a good time to run away, he dismissed the notion – one of the bar's bouncers was coming.

Coming from behind, the man with the security badge was tall, muscular, and confident in his ability to deal with anyone not carrying a firearm. Knives could be a problem, but he'd trained to disarm anyone stupid enough to sneak one onto the premises.

Gill watched, opting to lean back against the bar with a

confident smile on his face. When this was over, people would want to ask him what it was all about. His mind raced, trying to think of something cool to say.

The trio of flirty girls looked to be unattached; he would target them first.

However, watching the bouncer approach from the rear - what had to be the cloaked man's blindside – Gill's smile faltered.

"That's enough," the bouncer reached out with one meaty hand. "Time for you to be leaving." But when his fingers came close to the cloaked man's shoulder, a spark flew. It jumped through the air, bridging the gap to his outstretched hand with an audible snap. The bouncer collapsed as though someone had flipped his 'off' switch.

The man in the cloak never even turned his head.

"Gill Carlson," Zephyrus repeated his victim's name, this time in a low growl. "It is time for you to pay the price."

Gill's right eyebrow launched itself skyward, a question forming on his lips that he would never get to ask.

The wizard flung his arms in Gill's direction, launching the swirling orb of purple light across the bar.

It flew five yards, striking Gill in the chest, but not with any kinetic force that might have knocked him backward. Instead, it appeared to light him up from within. Purple light shone from inside Gill's open mouth while his whole body tensed.

The bar erupted into chaos. Screams and cries accompanied the patrons, most of whom were stampeding toward the exit. They had to take the long route to get around the man in the cloak, his very presence pinning some into the corner behind him where they were too afraid to move lest they get in his way.

Gill's body contorted, spasming on the spot, his arms

outstretched on either side until Zephyrus abruptly ended the spell. The man in the cloak dropped his arms to his sides, watching his victim.

Gill sagged, hung limply in the air for a heartbeat, then collapsed inward upon himself. Falling to the spill-strewn floor like a rag doll, he came to rest where he had stood. Only then did the wizard turn away.

Terrified people were still trying to evacuate the bar, pushing, shoving, and elbowing to get any advantage as they surged as one for the bar's main exit. Wisely, a few had gone out the back, opening the fire doors to escape, but most were still trapped when the man in the cloak began to stalk toward them.

Bouncers from the front door, there to prevent unwanted or unsavoury looking people from entering, had to fight against the crowd to get back inside the bar. The owner employed them to ensure The Vault was the top spot in Rochester High Street. They hadn't had an incident worth mentioning in over a year.

The attack was over and there was nothing they could do to fix that, but they were determined to stop the cloaked man before he could leave. They would hold him until the police came and at least the owner would know they had done all they could. Questions about how he got inside would need to be answered, but that was for later.

Approaching the cloaked man cautiously, the bouncers carried no weapons. Union rules prevented such things, but there were five of them and each knew their stuff.

"It will go easier if you surrender," snarled the nearest, genuinely hoping the fool in the cloak chose to resist so they could pummel him. There were still some patrons trapped in the bar and most of them were filming. They needed to be sure their use of force could be considered acceptable and measured, but that left plenty of room for a few broken bones.

Zephyrus raised his arms once more, pleased for the chance to demonstrate his power.

The bouncers formed a semicircle, pinning him in the middle. Or so they thought.

Flicking his sleeves to better expose his hands, the wizard shouted, "Incindair!" and thrust his arms outward at forty-five degrees to his body. Gouts of flame shot from each palm, lighting the room with such intensity that anyone looking had to turn away.

The fire struck two of the bouncers, igniting their clothes instantly. If further motivation to clear the bar was needed, their screams provided it.

The remaining bouncers dived for cover, terrified they could be next.

His path clear, Zephyrus strode in an unhurried manner to the bar's open doors. One was hanging off. Pausing just inside, he reached inside his cloak, fumbling briefly until he found what he was looking for. Returning to the bar, he found an area devoid of liquid and placed a small white card on the surface. There was nothing on it but a name: Zephyrus Frostwind.

Sirens wailed in the distance, the police responding at speed. They were far too late to save Gill Carlson though. And by the time they arrived, the wizard would be long gone.

Tentacles (I hope)

TUESDAY JANUARY 2ND 2031HRS

Two hundred yards from *The Vault*, Tempest Michaels heard the sirens and turned his head. Were they coming his way? He didn't think so, but regardless, he was running flat out and now was not the time to be distracted.

Ahead of him, a tentacled monster 'ran' as fast as it could, the tentacles blatantly not part of the creature's perambulation method. They flopped and flailed, shaking with its forward motion.

Tempest yelled, "Stop running!" an instruction he hoped the idiot would obey. It was just three weeks since he took a knife to the chest while solving the Grimm Fairytale case and saving his sister's kids. The stitches were out, and the wound was healed. More or less. However, strenuous exercise hurt, and he really didn't want to push his body before it was ready.

Predictably, the tentacled monster went faster, and from inside the suit, an alien voice made a noise much akin to a flatulent walrus expelling his excess gas underwater. Somewhere inside the odd sound were words, which made

Tempest believe he was hearing the voice of the fool inside the costume through a voice changing app.

It said, "You can go *something* yourself." The word Tempest couldn't make out was one he could guess.

Muttering obscenities of his own, Tempest pounded down the street to catch it. He could not see how the alien-looking thing was propelling itself along the street, but he didn't need to see them to know there were feet and legs doing the work. For years he'd lived by a simple rule when it came to tackling monsters: it's always, always a costume with an idiot inside it.

Only once could he ever recall being wrong in this assessment and the surgically enhanced polar bear he encountered in the French Alps still haunted his dreams from time to time.

Closing with the tentacled beast, Tempest couldn't figure out how to trip it – the tentacles stuck out in every direction. If he even tried to trip it, he would be the one sent tumbling. Instead of sticking out a foot, he threw his right shoulder into the middle of the thing's back.

Pushed off balance, it didn't get to stumble or fall for Tempest had chosen the timing and trajectory of his attack with care. As he bounced off and into some handy Georgian railings he grabbed to arrest his forward motion, the idiot in the costume collided with a lamppost.

A rather human "Ooooof!" reverberated out from within the alien being, followed swiftly by a groan of pain and the kind of language one might associate with a bar full of sailors.

Tempest sucked in some air, getting his breath back. Hands behind his head to maximise his lung capacity, he knew he needed only a few moments to recover. Regular fitness training during most of two decades in the British

Army ensured he was significantly fitter than the average person.

At six feet tall, he was just above average height, but muscle mass made him stronger. Not that he was a body builder. Far from it. However, like the fitness training, regularly testing himself with heavy weights led to muscular development.

The tentacled monster was on its side ... or was it the creature's front? Or back? Heck, did it have a front or back? There were no eyes that Tempest could see, but what it did have, now that it was no longer upright, was feet. Two of them stuck out from a central tube inside the costume and just in case there was any question left as to the human nature of the feet, they were wearing Nike basketball boots.

Tempest, his heartrate already slowing, was about to get started on the process of extracting the idiot, when a shadow caused his head and eyes to twitch to the right. There he saw two more tentacled aliens.

He didn't think they would prove particularly problematic, but as they closed the distance, coming to the aid of their fallen comrade, the idiot was wriggling free.

Dismissing the one he'd already felled, Tempest turned to face the new threat. These ones looked the same, but they each held two of their tentacles up like arms. Because that is what they are, Tempest surmised. A glint of light hitting something shiny suggested at least one carried a knife.

Lifting a hand to his throat, Tempest growled, "Ben? Where are you! I've got three of these things on me and they appear to be armed. A little assistance would not go amiss."

There was no time to say anything else for the creatures were arriving. They moved swiftly but were not running inside their suits. It was a measured approach, and they also seemed to have better control of their costumes than the first fool, all of which spelled trouble.

When the first creature abruptly split open, the man inside using a knife to cut it from head to ... um, tentacle, it really did become three against one, so Tempest chose the only sensible tactic available: he attacked.

Fight training and a career where he got to practice his moves on live targets who would fight back provided a level of confidence few possess. Knowing how few possessed it furthered Tempest's belief that he was going to do okay even though outnumbered three to one.

The man inside tentacled monster number one was still getting up and since he was closest, Tempest hit him first. He had a rough beard and ginger hair that was a grubby shade rather than the bright orange some people get. Darting forward just as Ginger tried to rise, Tempest ran through him, putting a knee to his jaw in a bid to dislocate or break it.

He heard the man's grunt of pain but couldn't spare the time to check if he was out of the fight. Tentacled monsters two and three were upon him and now they were closer he could see they both had a knife in each hand. The blades were the fold-out kind and about six inches in length – quite capable of killing a person if that was their intent. Their arms protruded through holes in their costumes. It gave them limited mobility, but enough that they were dangerous.

Tempest went left, moving into the middle of the street and making it so the monsters were now one behind the other instead of coming at him two abreast. They would correct that in a heartbeat, so he acted before they could.

"Think you're tough, do ya?" asked monster two,

advancing in a self-assured manner. Again the voice came with the underwater fart effect added.

Choosing to believe the question was rhetorical, Tempest watched and waited.

"I will carve you up with my testicles," the monster threatened, moving in for the kill.

Certain his ears had not deceived him, despite the alienesque voice alteration, Tempest felt his eyebrows rise in question.

"I'm sorry, your what now?"

He didn't get clarification and felt somewhat relieved when the monster slashed a knife-wielding tentacle in his direction. Stepping back, he surged forward as it lunged, and as the next arm swung in, he used an elbow to block it. That left the monster with both arms spread wide and its 'face' open for attack.

At such close quarters, Tempest had multiple options. He could step in to kick out a leg – kicking through a knee joint ends a fight fast, but the mass of confusing tentacles hid the targets – the man's legs were in there somewhere. He could deliver a hard punch to the solar plexus, another good move to wind an opponent, yet the costume dictated that his blow either wouldn't land at all or would miss its target.

Stuck for what to do next and with monster three coming around the side of monster two, he employed a move he could not remember ever using before: he head-butted it.

It was as his forehead connected that Tempest learned the costume, the head part of it at least, was not made from the same rubber as the tentacles. In fact, as his brain reverberated inside his skull, he wondered if perhaps it had been hewn from granite.

"Ha!" monster two burbled in its weird sounding underwater bubble voice. "Now you get all the testicles! We make mincemeat of you!"

Tempest staggered back, his vision blurring. His feet felt wobbly and disconnected. His arms were up to ward off the attack, but from the corner of his eye he could see Ginger getting back to his feet and knew he was in serious trouble.

He would be able to outrun them. Probably. He was a good runner, conditioned for long periods of exercise, but sprinting had never been a strength. If he turned tail and ran, there was a strong chance one might catch him if they were bright enough to ditch the costume. That was a risk, but it wasn't in Tempest's nature to run away, not from three idiots who had been terrifying people while burgling their houses for the last month.

His opponents spread out, Ginger coming into the middle so the idiots still in their costumes ended up to his left and right. They were all armed with knives and all Tempest had was his wits. His Kelvar vest would stop a blade, but it didn't cover his whole body so if they got him to the floor his survival chances were slim.

Ginger brandished his blade and sneered, "Maybe coming alone wasn't so bright, eh?" Now that he was free of his costume, Tempest got to hear Ginger's voice without the filter. It was eastern European for sure though he couldn't pin an exact country. "Probably should have brought a friend."

"But he did bring a friend!" yelled Big Ben, arriving at a run.

Like the three idiots, Tempest twitched his head around to see the newcomer arriving.

Big Ben got his nickname because he stands six feet seven inches tall and is almost as wide across his muscular shoulders. Unlike Tempest, Benjamin Winters *is* something of a bodybuilder and his physique is nothing short of startling.

Arriving at a run, he leapt into the air. Opening his legs like a pair of scissors, he hit the nearest monster with his groin, riding him to the ground and using his momentum to land with his right fist flying forward into Ginger's shocked face.

That left one final tentacled monster who, upon seeing what happened to his friends, chose to drop the knives.

"I surrender!" it burbled in the hard to decipher alien voice.

Big Ben punched it in the face, proving the hard shell covered the top half of the costume's headpiece only. "Did you say something?" he asked, standing over the now prone form.

"I surrender," the monster repeated.

Big Ben stepped forward, his giant right foot finding the softer, rubbery lower part of the costume. There, he guessed roughly where his opponent's testicles (not tentacles) would be and applied some downward pressure.

"Sorry, couldn't quite catch that. Can you try again without the stupid voice?"

Given a few seconds to recover, Tempest's head was clearing, and he rubbed his forehead, shocked not to find a dent in it.

As if noticing him for the first time, Big Ben continued to grind his right foot into the costume and raised his voice to be heard over the monster's squeals.

"You okay, little man?" he asked with a grin Tempest wanted to slap.

"Perfectly well, thank you. Shall I assume something

distracted you? Something more important than your colleague getting butchered by three idiots with knives?"

Big Ben nodded, utterly unashamed. "Yup. There were two girls and they both had massive t…"

Tempest's growl cut him off. "You were my back up! You were the cut-off man who was supposed to be in position to intercept them!"

Big Ben jinked an eyebrow. "Are you feeling okay? Would you like me to fetch you a chair so you can have a sit down?"

Tempest rubbed at his forehead again. "One day your need to pursue the fairer sex is going to get me killed."

Big Ben removed his foot from the monster's groin and twisted on the heel of his left foot to send a scything boot into Ginger's head. The idiot without the costume had been foolish enough to try getting up. Satisfied everyone was down for now, Big Ben put an arm around Tempest's shoulders.

"Someone has to satisfy the local ladies and since you are halfway to marital bliss with Amanda, I have to pick up your slack. It's not like I want to," he employed a wistful, hard-done-by voice that made Tempest wish he had a stun gun to hand.

Shrugging his shoulders to push Big Ben away, Tempest chose instead to ignore his annoying colleague and call the police. There were bad guys to collect.

The Problem with Big Ben

TUESDAY, JANUARY 2ND 2046HRS

The police took their time reacting to Tempest's call, but he knew they would. Like any large city, Rochester's law enforcers are stretched thin trying to cover all the calls.

"What's the story with these three?" asked Brad Hardacre, a police constable Tempest had come to know.

"They've been burgling houses across the Medway Towns for the last few months. Have you really not heard any of the reports?" Tempest didn't even try to keep the incredulity from his voice. There were more than a dozen incidents where victims reported their security system showed aliens outside their house. That the supposed aliens then disabled the security system and stole anything with any value should have been sufficient to tip people off that there was something screwy going on.

Brad shrugged. "You know what the chief inspector is like when it comes to strange and unexplained cases. He probably dismissed the reports without a moment's thought."

"Actually, he didn't. He forwarded the reports to me and left it at that." Tempest wasn't about to complain. It was an easy pay day. His relationship with Chief Inspector Quinn was adversarial at best, but his refusal to deal with cases that sounded like utter nonsense played into Tempest's hands.

A girlish giggle drew their attention to the other side of the street where Big Ben grinned at a young-looking female police officer.

Brad rolled his eyes. "Hey! McNally!"

The woman almost snapped to attention.

"Think you can tear yourself away from sorting out your social life for long enough to get a statement?"

Her cheeks flushed bright red, then turned crimson when Big Ben lowered his head to whisper something in her ear.

Brad asked, "Does he ever stop?"

"Only when he's asleep, but he usually does that under a pile of women."

There being nothing else to say, Brad helped the other officers at the scene to load the three men. Each carried ID in their wallets. It confirmed they were Romanian. Tempest promised to follow the cops to the station. He was required to give a statement and getting it out of the way was easier than putting it off.

Big Ben asked, "You want me to come with you?"

"No need. You gave a statement to the PC?"

"And got her number in return. Would you believe she hasn't heard of me? I feel slightly insulted."

"Well, I'm sure she will learn all about you very soon. In fact, I would imagine her colleagues are warning her as we speak."

They both turned to find PC McNally getting advice from two female colleagues.

"Ah, yes. Sally and ... I want to say the blonde one's name is Misty, but I could be wrong about that. I will consult my journal later."

"You have a journal?"

Big Ben frowned. "How else am I supposed to remember them all. Misty, or whatever her name is, will be listed under 'girls in uniform' as well as under 'blondes'. If I recall correctly, she has a big tattoo of a lion on her back."

"Well, she appears to be telling your latest mark what you are like." Tempest clapped Big Ben on the shoulder. "Better luck next time."

"Next time? What are you talking about?"

Tempest's grin froze in place when both Sally and (probably) Misty looked at Big Ben with absolute hunger.

"Now I wonder if I can convince all three of them to ..."

Tempest walked away. His friend's ability to score with virtually every woman on the planet was annoying, but not for any good reason. If asked, he would happily claim to be done in his search for a partner. Amanda Harper was everything he could want and probably better than he deserved. He wasn't about to mess with the best relationship he'd ever had for a little action on the side.

Smitten from the moment he first clapped eyes on her, Amanda ticked every box. Multi-tonal blonde hair with a natural wave fell below her shoulders. Her blue eyes and perfect teeth were framed by a face he could spend eternity just looking at. Regular exercise kept her figure trim and toned, but the physical attributes were only a small part of the package. Intelligent, educated, determined, sensual ... Tempest knew it would take him a while to run out of superlatives.

Knowing she was at home waiting for him was all the

motivation he needed to close out the final elements of what had been a relatively easy case. It left him with a blank slate, but if the last couple of years as a paranormal detective had taught him anything, it was that new cases are never very far away.

New Client, New Case

WEDNESDAY, JANUARY 3RD 0811HRS

Tempest and Amanda ate their breakfast together at the breakfast bar in his kitchen. They were not living together or, at least, they were yet to define their arrangement as such, but Amanda brought a suitcase of things to his house to stay over at Christmas and simply hadn't gone home since.

Swallowing the last of his ham and mushroom omelette, Tempest picked up his plate, collected Amanda's, and dumped them both in the dishwasher. He wanted to confirm she was moving in and to raise the topic of what she wanted to do about her flat in town. His place was bigger and more comfortable, but he'd always imagined he would have popped the question before he asked her to move in and he was yet to find the right time.

Christmas came and went, as had New Year's Day, but neither occasion felt like the right time to bring out the ring he'd been carrying in his pocket. He could drop to one knee right now in the kitchen and it would be done. He could follow her acceptance up by discussing their living arrangements, but the kitchen was hardly a memorable location to ask Amanda for her hand.

Three times he booked a suite at the Ritz in London, each occasion intended to be the perfect setting for 'the question'. Yet work intervened the first time, he was injured and had to cancel the second time, and most recently his plans were scuppered when Amanda's stepfather had a mild heart attack. He recovered quickly enough, but not before the third booking came and went.

Fingering the ring in his pocket through the material of his trousers, Tempest's thoughts were a million miles away when Amanda spoke.

"I'm sorry, what did you say?"

Amanda had her phone under her nose. "I said, Jane is spending the day with Cassie again. She says she has something to tell us later. Something too secret to put in a text."

"That's cryptic. I wonder what it could be."

"Maybe they finally have a lead on who is behind the recent deaths."

They both knew Detective Inspector Cassie Munroe from a case the third detective at the Blue Moon Investigation Agency attended. Jane Butterworth started out as Tempest's assistant but soon proved she had skills going to waste on filing and admin. Cassie worked in Buckingham Palace as part of a two-person team permanently assigned there to deal with any problems that might arise and to be the liaison officer in case of an emergency.

The case that drew Jane into the royal circle was to do with a dragon. It turned out to be the eldest son of a duke in a prototype flying suit fitted with a flame thrower. He crashed and burned to death in the castle grounds, but not without leaving behind a whole bunch of questions. The suit was peppered with bullet holes where the soldiers assigned to the palace opened fire, but the bullets didn't hit the body inside. It made no sense.

Unless one assumed the body was a plant.

DI Munroe suspected the duke's youngest son but had not one jot of proof. More deaths followed, the line of succession suffering multiple fatal accidents. Some could be dismissed, but others were highly suspicious. An investigation was underway, but according to Jane, Cassie wasn't included.

There were reasons behind her exclusion, but whether they were justified or not, they led to Cassie bringing Jane into her own investigation. There was something screwy going on with the royal family and a giant spectacle of a wedding just a few months down the line.

Jane wasn't being paid for her hours with Cassie, but Tempest didn't care. After his time in the army, there was no question where he sat on the patriotism question. If the royal family needed his help, he would drop whatever he was doing.

Silently contemplating what secret Jane might have to share, he checked his pockets, picked up his keys, and whistled for his dogs. The duo of miniature dachshunds skidded to a stop by his feet half a heartbeat later.

"Sorry, boys. I wasn't calling you for second breakfast. It's time to go to work." One of the many joys of being his own boss was the ability to take his dogs to the office. He took them on cases sometimes, too, though it was their habit to get in the way, chase the wrong person, and generally cause trouble.

Amanda picked up her coat, hanging it over one arm because the seat in her Lotus was a little too snug to be comfortable with an extra layer. The engine was already running, so she would be warm enough in the car without it.

Though they lived in the same house and were heading to the same office, they took separate cars. Typically, they worked separate cases and that often meant going in different directions, necessitating separate modes of transport.

Most days Jane would beat them there. Hence the text message to let them know she would be working away. Marjory, the office administrator, kept to the clock, so they would be first and second to arrive. In her sixties, ruthlessly efficient, and not to be messed with, Marjory had stapled Big Ben's hand on more than one occasion. The office was dark when they arrived and devoid of the unctuous scent of freshly brewing coffee that would usually waft out to greet them.

"Coffee?" Tempest asked, already striding toward the high-end machine he bought not long after moving into the plush office. The dogs charged along in front of him, their youthful exuberance manifesting in a burst of playful energy.

Amanda turned right to get to her office, calling, "Sure," at Tempest's back.

He was almost at the machine when someone rapped their knuckles on the glass entrance door and the dogs exploded in a fit of barking. He knew without looking that it was nowhere near opening time, but if a client felt desperate enough to queue outside his door in January, he wasn't going to make them wait until 0900hrs.

A quick glance showed a set of eyes and the top of a woman's head peering through the clear glass that started about five feet off the ground. The lower portion was frosted for privacy.

Fetching the key from Marjory's drawer, he used his right foot to unlock the deadbolt in the floor and reached up to remove the one at the top before inserting the key. Rochester High Street is a great place to have an office, but the city suffered from crime like anywhere else.

Scooping the dogs, one under each arm, he managed to hook the door handle to get it open.

"Good morning, please come in." He stepped back to let the lady outside get in from the cold. She looked to be in her early thirties, and her clothes told Tempest she thought about her appearance and had enough money to buy designer labels. Passing him to get through the inner door where it was warmer, Tempest noted her height, hair colour, eye colour, and that there was no ring on her left hand to indicate she was married.

"Sorry. I suppose I'm early, aren't I?" She shivered and hugged herself.

Closing the doors to keep the cold at bay, Tempest said, "That's perfectly all right. I hope that I can be of assistance. You look cold though. Can I offer you a hot beverage?" The dogs were struggling to get free, their little tails wagging as if to propel them through the air.

He placed them back on the carpet and was already moving toward the coffee machine when she replied. "Yes, thank you."

While the machine got busy, he settled into one of the plush chairs next to it and indicated that she should sit. The dogs fussed around her feet but knew better than to jump up at her legs. She appeared unbothered by their presence, so Tempest continued as though they were not there.

"I'm Tempest Michaels, owner of Blue Moon Investigations. How may I help you today, Mrs ...?" The lack of a wedding ring ought to have dictated he address her as Miss, but there were little clues. An unnoticed smear of food on the lower hem of her coat suggested a child had left their sticky mark. Pulling into the carpark behind the office, he'd noted an Audi Q5, a vehicle designed to carry multiple persons. It was one a mum with money might pick for reliability and other reasons. The nervous looking woman taking a seat diagonally across from him held an Audi key fob in her right hand. He couldn't see her ring finger in enough detail, but suspected he would find a thin line where a wedding band once sat.

"Legg," the lady replied without correcting him. "Valerie Legg." Warming up now that she was out of the cold, she reached up to unbutton her coat. "As for what help you can give … the truth is that I don't know if you can. Or if anyone can."

This was a line Tempest heard all the time. The firm's clients fell into two distinct categories. The ones with a serious problem to resolve and the absolute nutters. The nutters would see a shadow in their house and automatically assume it was their great aunt come to haunt them for wetting the bed when they went to stay with her in 1973. Or next door's cat would regurgitate a slow worm on their door mat which could only be the work of the devil. The people in the nutter category would run to the Blue Moon door, foaming at the mouth with their need for an exorcism or hopeful demands that he drive a stake through the heart of their neighbour whose canines were definitely longer this week than last.

The ones with serious problems were almost always quiet and apologetic. Just like Valerie Legg.

When the twin spouts filled the first cup, he placed it on the coffee table in front of Mrs Legg and offered her an earnest expression.

"You are probably thinking that the tale you have to tell will sound fanciful or ridiculous, but I spent last week investigating water sprites at a farmhouse in Barming. Whatever you have to tell me will be treated in the strictest confidence, and in all likelihood it won't be the first time we have been called to investigate whatever it is you have to report."

Mrs Legg sighed, a mournful exhalation that let her shoulders slump. Tempest wondered if she would need further encouragement, but she started to speak a moment later.

"I got this through the post." She reached into her bag to withdraw a business card which she offered to Tempest.

He took it, turned it over to find the reverse side blank and turned it back again. The small, white, rectangular piece of card bore a name and nothing else: Zephyrus Frostwind.

He said the name aloud and asked, "Does that mean anything to you?"

Valerie's eyes had been firmly glued to the surface of the coffee table until he posed the question, at which point she snapped them up.

"I expected you to be better informed."

Amanda's voice echoed across the office. "That's the name of the wizard, Tempest. That's what the press are calling him. I've just seen it online. It was announced on the news this morning. Of course we missed it." Amanda didn't need to remind Tempest they had too little time to watch the news that morning because they chose to stay in bed and fool around instead.

She walked across the office to join Tempest and his client, extending her right hand so she could introduce herself. Task complete, she took the seat opposite Valerie and filled in some of the blanks.

"There was an attack last night. A man in a cloak walked into The Vault and killed a man in front of dozens of witnesses who say he used magic to do it. There are a whole bunch of videos online. Taken by people in the bar no doubt." Producing her phone, she set it on the coffee table so they could all see it, and played one of the clips. It showed a hooded figure in a black cloak standing in the middle of the bar with a wide circle around him. Pumping music made it hard to hear what he was saying, but they saw when a bouncer placed a hand on his shoulder and recoiled as though shocked.

Raising his hands, the cloaked figure fired a purple orb at his victim. It lit him up from within, making sparks jump and dance across his skin and the person holding the phone clearly moved because the next shot was a panicked blur of ceiling, floor, and people running to be elsewhere.

"The bouncers tried to stop him from leaving and he set fire to them. There is footage if you really want to see it."

Amanda's question was meant for Tempest, but Valerie shook her head emphatically. It was not something she wished to see.

"Then he left a calling card on the bar with nothing but a name."

"Zephyrus Frostwind," Tempest supplied, looking down at the business card in his hands. "And you say you got one through the post?"

Valerie nodded. "Eight days ago. I don't know anyone called Zephyrus Frostwind and that's not exactly a name a person would forget hearing. They are saying he's responsible for three deaths now."

"That's right," said Amanda. "The first two victims weren't identified until this morning, though. The first happened weeks ago. Before Christmas, anyway. They found the business card tucked into the pocket of a woman impaled by steel bars near to a construction site in what was previously listed as a freak accident. The second is a guy who they thought to have been hit by lightning in a carpark. So, yes, that makes three deaths. Three murders, I guess. The local news showed the business card on the TV this morning."

"And that's why I am here," said Valerie.

Tempest asked, "Have you spoken with the police?"

Valerie made a grumpy face. "Yes. They told me not to worry. Said they would send someone around to ask me about it later."

Tempest expected little else. "Mrs Legg, I will take your case. The unexplained is our specialty. I need to ask you some questions. Quite a few of them probably, because unless this person has selected you completely at random, there will be a connection, a reason why you received a card."

"But I don't know who it could be," she protested, fear straining her words. "And I don't know any of the other victims. They gave their names on the news this morning and I've never heard of them."

"Nevertheless," Tempest persisted, "I expect to find there is a reason why this Zephyrus Frostwind chose to single you out. If he intends you harm, the best course of action you can take is to remove yourself from the area. Do you have somewhere you can go?"

"Go? You mean like I should stay with my mum in Cleethorpes? I guess I could, but I have two kids. What do I do about their school?"

Tempest took a second to consider what he wanted to say. He did not want to scare the woman unduly, but part of his self-imposed responsibility in taking the case was keeping her safe. By extension that meant her children too. However, he perceived the possibility that the wizard might attack her at home.

"Valerie, I wish to stress that despite what you have seen and whatever conjecture you might have heard, there is no such thing as magic. The person behind this is using clever tricks to create the effects filmed in the bar last night. He is killing with unconventional weapons, but there is nothing magical about it."

Frowning, Mrs Legg asked, "How can you be so sure?"

"Because there is no such thing as magic. Amanda will back me up. We are called to investigate supernatural creatures, ghosts, demons ... name it and we have probably come across one. None of it is ever real. The same will be the case for this man."

"Okay. Let's assume I believe you. How does that help me? If he attacks me with magic or what you called 'an unconventional weapon' I will be just as dead, won't I? Can you protect me? Can you protect my children?"

Thankful now that he had no other cases, Tempest said, "I am certain I can, but we will need to take some steps. I can arrange a bodyguard ..."

"Big Ben?" Amanda questioned if Tempest was being serious.

Tempest nodded and Amanda rolled her eyes. Big Ben was very good at what the industry calls close protection – the art of bodyguarding an individual. In Valerie's case, he would likely do it by laying on top of her. In bed. After seducing her.

Very close protection indeed.

Ignoring her, Tempest said, "What I said earlier about staying safe by going away remains my best advice."

"But I don't want to take my kids out of school. My

eldest has her exams this year. And I work from my house. If I go away, I stop earning money. If I am there, I shouldn't need to go out other than to take the kids to and from school."

"Noted. Then I want to go from here to your house, Mrs Legg." If Big Ben agreed to the bodyguarding work, which Tempest believed he almost certainly would, the risk to Mrs Legg and her family diminished sharply.

"Can you protect me there?"

"Yes, I believe so, but before we go any further, we need to discuss rates. This is an investigation agency. I'm afraid personal protection will cost extra."

Mystery Men Occult Bookshop

WEDNESDAY, JANUARY 3RD 0902HRS

When Mrs Legg left the office to head home, Tempest picked up his phone.

Eyeing him, Amanda asked, "You're calling Big Ben?"

"Yeah. I need to get him up to speed and deployed."

Amanda reached out to grab Tempest's hand so he couldn't hit the dial button.

"You know he'll have her knickers off in under ten minutes, right?"

"Entirely possible, but he'll do the job all the same."

"It would be better if you did it, Tempest."

Quirking an eyebrow, he asked, "The protection thing or the bit with her knickers?"

Amanda scowled at him in a manner convincing enough for his testicles to try hiding behind each other.

"Just making a joke, darling."

"Uh-huh. About sleeping with another woman."

Sensing he'd stepped over some invisible line, Tempest managed to say, "Um."

Amanda stepped a little closer. "That worried sensation

you're feeling right now. Imagine how this would go if you were actually stupid enough to get a little on the side." She held his eyes with hers, boring into his soul like a puppet master holding his strings.

Then she kissed him. "Just kidding, babe. I know you would never."

"That's right," Tempest agreed emphatically. "I would never."

Moving back to her office, Amanda said, "You should still do it yourself. You need to quiz her anyway. I expect you to be right about the connection. This wizard character must know her."

Putting his phone back in his pocket, his fingers brushed against the ring. Was now a good time to get down on one knee? Hardly. A cold Wednesday morning at the office? When he did it, he wanted to be able to kiss her and bask in the moment, holding her hand and talking about their future. There was no time for that now.

With a deep breath to centre himself, he collected his coat and called for the dogs.

"Come along, boys. It's time to speak with Frank."

Frank Decaux, the owner of an occult bookshop a few yards around the corner from the Blue Moon office had served as the font of knowledge for all things supernatural since the day Tempest opened his business. He considered Frank to be more than a little eccentric, but rather than label him as harmless, Tempest considered the short, scrawny bookshop owner to be an important ally.

Together, they had survived several life-threatening situations where the smaller man proved himself worthy in every sense of the word.

The bookshop could be found on the first floor above what was now a florist shop. Accessed through a door on the side of the building, a flight of old wooden stairs led up to the shop. Inside, shelves lined with comic books, graphic novels, and non-fiction titles were complimented by collectibles, weapons fake and real, such as crossbows and swords, and all manner of paraphernalia pertaining to the occult.

Want a vampire hunter's kit? No problem. A silver-lined container in which to collect and store ectoplasmic slime; special offer on those today.

Tempest let himself in, the dogs bounding ahead to scurry behind the counter.

"Boys!" squealed Poison, Frank's primary shop assistant. At nearly twenty-one she was stunning in a crop top to show off her muscular midriff. Today she wore a streak of sky blue through her jet-black hair, which vanished behind the counter when she dropped to greet the dachshunds.

Following them, Tempest said, "Good morning, Poison."

She didn't answer until she had hoisted first Dozer, then Bull onto the countertop. Using both hands to scratch the fur behind their ears, she looked up through her fringe to pierce Tempest with a sultry look.

She said, "Hey, gorgeous."

There had been much flirting in the past; almost all from the young Chinese woman who was most definitely too young for Tempest, in his opinion, even when he was still single. That he once saved her life earned him a reward he was still opting not to claim.

Unsure what an appropriate response might be, he was saved by Frank.

"Is that the Dangerman I hear in my place of business?"

"Hello, Frank."

Frank appeared a few moments later, arriving in the

shop through a door behind the counter. It led to his storeroom and office in the back.

"You'll be here about Zephyrus Frostwind I assume."

"On the ball as always, Frank." Tempest had learned not to be surprised by the perceptive bookshop owner a long time ago. He might come off as completely bonkers, but he was making a fortune with his business and was nobody's fool. "What can you tell me about him?"

Frank scratched his skull with one hand and pulled a worried face.

"Well, he's the real deal. I think we should start with that. This guy is about as dangerous as a tornado and just as likely to destroy your house."

"There's no such thing as magic, Frank."

"Ha! That's what the government wants you to think! Witchcraft and sorcery once ruled these lands, but purges against those imbued with the power to wield the earth's elemental forces caused a decline. Death sentences without trial forced innocent witches into hiding, and the most powerful among the magical community simply fled our shores to pursue a peaceful existence elsewhere."

Tempest kept his mouth shut. Frank ranting utter nonsense was nothing new and he quite enjoyed hearing the bookshop owner's alternative views.

"The Salem Witch Trials in America are perhaps the best known, but they are just one example of a practice that became rife. In the last century or so, as murdering women in the street became less palatable, the magical community slowly began to reform. Witchcraft and sorcery returned, but the government saw danger in allowing it to go unmanaged."

"You think there are clandestine government organisations directly involved in managing the magical community in Great Britain?"

"Goodness no."

"Oh."

"Not clandestine. They do it in plain sight."

Tempest fought to keep his amusement inside.

"Do you really think there is such a position as a Culture Secretary? What do you think the Minister without Portfolio does? It's right there in our faces. It couldn't be more blatant! Anyway," Frank waved a dismissive hand to move the conversation on, "I, for one, am glad to see such a powerful practitioner back in England. I just wish he was using his mastery of magic for good and not whatever vengeance mission he is on."

"So, you don't think he is using special effects to create his illusions?"

Frank's eyes almost popped from their sockets. "Haven't you seen the footage from the attack last night? My word I wish I had been there. I might have been able to reason with him, to convince him to join the newly reformed Kent League of Demonologists ..."

"Wait." Tempest raised a hand, palm out, to stop Frank talking. "Those psychos are back?"

"Newly reformed, Tempest. Most of the old order went to jail, remember. Or were charged and released under caution. Those of us who were left have been recruiting fresh blood. The county sits on a confluence of ley lines that draw supernatural forces like iron particles to a magnet. Rochester has been a hotbed of paranormal activity for centuries."

With Frank heading off on another tangent, Tempest posed the question he really wanted to ask.

"Do you know who Zephyrus Frostwind is in real life?"

"In real life? Like, you think he has another name?"

"Yes, Frank. That's what I mean. What are the chances he is one of the new loonies in your league of demented ologists?"

Tempest received his second scowl in half an hour. "They are not loonies, Tempest, and neither am I. As for Zephyrus Frostwind, I have no idea who he is and there is no mention of him in any of the online forums beyond this last week. Whoever he is, he's powerful enough to stand alone. Please tell me you haven't taken a case that will put you in his path."

"I have a client, yes. She received one of his business cards through the post and is worried he might plan to attack her."

"I should say that is exactly his plan, Tempest. But you must know you can't stand against him. He commands the elements, for goodness sake!"

Knowing there was no point arguing, Tempest said, "Please keep your ear to the ground, Frank." The request was his other reason for visiting. If weird stuff was happening, Frank tended to hear about it first. "Let me know if you learn anything that might help me."

Frank bowed his head, his expression one of disappointment. "Okay, Tempest. The League have already left messages for him on a bunch of dark web boards. If he makes contact, I'll let you know, but I have to beg that you reconsider involving yourself in his business. If you go up against him, you will not survive."

"Understood." Tempest reached out to pluck Dozer from the counter. With Poison still massaging his head with one hand, he was barely awake. Bull was no different, and they looked disappointed to have their affection session interrupted. "Time to go, boys."

He turned to go only to have Frank grab his sleeve. "Tempest, you said your client got a card through the post, yes?"

"That's right. Seems likely Mr Frostwind hand delivered it through her mailbox." As he said the words, Tempest questioned if Mrs Legg had a doorbell camera. It could provide a breakthrough and would need to be explored, but Frank was still trying to make a point.

"Tempest, how many other cards did he send?"

Mrs Legg's House

WEDNESDAY, JANUARY 3RD 1032HRS

Judging the dogs to have had enough exercise and excitement, Tempest dropped them at home where he knew they would sleep in their bed or on the sofa until he returned. From there he pushed onward to Chart Sutton, a small village on the other side of Maidstone, and the address Mrs Legg provided.

He could not tell just from the street name, but Tempest knew Chart Sutton to be a picturesque village where the house prices were higher than the surrounding area and properties outside of the very centre tended toward the larger, more desirable side. So it came as no great surprise when his satnav announced his arrival and he turned off the street into a sweeping driveway.

The house was a mock Tudor recreation detached property with fake wooden beams inset into the front façade. Painted white across the upper floor, the bottom eight feet were left to brick. To the left, a double garage and car port housed the Audi Q5 he guessed to be hers when he first saw it.

Stopping in front of her door, he was only halfway out of the car when it opened inward and Valerie appeared.

She waited on the doorstep with the door pulled to but not shut - keeping the cold outside.

"Found the place easily enough?" she asked.

"Satellite navigation is a modern wonder."

She pushed the door open and went inside, holding it until he came through and shutting it once more.

The interior of the house was modern and plush. The carpets were cream wool with thick underlay to make them soft underfoot. The doors were bespoke items in solid wood and the furniture he passed as she led him through the house were not the kind of pieces one can buy just any old place. Some looked like antiques.

"My husband was a plastic surgeon," she revealed though Tempest had not asked. "We've been divorced six months but separated three years ago. He lives with his new wife in Canterbury."

Tempest remained tight lipped. He didn't need to know her marital position. Nor did he wish to discuss the subject. Valerie had more to say, though.

"When I discovered he was cheating, I took him for every penny I could get. This was the house we were living in with our kids and I refused to leave. I'm only telling you this so you can understand why I am selling things on the internet to bring in money. I have a small business making t-shirts, and mugs, things like that. Anything with a label or logo, really. If you wanted branded stationery for your office, I could supply it."

"Thank you. I'll keep that in mind."

"What I'm trying to say is that despite the car and the house, I don't have a lot of money. In fact, it would be accurate to say I don't have any money because of the house and car. I should probably sell both and downsize, but I want to hold on to this place until the kids have left for university. It feels more acceptable to claim I am downsizing because I have an empty nest than because my husband was the breadwinner."

"Understood. I will try to be budget conscious. I have dispensed with the additional bodyguard and will provide that role myself."

Valerie released a breath she'd clearly been holding. "Thank you. I don't want to come across as cheap, or to suggest you shouldn't charge for your services, but I do have a limited budget."

Feeling the subject of finance could be put to bed, for now at least, Tempest said, "With that in mind, we should move forward. I have some questions." On the way in, Tempest looked for but could not spot a camera doorbell. He hoped that didn't mean there wasn't one.

Except it did. It was a thing Valerie said she wanted to get, but again her budget, because the big house wasn't cheap to heat or maintain, denied her the option of buying things she could manage without. Tempest guided her through her past, asking questions about her husband, any partners she might have taken and subsequently rejected since the breakdown of her marriage, and quizzed her about phone calls, text messages, and mail, specifically any that were cryptic or threatening.

Throughout the interview, Valerie maintained that she had no reason to believe anyone in her life could be Zephyrus Frostwind. Her husband couldn't care less, she'd taken two lovers in the last three years, neither lasting very long and both ending the relationship before she could. She showed Tempest her email and text messages, promising that she was holding nothing back.

She wasn't aware of any debt her husband might have failed to declare and which could, possibly, explain why someone might hold a grudge, and she had no enemies, not even among the school mums who she said could be quite bitchy. She went on to say they were another reason why she wanted to stay in the house and meet the monthly car payments. Moving to a smaller property and driving a ratty car would result in her kids being snubbed. Party invitations would dry up and invites to evening drinks with the mums would evaporate because no one would want her car on their driveway.

It was just that kind of community.

They talked for more than an hour with Tempest leading. Ultimately, there was nothing to learn. She didn't know Gill Carson, Diane Meacock, or the second victim, Wayne Lawson, and there was nothing to indicate she should. They were of different ages, lived in different parts of the county, and worked in different sectors.

"So what do you think?" Valerie asked when Tempest ran out of questions. "Am I worried about nothing?"

Tempest pursed his lips and thought about what he should say.

"That is hard to judge. I am short on information and need to figure some things out. The card you received could be random, or even a mistake, but I don't think it is. The story about the cards didn't break until this morning, so we can dismiss the notion that it could be someone playing a trick on you because you got it more than a week ago. I think the threat is genuine. What I cannot guess is whether he will target you here if this is where you remain."

As if the thought had just occurred to her, she gasped, "Do you think he might go after my children?"

It was another tough question for which Tempest had no answer.

"That is not something he has done so far, but I'll tell you what – they have phones, yes?"

"Of course."

"Do you usually pick them up from school?"

"No, there is a bus service laid on for them."

"Then message them and collect them yourself. You will feel better and can be wary and watchful without scaring the kids. Come straight home and I will be back before it gets dark. Staking out your property in case he comes here is almost certainly a waste of my time and to that end I won't charge you for it. It will mean you can sleep safe tonight, but I stress again that safety will come with distance. Please give some more thought to taking an impromptu vacation. The kids' teachers can give them work to take with them."

Valerie gave a sad nod of acceptance. "You're right. I will think about it."

There being little more to say, Tempest got back into his car. He had work to do. Leaving her felt risky, but he still had no good reason to believe she was in any immediate danger. Offering to watch her house and grounds for the night was almost certainly overkill that would result in a stiff back, aching joints, and a foggy mind from lack of sleep.

Too late to back out now, though. He'd offered and she accepted.

Still thinking Big Ben presented a better option, despite Amanda's misgivings, Tempest pulled off the drive and steered his car for home.

Research

WEDNESDAY, JANUARY 3RD 1211HRS

What he needed more than anything was information. All he had so far was the names of the three victims along with some basic details. He could do that back at the office, but there he would suffer constant interruptions. Marjory would have questions and things for him to sign, and if Amanda was out he would have to handle all the calls and any drop-in clients who showed up.

The business regularly attracted more work than the three detectives could handle. Tempest knew that was no bad thing, but any new clients were going to have to wait until he had more time to deal with them.

Arriving home, he fought the dachshunds to get into the house. They were excited and trying to squeeze out through the gap to greet him outside even as he tried to step over them to get in.

"Honestly, boys. We do the same thing every single time I come home. If you just wait inside, I will come to you."

They pranced in his wake, bumping against one another until his hand touched the treat jar. The sound of the lid rattling acted like a freeze ray to stop them dead in their tracks. Until he tossed two gravy bones in different directions and they exploded into action once more.

He flicked on the kettle and opened the fridge.

Five minutes later, he was sitting in front of his computer with a steaming mug of tea to his right and a plate to his left. Taking a bite from a ham and mustard sandwich, he opened a search bar and got to work.

The first victim was a forty-seven-year-old woman called Diane Meacock. She worked at a pharmaceutical firm as a senior executive. He found the details reading a report in The Weald Word, a local rag that would report anything from murder to funny shaped turnips so long as the story fell within the area known as the Kent Weald.

Diane left behind a daughter and a husband. Her untimely death came when she was impaled by steel construction rods. The kind they use to reinforce concrete, Tempest guessed. There were no witnesses.

The second victim, Wayne Lawson, suffered a fatal heart attack. Like Diane, tucked into his clothing was a business card with Zephyrus Frostwind's name printed on it. It was ignored by the police until the card left at the scene of the third murder made it very clear they were all linked.

Like Diane, Wayne met his end without anyone to witness what happened. Found in the carpark behind the office where he worked, his car was unlocked and the door was open, but he didn't make it inside. A CCTV camera covering a different area of the carpark captured flashing lights that looked like lightning, but it was an old black and white feed and it failed to show the figure, if there was one, at any point.

Wayne worked as an estate agent. He was sixty-two years old and had a heart condition. The last factor suggested the killer knew his victim. Possibly even knew him quite well, if one took the leap to believe the heart attack was deliberately induced, but there was nothing in any of the reports Tempest found to indicate how the wizard made it happen. Nevertheless, an electric shock of sufficient magnitude would do it if the man had a dicky ticker.

Tempest made a note to find out who performed the autopsy. The light show sounded like a good way to disguise the use of a taser.

The most recent victim, killed less than twenty-four hours ago, was too fresh for there to be much detail in the papers. What little existed, and the fact that he'd been named, came down to the footage shot in the bar. Livestreamed to the internet as it occurred, the person with the phone undoubtedly scored a million new followers when the video went viral. Putting to one side how scummy that made the person, Tempest learned Gill was forty-three and divorced. He had no kids and worked at a men's outfitters in Rochester.

Three victims, their ages all far enough apart they couldn't have gone to school together. Working in vastly different industries, it was hard to see what could connect them. However, Tempest doubted their selection could be entirely at random and that meant there was a commonality somewhere. He just had to find it.

Picking up his mug to finish his tea, Tempest discovered it had long since gone cold. He could make another but placed the mug back on the coaster to think. Frank asked a critical question about how many other people might have received a card.

The number was impossible to know. Unless he found a way to encourage potential victims to come forward. From a business perspective, taking on multiple clients for a single case had the potential to lead to a big pay day. But how to get them to come forward?

From its charging cradle in the kitchen, his phone rang, trilling through the quiet house.

Taking his half full cup of cold tea with him, Tempest went to find it. The dogs followed, just in case he was going to fetch them some food.

Displayed on the screen, the name 'Marjory' dictated he answer.

"What have you got for me, Marjory?"

"A client. He's got one of those cards. I called Amanda first, but she said you had already taken the case."

And there it was. Frank had called it right.

"Can you come to the office? The gentleman is here now."

Tempest didn't need to think.

"I'll be right there."

The Blue Moon Office

WEDNESDAY, JANUARY 3RD 1348HRS

Content the dogs had relieved themselves in the garden and would happily sleep the afternoon away on the couch, Tempest left them behind when he returned to Rochester.

The allotted spaces behind his office were all empty; Amanda and Jane out to leave the business solely in Marjory's care. Such was the nature of the firm that they would often all be out during working hours. Not that any of them really kept working hours. More than fifty percent of their cases demanded nighttime activity with the inevitable knock-on effect that they needed to grab some sleep the next day.

The business continued to flourish, not least because Tempest elected to franchise the firm more than a year ago when he discovered other detectives performing a similar service in the US. They were disorganised and operating individually, but each possessed great potential. Leveraging his infamy – some of the firm's past cases made global news headlines – Tempest recruited two detectives in America plus an old army buddy in Australia. On top of those, Jane's uncle asked for permission to use the firm's name for a division of the Boston PD charged with investigating the wonderful and weird.

The time to recruit a fourth investigator at the home branch was already nigh, but it was also a task he could put off and that was exactly what he'd been doing for months.

Arriving through the back door, Tempest sought out Marjory at her desk.

She dipped her head toward the private offices to Tempest's right. The client waited for him there.

Wasting no time, Tempest walked into his office with purposeful strides.

"Good afternoon." He thrust out his hand. "Tempest Michaels, owner of the Blue Moon Investigation Agency."

The man took Tempest's hand reluctantly, and perhaps only because not doing so would be extremely rude. He was tall at six feet five inches and broad across his shoulders with a large belly to match. Somewhere around sixty, his hair was almost non-existent and what little remained clung to the sides and back of his skull like a herd of tiny mountain goats balancing on a ledge. His chin tiered into his neck which morphed into his chest. Tempest figured his weight to be around the three-hundred-pound mark, but the man carried it well and could have been a rugby player or a wrestler in his younger years.

"Richard Cowell," the man introduced himself. "You investigate ghosts and weird stuff, right?" It wasn't so much a question as an accusation and far from the first time Tempest found himself confronted by a client who questioned why they had chosen to waste their own time on such nonsense. His attitude was gruff, his body language annoyed. He didn't want to be in Tempest's office and was making it quite clear without needing to articulate the fact.

"We prove they don't exist, yes. Our clients are generally people with problems they cannot explain and ones in which the police have no interest. There is always a vanilla human behind whatever we investigate, and the same will be true of the wizard plaguing the city. I believe you received one of his cards."

Walking around Richard now their introductions were complete, Tempest dumped his car keys on the desk, shucked his jacket, and settled into the chair behind the desk. Richard had been sitting in the chair in the corner of the room, only rising when Tempest entered. He retreated to the chair where his thick winter coat rested over one arm.

From it, he produced his wallet and from that the Zephyrus Frostwind business card. It was stained.

"It came through the post a couple of weeks ago. I had to go searching through the bins to find it. Fortunately, I suppose, my wife insists that we separate all our rubbish, so it was in with the cardboard and paper and not the general waste. I wouldn't have gone digging for it there."

He was offering it for Tempest to take.

Tempest politely declined the icky piece of card.

"What prompted your visit today, Richard?" Tempest suspected he knew the answer but wanted to get the prospective client talking.

"The news this morning. They showed one of these cards and said it was linked to the murder in The Vault last night. In fact, they said the man last night was the third victim. I don't feel like being the fourth."

Convinced Richard was now on the hook and primed to be reeled in, Tempest said, "Would you like me to investigate the wizard for you, Mr Cowell?" It was a yes/no question and thus would move their conversation forward quickly or end it abruptly.

Despite that, Richard took his sweet time answering. His eyes were down, aimed at the carpet as if it might yield an answer.

Ten seconds passed before he looked up to meet Tempest's gaze.

"What will it cost?"

It wasn't the response Tempest expected, but his reply came smoothly. Outlining the firm's rates, and explaining how he could not predict how many hours or days it might take to achieve a result, he arrived at a ballpark figure.

Richard's lips twitched in time with a generic shoulder shrug that Tempest took to mean the fee was acceptable.

"You think you can catch the guy?"

Drifting in from the main office, Tempest heard Marjory greet someone coming in from the street. It was a woman. Another potential client, perhaps.

Focussing his attention on the man sitting opposite, Tempest said, "It's what I do. To be clear though, I am an investigator. I have no powers of arrest beyond that which any citizen can claim. When I find him, it will be the police who take him away. He is suspected of three murders."

"Why do I need you then?" Richard's question came in a gruff manner. "Why don't I just leave the police to catch him and save my money?"

Tempest leaned forward in his chair, piercing Richard with his eyes. "You have every right to do precisely that if you believe they will get to him before he strikes against you. You said you had no desire to be the fourth victim. That is your concern, is it not?" It was an ultimatum. *Decide to hire me or stop wasting my time.*

Richard was a bullish man who Tempest gauged was used to getting his way by using his size to intimidate others. It was why he responded in an equally bullish manner.

It had the opposite effect.

Hooking his coat with one arm, Richard got to his feet. "I've made a fortune from having a nose that can sniff out nonsense from a mile away."

Marjory appeared at the door. "Sorry to interrupt, Mr Cowell's wife is here." She stood aside to let a petite woman enter.

Dressed for the cold, Mrs Cowell had to be ten years her husband's junior and one third his mass. Long, chestnut brown hair fell in flowing, loose curls around her shoulders. Blessed with high cheek bones, twinkling dark brown eyes, and a set of perfect white teeth, she was stunningly attractive.

"Oh, super," she said, looking from Tempest to her husband and back again with a pleased expression. "You've already hired him then."

Tempest swung his gaze from Mrs Cowell to Mr Cowell to find his angry face replaced by one of embarrassment.

"Ah, we were just getting to that, my love."

Sensing triumph, Tempest rose from his chair to greet the lady. Richard's inexplicable attitude – coming to the office when it was clear he saw no need – was now explained. His wife made him do it.

She took Tempest's offered hand and gripped it tightly with her tiny digits.

"Thank you so much for taking our case. The police won't be able to solve this one. I've been following your exploits ever since that vampire case two years ago."

Fighting to keep the grin from his face, Tempest said, "Please be assured this case will have my personal and undivided attention."

The Cowells

WEDNESDAY, JANUARY 3RD 1403HRS

With the Cowells in his office, Tempest went through the names and details of the previous victims, again looking for any indication they might know them. He also told them about Valerie Legg and the business card she received.

He drew a blank on all counts. When asked to provide more details about themselves, Tempest learned Richard owned the Casino Rooms, a nightclub less than a hundred yards from his office. It featured various cabaret acts, male and female strippers, a casino, and other events to keep the punters rolling in. Tempest had never ventured inside but was familiar with the operation.

Mrs Cowell, whose first name was Carol, met Richard when she took a job as one of the exotic dancers almost thirty years ago. They lived together in a large, detached property in the village of Aylesford, just a couple of miles from Rochester.

"Richard, there exists the possibility that this Frostwind character has targeted you at random. However, I think it more likely you have made an enemy out of him at some point in the past. Can you think of anyone with whom you had a business deal go wrong? Or someone who might hold a grudge and want to do you harm?"

Carol looked across and up at her husband with expectant eyes.

Richard grunted, "You want a list? In my line of work upsetting people is part of the job. I must have fired more than a hundred people over the years. Some for stealing, some for being lazy, others for pure incompetence. There have been plenty of business deals that went sour; that's just the nature of business. You don't win them all but if you win more than you lose you're doing okay. I never bothered to hold a grudge."

His wife's eyes argued.

"Well, not for very long, at least. My point is, I have made *lots* of enemies, but if you want me to name someone who might go to all this trouble just to get back at me, I'm afraid I draw a blank."

There were a lot of blanks so far. Tempest asked about strange occurrences other than the unexpected business card, and whether either of them had noticed anyone watching them or the house in recent weeks.

They had not.

Marjory took over for the exercise of paperwork to formally engage the firm and took a deposit to get Tempest started on their case.

"Now that's complete," said Tempest, "I need to ask about your plans for the coming days. Frostwind has killed three times, and I see no reason to believe he will stop. Whether he genuinely intends to target you and how soon he might do that I cannot guess, but the prudent move on your part would be to take a vacation. He cannot attack you if you are not here."

Mrs Cowell grabbed at her husband's arms. "Oh, yes, Richard. Let's go on holiday! We could go back to Hawaii."

"No chance," he shot her down in an instant. "I can't go anywhere right now. The business won't run itself."

"You must have staff on whom you can rely," Tempest pressed.

Carol said, "Ha! He fired his club manager last week."

"Because he was continually drunk, darling. It's not like I wanted to."

Tempest took the man's name for good measure, though the dates didn't stack up if he was fired the previous week and Richard got the business card the week before that.

Guiding them to the door, he said, "If I cannot convince you to leave, I want to place a guard on your house tonight. Will you agree to that?"

Richard asked, "Will it cost me extra?"

He got an elbow in the ribs from his wife, who said, "Yes, please, Tempest. Whatever protection you can offer us."

When Richard offered no argument Tempest accepted Carol's decision and let them go.

Returning from the door, Marjory said, "Aren't you already guarding Mrs Legg's property tonight?"

"Yup."

It presented a quandary for which Tempest hoped there was a simple solution. Big Ben had always been his pick to guard Valerie's house, but Amanda made a fair point that he would likely end up inside the house, inside her bed, and inside … well, best to leave it at that. Tempest could manage Valerie's place, but he couldn't be there and the Cowells' at the same time.

When his phone rang, Big Ben was naked and lying face down on a massage table in the living room of his apartment. On his TV, Jason Statham did his best to kick a giant shark in the trousers while two scantily clad women kneaded and worked the muscles in Big Ben's back, one from each side.

Big Ben lifted his head, turning it slightly to the right to ask, "Can you grab that for me, please, Darla?" Letting his head drop back into the hole designed for it, He held out his right hand until the phone appeared in it. "Thanks, babe," he purred, only too aware what was going to happen when they finished on his back and asked him to turn over.

Eyeing the screen, he saw the name and tapped the green icon to connect the call.

"Hey, Temp, whad'ya need?"

"Protection gig. You've seen the wizard on the news?"

"The one who killed a guy at The Vault last night?"

"Yup. That one. Got two different clients who need their houses watched tonight."

"And you want me to take one. Let me guess, one is a hot woman and the other is an ugly bloke and you picked me for the latter."

"Very astute of you. However, both houses contain attractive women, if you must know. Yours just happens to have a husband. Are you in?"

Big Ben grinned, thinking about the two sets of hands already on his bare skin. He was in all right.

"What time and where?"

Tempest provided the details.

Like any other night of the week, Big Ben had a date arranged. However, his sex life was such that he got more than he really needed, so the opportunity to do something different appealed.

"Sure thing. I'll be there. Are we meeting first?"

"Yeah. I'll see you on site at 1800hrs to introduce you to

the clients. I judge the likelihood of action to be very slim, not least because the wizard might have given out dozens of his calling cards."

With the call complete, Big Ben on board, and a sleep-deprived night ahead, getting in a swift nap elevated itself to the top of Tempest's to-do list. He would attend to it shortly but first turned his attention to the map on the wall in his office.

The three victims all lived inside the Medway Towns area, as did his two clients. Using green thumbtacks for the attack sites, and red thumbtacks for the places of residence, he marked eight positions. The question of how many other business card recipients there might be continued to itch at his skull. It was all very well protecting the two he knew about as he looked for clues that might lead him to identify the wizard, but Tempest knew he would feel not just woefully ineffective, but also guilty if the killer struck elsewhere to claim a victim he might have been able to prevent.

Reaching for his phone, he brought up a contact he believed would be able to help, then hesitated with his index finger hovering over the dial icon.

As a local reporter for the Weald Word, Sharon Maycroft could not only run a front-page article showing the business card but also had a segment on the local TV news. Warning people via their TV screens would be more effective and likely to garner instant results. If Zephyrus Frostwind had sent more cards, an appeal was the best way to get them to come forward.

But Amanda narrowed her eyes every time Sharon showed her face. Tempest suspected she wasn't actually threatened by her, but she knew he and Sharon had 'history' and Sharon made things more complicated by openly flirting with him every chance she got.

Huffing out a breath of frustration, Tempest thumbed the button and set his phone to speaker. It rang at the other end until it switched to voicemail.

He'd expected her to answer. She was a reporter after all. In his head reporters always answer the phone.

Invited to leave a message, he composed one in his head and started talking.

"Sharon this is Tempest. Um, Tempest Michaels." He winced. How many other Tempest's could she know? "I need a favour." Did that make it sound like he was flirting? Beginning to sweat, he pushed on. "I'm sure you've heard of Zephyrus Frostwind. I have reason to believe he's sent a bunch of his business cards or calling cards … whatever you want to call them, to the people he plans to attack. I have two clients already and I'm worried there might be more. Can you get something out in the paper and online? I know you have an online edition now that gets updated all the time. Also TV, if you can put it in your segment? Whatever you can do, really." Sensing that he was now rambling, Tempest rallied his braincells to wrap things up. "Um, well, that's it. Just that. Call me if you need to discuss anything."

Jabbing the red button to end the recording, he sucked in a lungful of air and prayed she would never listen to it.

"Call me?" he echoed, convinced Amanda would somehow already know he'd phoned his former lover and would thus offer him a cold shoulder for the next few days.

Unable to understand why he found relationships with women so challenging, Tempest gathered his things and let Marjory know he would be out for the rest of the day. He would be working the entire night and probably not available until mid-morning – things she needed to know. Content he was ready, he left via the back door.

Valerie Legg's House

WEDNESDAY, JANUARY 3RD 1823HRS

Having introduced Big Ben to the Cowells, Tempest left him to settle in and made his way back to Valerie Legg's house. He very much doubted the wizard was going to come to her home – his attacks thus far had all occurred on the streets, but he couldn't rule it out.

The point was to make her feel safe, and to watch because the one thing he could gauge from the three murders was how well planned they had to be. In the case of the first two victims there were no witnesses. Unless he was very lucky, the killer knew where his targets would be and when. The third victim, Gill Carlson, differed in that his death was a public act. To pull that off and get away had to require even greater planning. Escape routes, how many members of security he would have to face, police response time ... not to mention being able to time his grand entrance to coincide with his victim's arrival.

Tempest believed it indicated a person who was meticulous. Would he be watching the property tonight? Probably not, but if he intended to attack Valerie Legg, it was reasonable to expect he would study her. Perhaps that task was already in the bag, maybe it was yet to come.

Maybe he'd had enough and would go to ground never to be heard from again. Tempest had no way of knowing but was ready to spend the next few hours observing Valerie's property in case someone showed up.

She knew Tempest would be outside and had promised to pretend he wasn't there. No need to tip Zephyrus off if he was watching.

Heading into Chart Sutton, he slowed the car in deference to the rural roads. It was a quiet area which worked in his favour. Apart from people who might be out walking their dogs, the residents would be locked securely inside their nice warm houses. Spotting anyone sneaking through the streets would therefore be that much easier.

Turning into Valerie's road, he was yet to see a single soul, but that changed when he angled his car into her driveway and his headlights picked out a black figure. Shrouded in shadow next to her front door, it became visible only when his headlights pointed that way.

Clad in a full-length robe that covered the figure's head and fell all the way to the ground, there was no doubt in Tempest's mind that he'd hit the jackpot, but he was still mentally punching the air when the figure spun around to face him.

The cowl on the robe covered the top half of the man's face and a beard covered the rest. As the headlights swept across the figure, Tempest caught a flash of teeth. They were there one moment and gone the next, replaced by glowing light in the man's hands.

Tempest had just about enough time to realise he was about to be hit with something when the wizard launched his attack. What he could only describe as a firebolt left the wizard's hands, racing across Valerie's front lawn on an intercept course with his car.

Yanking the wheel to one side, he gritted his teeth and held on. The fireball narrowly missed, blazing a trail past the passenger's side of the car. Tempest cut his eyes to his rear-view mirror in time to see it hit a tall hedge between Valerie's garden and next door.

Not looking where he was going, but largely out of control anyway, the Porsche ploughed through a clipped, round Buxus, destroying it completely before Tempest stomped the brakes and slewed the car to a stop on the front lawn.

Expecting more of the same, Tempest rolled out of his car using it as a barrier. Two steps to his right he hugged the ground and bear-crawled at speed to find cover behind another shrub. In the dark, with the headlights now off, the only light came from the moon. It was an environment in which Tempest felt quite comfortable. His all-black outfit made blending into the shadows simple and instant. To disappear all he had to do was stop moving.

In contrast, his opponent couldn't have been more visible. Nevermind that standing in the open made him visible even with the limited ambient light, he had another glowing orb in his hands.

"Hey, Zephyrus!" Tempest called. "That's a neat trick you've got there. Do you do parties?" Speaking gave away his position, but Tempest was ready when the wizard launched his next salvo.

The ball of flame whipped through the air with a sizzling, crackling sound to slam into the shrub and set it alight. Tempest was moving before it got halfway. He'd taunted Zephyrus to get a better look at the flaming orb, but seeing it properly for the first time, he couldn't figure out how it was produced. The stench of burning accelerants filled the night air, accompanied by the scent of burning from the hedge and now the shrub. Drifting smoke fogged the garden.

Thankful the garden had mature trees to give cover, Tempest ducked behind a silver birch. The trunk wasn't thick enough to hide him, but he wasn't trying to get away. He wanted to get closer and used the trees to disrupt the wizard's aim.

"What else can you do?" Tempest teased, sprinting to the next tree. "Can you do the one where you saw the woman in half? I've always been a fan of that one."

Zephyrus advanced, his hands weaving patterns at chest height. "I am about to kill you. Now would be a good time to tell me your name." His hands flicked outward, palms open and extended.

Tempest flinched, expecting a gout of flame or a lance of lightning, and was caught by surprise when a dozen or more tiny barbs struck his flesh. Recoiling, he swiped at his face where he found a thin spike sticking from his flesh. Ducking and running, he plucked it free. There were more in his arms and across his chest, most of which hadn't penetrated to his skin, but some had.

Holding one so he could see it, Tempest called out, "Nails? You're throwing nails?"

"I can conjure the elements, little man. Commanding steel to obey my will is child's play." As though to prove his point, he launched a jet of blue/green flame from his left hand while swirling the right to produce orange sparks.

Too close now, Tempest saw the fire coming and had to throw himself at the ground to get away. Landing, he forced more of the nails through his clothing and into his flesh, but they were a minor concern because his legs were on fire.

Made from ripstop fabric, his trousers were hardwearing and perfect for the kind of rough treatment they would get in a fight, but they were not fireproof. Feeling the heat through the material, Tempest scrambled to get up. He had to get some distance between them before Zephyrus could turn him into a fireball, but he also needed to stop, drop, and roll to put out the flames.

Sensing now that he was outmatched, and unable to explain the wizard's 'magic' tricks, he narrowly missed the next barrage. Fresh flame, this time from the wizard's right hand, set fire to a patch of lawn a fraction of a second after Tempest left it.

Looking about for anything he could use as a shield, Tempest spotted the bins to the side of Valerie's house. To stand a chance he needed something to deflect the flame and whatever else Zephyrus sent his way.

But the wizard knew he was winning. With his opponent on fire and scrambling to get away, he stalked forward, hands raised to deliver a death blow.

Until the front door opened.

Light inside silhouetted Valerie in the doorway. "What on earth is ..." She didn't get to finish her sentence.

Zephyrus switched his aim. Swinging both arms around he sent his next lance of flame at the house.

Valerie screamed; her face illuminated by the onrushing fire.

It hit the open door as she fell backward to land on the carpet. Bouncing off, the liquid accelerant fell to the floor inside her house, setting fire to the carpet before she could kick the door shut with a resounding bang. Fire clung to the door, eating the material.

Zephyrus swirled his arms through the air again,

conjuring another spell, his opponent in the garden momentarily forgotten.

Until the wheelbarrow hit him.

Valerie's interruption bought Tempest the seconds he needed. The flames on his trousers were out, though they continued to smoulder and smoke, but he'd wasted no time inspecting the damage. Heading for the bins, he spotted the empty wheelbarrow parked against the side of the detached garage.

Swinging his whole body like an Olympic hammer thrower, it flew better than he'd expected.

The wizard cried out in pain when the wheelbarrow bounced off with a dull clang. It was enough to make him stagger, but he didn't fall as Tempest hoped he might.

Nevertheless, this was his first opening, and he had to make it count. Holding the lid of an old steel bin employed for composting, Tempest charged. In his right hand, he held a leaf rake. It wasn't exactly the weapon he would have chosen, but it was the only one he could find.

Planning to run right through Zephyrus to flatten him before following up with disabling blows, Tempest saw the wizard recover. The blow from the wheelbarrow stunned him, but not for long enough.

He was three feet from getting properly into the fight when Zephyrus unleashed a new weapon.

Magic Battle

WEDNESDAY, JANUARY 3RD 1828HRS

Tempest heard a pop of something before a concussion wave of sound and light hit him. The effect was much like having his brain switched off and back on again. He was conscious and could see, though his eyesight had shut down for a nanosecond, but everything needed a moment to reset.

Sprawled on the cold grass and completely vulnerable, there wasn't a thing he could do to stop Zephyrus from ending the fight. Dazed, Tempest couldn't work out why nothing was happening.

A groan from the vicinity of his feet provided an answer.

He couldn't exactly remember it happening, but he'd been running to shoulder barge through the wizard when the flash grenade went off. Whatever the heck Zephyrus used, it did the trick but failed to stop Tempest who'd been too close and moving too fast to miss.

Like *Slyvester Stallone* and *Carl Weathers* at the end of the second *Rocky* movie, they were in a situation where whoever got to their feet first won.

Tempest shook his head, trying to clear it, but the action only made it feel like his eyeballs had come loose. He could taste blood, and his ears wouldn't stop ringing. Movement by his feet told him Zephyrus was conscious and moving. If the wizard could raise his hands, he would be able to deploy whatever weapons remained in his arsenal.

With a scream of rage that split his head in two, Tempest forced himself off the ground. Pivoting off his knees, he threw himself at the robed form.

Zephyrus was on his front and gasping for breath. When Tempest hit him, it drove all the air from his lungs. He was dazed and winded, but equally aware of his need to get moving when Tempest landed on his back.

"Who are you?" Tempest snarled, grabbing at his robe. His uncoordinated limbs wouldn't obey his commands, yet if he could just get the wizard's hood off he would be able to see his face. If he could get him into a choke hold or an arm bar, he could keep him pinned until the police arrived, but a flailing arm caught him under the chin.

Fighting to get out from underneath the man on his back, Zephyrus bucked and struggled, landing a solid but unaimed blow that caused the weight pinning him to roll away. It was momentary, though.

Tempest came again, grappling to get hold of an arm only to find he was too late. Zephyrus had managed to swivel his body around and this time when Tempest tried to grab his arm, he kicked out with both legs. His boots hit the Kevlar plate covering Tempest's chest, driving him back.

Staggering to his feet, the wizard wheezed, "She has it coming. They all do. I will be avenged."

Tempest got his knees under his body but could tell he wasn't going to be able to stop the next assault. Zephyrus was on his feet and though hunched over and breathless, his arms were already raised to conjure a spell.

When nothing happened, the wizard swore and stared at his arms. Using his right hand to feel his left forearm he swore again.

Tempest stood up. His head hurt more than he thought it ever had. He felt nauseous and weak, but the fight was still on. If he judged the situation correctly, the wizard's bag of magic tricks was either exhausted or broken, but whichever it was, they were now man against man and Tempest fancied his chances.

Zephyrus spun off his right foot and bolted.

Tempest, his fists up and ready to fight, huffed a defeated breath and tried to give chase. Zephyrus wasn't moving fast. In fact, his lumbering escape could hardly be called running at all, but he was still going faster than Tempest could manage.

He ran down the side of the house, passing the garage to reach the rear garden. Tempest staggered after him, using his hands on the side of the house to keep himself upright on more than one occasion. He felt like *Pepe Le Pew* chasing after the cat, except his slow pace wasn't going to result in catching the target.

The wizard's robe flapped in his wake as he stretched the distance between them. Valerie's back garden was just as impressive as the front, only many times bigger. Zephyrus reached the end of the lawn where it gave way to trees and there he vanished into the shadows.

Tempest followed, cautious in case Zephyrus waited to ambush him with a counterstrike, but a few minutes later it became clear he'd reached the back fence and was gone. Beyond the fence, woodland stretched for miles until it reached Staplehurst.

Cradling his head, Tempest wandered back to the house, and around to the front door where he lowered himself to rest on the step. Feeling beaten, he spat out some blood and used an elbow to knock on the door.

"It's okay," he managed to call out, his head resting against the doorframe and his eyes closed. "He's gone. Are the police coming?"

A reply came a few seconds later when Valerie spoke through the door. "Yes, the police are coming. Are you sure he's gone?"

Tempest drew in a deep breath. He hurt all over. Far from being his first fight, it was perhaps one of his worst in terms of how he felt afterwards. Talking made his head ache, but he forced himself to say, "Fairly sure. He's hurt. I believe he has withdrawn."

The front door opened with such abruptness it made him flinch, but it was the sound of Valerie yelling at him that made him recoil.

"You told me none of it was real! You said he was just a guy with some tricks! I saw him do magic! There were flames coming out of his hands!"

Tempest had his hands over his ears to protect his throbbing brain but opened his eyes and looked up when Valerie suddenly stopped yelling.

"Oh, God, are you all right? You're covered in blood! Is that … is that a nail sticking out of your head?"

Aftermath

WEDNESDAY, JANUARY 3RD 1943HRS

The police arrived a few minutes later, a duo of constables in a squad car skidding to a stop on the gravel drive followed shortly by two more. By then the adrenaline was leaving his body and the cold was seeping in. Tempest shivered, raising his hands to show they were empty. The cops were responding to a panicked call for help from a single mother at home with her kids. The sight of a man in combat gear was going to make them wary until they figured out he wasn't the bad guy.

The first officers checked the back garden, calling in additional units to help search the area though it seemed likely Zephyrus would have doubled back through the woods to a car parked somewhere nearby.

They checked on Valerie and her kids and formed a cordon at the edge of the property to keep neighbours back as they began to appear, though they let a woman from across the street through when Valerie asked them to.

More and more arrived over the next ten minutes,

including Chief Inspector Quinn who immediately seized control of the scene.

Paramedics arrived, summoned to the scene when the first cop saw the state of Tempest's face. There had indeed been a nail sticking out of his skull, but it was only a tiny thing roughly half an inch long. He plucked it out the moment Valerie identified it.

His wounds were superficial and by the time the paramedics got to him, his headache was subsiding. The nausea had passed. So too the ringing in his ears, and when he gingerly got back to his feet, he found he could move around without feeling like he might fall over. His trousers were ruined and the skin on his lower legs was tender to the touch, but no worse than a mild sunburn.

Tempest watched Quinn giving orders and coordinating with a helicopter that had appeared overhead just a few minutes earlier. The chief inspector avoided Tempest, sending a detective sergeant to get his statement rather than do it himself.

Tempest provided all the detail he could, which was plenty, but did not include a description of the wizard's face. He was able to state that the man in the robe was white, probably in his fifties, of muscular build, roughly six feet tall, and had a black beard. He also described the voice, which had a local accent and was a little nasal. Beyond that there wasn't much to tell.

The crime scenes guys, two men Tempest had met numerous times, would figure out what was in the napalm-like gel Zephyrus used to throw his fireballs around and they would comb the front garden for any other clues that might aid them to figure out the wizard's identity. Not that the information would be shared with the local paranormal investigator.

To that end, when the paramedics accepted his refusal to go with them to the hospital, he returned to the general location where the concussion device went off. He'd seen flash bangs used on TV and in films and had used similar devices during training exercises in the army where they were employed to simulate grenades. It was, however, the first time he'd been subjected to one at such close range and he wanted to be sure what it was.

Crouching with one knee on the ground to run his hands through the grass, he found a jagged plastic fragment. Picking it up, he held it to the light for a better look.

"Hey!" shouted Chief Inspector Quinn. "What's he doing? Get him away from there!"

Without bothering to look his way, Tempest rose to his feet, saying, "It's called evidence, Ian."

"Evidence that you are now tampering with."

Unable to continue his policy of ignoring Tempest in the hope he would simply cease to exist, Quinn strode across the lawn to get to him.

"Hand it over."

Tempest threw it in a lazy arc for the chief inspector to catch. He smiled when a sharp edge bit into Quinn's flesh causing him to wince.

"I think it's part of a stun grenade. It's what he used when I got too close."

"So you claim."

Tempest didn't rise to Quinn's bait. "If you can find enough pieces, there is probably a serial number on it. That can be used to trace where it was made and who it was sold to. If you're lucky, that is."

Quinn scowled. "Yes, thank you, Mr Michaels. I know how to conduct an investigation. You've given your statement, so I see no reason for you to still be here." He clicked his fingers and gestured for a constable who jogged over. "Escort Mr Michaels from the premises."

"Yes, sir."

"Not so fast, Quinn. That's my client in the house. I am going to check on her before I go anywhere."

He hadn't realised it, but Valerie was within earshot.

"There's no need, Tempest. I won't be needing your services any longer."

Quinn's smile was so broad it almost touched his ears.

"I'm doing what you told me and leaving the area as soon as the chief inspector clears me to go. They are on the case now. Thank you for stopping the wizard tonight. I'll pay you for your time and I'm sorry you got hurt, but you were wrong about him. I saw what he did, and you endangered me and my kids by underestimating what he was capable of."

Tempest didn't bother to argue.

"Right," said Quinn. "Well, I think that confirms the end of your business here."

Tempest started walking. They would open the cordon to let his car out, but he wasn't going far. Not yet. He'd just spotted someone he wanted to talk to.

Interview

WEDNESDAY, JANUARY 3RD 2008HRS

The police had to work to get the onlookers to move out of the way, but they parted slowly to let Tempest drive from the property. Flashes from cameras robbed his sight. Photographers snapped pictures through his window and shouted questions followed him until he pulled to a stop on the opposite side of the street.

They had all assumed he was leaving, but Tempest exited his car and locked it, searching the crowd for the face he wanted as the journalists among them flooded his way.

"Sharon!" he shouted her name when his eyes couldn't find her. "Sharon Mayfield?"

A hand went up, rising above the shoulders of people blocking her from view.

"Over here!" She barged her way through, a photographer hard on her heels. A smile pushed her cheekbones higher. "Going to give me an exclusive, are you, Tempest?"

He hooked her left elbow with his right hand, using it to steer her away from the neighbours.

"Sure. A little quid pro quo. I need your help."

"Yeah, I got your message," she grinned. "I already spoke with my editor and with the TV station manager and they both agreed. My editor is waiting for me to produce the article. I called you, actually."

"You did?" Tempest patted his pockets, looking for his phone.

"Yeah. About an hour ago. I thought it was strange when you didn't answer or call me back, but I guess I know what you were doing now."

"It's in the car," Tempest realised. His habit was to remove it from his pocket before getting behind the wheel. It dug into his butt otherwise. Arriving at Valerie's to an attack by the wizard, it stayed in the centre console and was still there now.

Sharon was half listening, her focus more on getting her recording device set up and directing her photographer to take the shots she felt they needed.

"You're okay to do this here?" she asked. "We can go somewhere else if you want. You look a little battered."

There were sticking plasters where the nails made holes in his forehead and his bottom lip was swollen. He was about to say something suave and brave to make the injuries seem insignificant when a car stopped right next to where they stood. The window powered down to reveal Frank Decaux's face.

"Cor, that was some show you put on, Temp. How the heck are you still alive?"

Confused, Tempest frowned. "Quite the show? How would you know?"

Frank's eyebrows climbed his face. "It's all over the internet! You didn't know? Two kids filmed the fight. I mean, they missed the start of it," he explained, pulling his phone from an inner jacket pocket, "but they got some great footage."

Sharon barged Tempest out of the way to see it, her own phone in her hands so she could search for the same video.

Tempest watched himself on the tiny screen of Frank's phone. Whoever filmed it had to have been standing at the edge of the driveway and looking around the tall hedge that caught fire. He could see the flames dancing to light the garden just out of shot. For the most part, the video focused on Zephyrus, capturing the light coming from his swirling hands and the fireball that followed.

Sharon murmured, "This is amazing," then clicked her fingers at the photographer. "Find out who these kids are. They must be local."

Handing Tempest the phone, Frank got out of his car and came around to stand beside him so they could both watch. When Zephyrus ran off with Tempest staggering along behind him, he adopted a serious voice.

"You could have been killed, Tempest. This is a seriously powerful mage you are dealing with. You must see that now."

From his pocket, Tempest produced a second piece of jagged plastic from the concussion grenade, the one he palmed when Quinn saw what he was doing.

"This is what he used to beat me, Frank. There's nothing magical about it. Whoever this guy is, he's got some good tricks, but that's all they are. I'm going to catch him, Frank."

"You're going to get yourself killed, Tempest. You always think you can explain everything, but magic is as real as you and me. The League is reaching out, trying to make contact. He can't be stopped, not by conventional forces, but if we can convince him to join us, we can harvest his talent for good."

"He's killed three people, Frank." Tempest sounded exasperated because he was. "And tonight he came after a mum in her house with two kids. If he makes contact, you need to tell me. In fact, hold on. What do you mean the League is reaching out? How, exactly?"

"Yeah," Sharon joined in, "How are they involved and who are they."

"The Kent League of Demonologists," Tempest supplied. "A total bunch of delusional nutters who believe they form the last line of defence to keep the people of the county safe against supernatural dangers."

She kinked one eyebrow. "Seriously?"

Ignoring her, Tempest pushed Frank for an answer.

"Through the usual paranormal forums and online services. I told you about it when you came to the bookshop."

Tempest's eye rolled upward as he consulted his memory. "That's right," he nodded. "You did."

"Yes, I did. He's bound to be listening, Tempest. The question is whether he will respond."

"Wait," Sharon pushed her way into the conversation again. "You said something about a bookshop?"

"That's right," said Frank, spotting the chance for some free publicity. "The Mystery Men bookshop on Northgate in Rochester. We specialise in all things …"

Tempest stopped listening. Feeling weary and with the need to watch Valerie's house now gone, he could head home. Well, as soon as he'd given Sharon her promised interview.

It was almost thirty minutes later when he flopped into

his car. Further exhausted by Sharon's quizzing, he was ready for his bed. The dogs were with Mrs Comerforth, his next-door neighbour, who would be disappointed to have to give them back so soon, but he needed a bath so perhaps he would leave them with her until he was almost ready for bed.

With a twenty-minute drive to get home, he tapped the phone icon on the centre console and told the voice activated software who to call.

Big Ben answered with a single word. "Speak."

"The wizard attacked the client at my location. Or rather, he would have if I hadn't turned up."

"You're still alive, so I'm guessing he's in custody and I can stand down."

"I wish. Sorry, he got the better of me."

Expecting a snarky response, Tempest was surprised to hear Big Ben's voice turn serious.

"You're okay?"

"A little banged up, but yeah. Client ditched me, so it's just the Cowells we are protecting now. All quiet there?"

"Quiet as a graveyard."

Tempest outlined events in Chart Sutton, listing the weapons Zephyrus deployed and advising Big Ben should find himself a shield just in case. He also told him to look for the footage even though it made him look like an idiot scrambling from tree to tree and running around with his trousers on fire.

"I doubt he'll try to hit a second target in the same night, but who knows. I'm heading home to get cleaned up and do some research. I want to know how he can do some of the things he does. He threw a ball of fire at me and I intend to be ready next time we meet.

The call ran for most of the journey, ending just before Tempest pulled into Finchampstead. By chance, Mrs Comerforth was outside letting the dogs 'water' her front garden when he pulled onto his driveway.

"Home earlier than expected then?"

Tempest nodded. "Things did not go entirely to plan. Boys behaved themselves?"

"Of course. They're little angels."

Bull and Dozer were at Mrs Comerforth's gate, tails wagging and eager to rejoin their human. When she let them out, they ran back to their own door, keen to get inside where they knew Tempest had gravy bones.

Tempest thanked his neighbour, apologised for collecting the dogs early, and bade her a good night.

Inside the house, he set the bath running, poured himself a rum and coke, and was about to take stock of his injuries in the bathroom mirror when his phone rang.

It was Amanda's name displayed on the screen.

"Darling." He turned around to sit on the edge of the bath.

"I just saw the video. Are you all right?"

"Yup. I'm home and about to go for a soak."

"You were on fire."

"My legs were, not the rest of me. My trousers are trashed, but I'm fine. Honest. Where are you?" he asked to change the subject.

"Out with my mum. I told you like five times."

"Sorry. Forgot. I knew you were out."

"I'll be back soon, okay. Don't drink too much rum. I want to hear more about the wizard."

Tempest's hand had stopped halfway to his mouth, the glass of rum hanging guiltily in the air. How did she know?

She blew him a kiss and reaffirmed her promise to be home soon. She said 'home' as in the place where they lived together. It made him feel good and he sunk into the hot, steamy water, with proposal thoughts in his head.

Home Invasion

THURSDAY, JANUARY 4TH 0113HRS

He closed the door silently and listened. A gentle hum from the refrigerator to his left was the only sound to be heard. Upstairs, they would be asleep, and when he got closer, Zephyrus knew he would be able to hear them breathing. It excited him to be so close to ticking another pair of names from his list.

He waited a full minute, his feet planted and motionless on the kitchen tile. If they had heard him enter, they would have reacted by now, so he crept forward, easing through the house to the foot of the stairs.

They presented another challenge, for what set of stairs could be ascended silently? They would creak and groan just like the stairs in every home in every house in England. But if the residents woke, it wouldn't matter now. He could kill them in the hallway just as happily as in their beds as was his plan.

Of course, it was the children who caused his need to kill. They were the ones who insulted him. Had their parents berated them as he knew they should, there would never have been a need for him to visit their house a second time. Yet they sided with their spoilt brats and for that he was happy to condemn them.

Keeping to the very edges and striding out so he only placed a foot on every third step, he ascended as quietly as he could. The next to last stair creaked under his weight, a groaning noise that sounded loud in the silent house. He froze, waiting for someone to say, "What was that?" but the family continued to sleep.

On the landing, Zephyrus turned toward the front of the house where he expected to find the master bedroom.

Walter Freeman opened his eyes, his senses twitching. Lying still in his bed, he listened. If anyone asked, he would tell them he was a light sleeper, but he knew it wasn't really true. Regardless, something had awoken him and with dread creeping across his skin, he accepted what his ears were telling him: there was someone outside the bedroom door.

Reaching out, he touched his wife's arm and propped himself up on one elbow.

Vanessa wiggled away, unwilling to be woken at this time of the night, and most definitely not interested in whatever it was her husband wanted.

Gripping her arm, he shook it to wake her and whispered, "Nessa. There's someone in the house."

Thoughts swirled and collided in his head, arguing whether he needed to find some underwear first and questioning what there might be in the bedroom that he could employ as a weapon. Vanessa's hairdryer appeared to be the only viable option. At least he could swing it around.

The 'barely there' sound of movement outside the

bedroom door ceased, silence returning to claim the night once more as though it had been nothing more than his imagination.

Grumpily, and without lifting her head from the pillow, Vanessa said, "Did you forget to lock the cat in the kitchen again?"

Was that it? Was his heart beating so fast for nothing more than their daughter's pet. The stupid thing liked to sleep on their bed, so they had taken to locking it in the kitchen before they retired for the night.

But he'd done that. Walter was sure of it.

Questions about cats and weapons and underwear vanished in the space between heartbeats when the bedroom door exploded inward, showering the bed and its occupants with wood and splinters and dust.

Instantly galvanised into moving, Vanessa sat up and screamed. Beside her Walter found himself frozen. He wanted to move. He knew he ought to be out of bed and running to check on the kids, but he couldn't get his limbs to respond. The terror he felt trebled when a cloaked figure strode through the choking dust.

"Time for you to pay for what you did," the figure rumbled, his deep bass voice muffled by the mask he wore. Not that his victims could see it, the hood of his cloak hid his face completely.

"Hey," Walter started to get up. "Hey, I know you."

Zephyrus made weaving motions with his arms, gathering his magic to deliver the spell he'd selected specially for his latest victims. From his hands came a fine mist that filled the air.

Walter leapt out of bed, his wedding tackle on display.

"Remember him, Vanessa? He's that …" Walter's breath caught, and he found he couldn't speak. Gasping like a fish on dry land, he twisted his head to beg his wife for help, but Vanessa's eyes bugged from her face, and she clawed at her throat.

"Time to die," said Zephyrus, his fingers trailing tiny sparks in the air.

Ride You Like a Fairground

THURSDAY, JANUARY 4TH 0358HRS

Tempest had tried to sleep, but the bliss of slumber seemed determined to evade him that night. Waking almost constantly after a brief hour of initial rest, he accepted defeat before 0400hrs.

Leaving Amanda asleep in the bed, he hooked first Bull and then Dozer from under the covers on his side of the bed, slipped on a pair of house slippers, took some slouchy sportswear from a drawer, and made his way downstairs.

The chief culprit for his insomnia was the need for knowledge. He couldn't explain how Zephyrus conjured light from the air, or how he sent jets of flame from his hands. In fact, he was struggling to explain any of it and wanted answers.

With a steaming mug of tea in his right hand, he slipped into his office chair. Starting with the video of their fight, which he rewatched three times, Tempest examined Zephyrus and the way he moved. Reason dictated the 'wizard' employed devices hidden about his person to produce the light effects and to create the fire, but it was too dark in Valerie's front garden to make out any detail.

The video had more than two million views and many thousands of comments despite only going live a few hours earlier. There were tens of thousands of comments which fell into a few distinct threads. A lot of the comments were to do with the wizard and his awe-inspiring display. In contrast to those who thought it to be real were those who debunked it, claiming to have seen better effects on low-budget B movies. Tempest sided with them, but the third thread was about him. It started with someone making fun of the hapless idiot running toward danger instead of away from it. Viewers laughed at his efforts, but then someone identified who it was, went on to explain what Tempest Michaels did for a living, and finished by providing his work email.

Tempest thought it was grossly unfair. Essentially unarmed, he'd gone up against a man wielding fire and throwing nails. He rubbed at the sticking plaster on his forehead, sucking a little air through his teeth when the wound sites rewarded him with a jolt of pain.

Admittedly, the footage did not reflect his efforts in the best light. He ran from tree to tree looking like a frightened rabbit, and when Zephyrus set fire to his trousers, he flailed and scrambled around on the grass only surviving because Valerie opened her door.

Curious, he opened his business emails to find a deluge of abuse in his inbox. Having been outed, those with nothing better to do – what the industry likes to call trolls – filled their lives by hurling abuse his way.

Unable to change it, Tempest deleted more than a thousand emails, closed the tab, and started a new search. Looking for 'magic tricks revealed' he found and dismissed a lot of pages showing close-hand magic with cards and rubber bands before finding something more promising.

Two hours ticked by with Tempest's eyes glued to the screen of his laptop. The only time he moved was when his bladder demanded to be emptied. He pressed the kettle into service again before returning to his chair with a fresh mug of caffeine.

Not that it worked.

He could not recall his eyes getting heavy, or making the decision to lay his head back, but when his phone went off at 0612hrs, he was asleep in his office chair with a line of dribble running from one corner of his mouth.

Bull and Dozer were asleep on the sofa, their bodies a single dark blob against the lighter material of a cushion. The ringtone woke them, but neither dog thought it necessary to raise their heads. If the human moved, given that it was now nearing breakfast time, then they would find the energy required to leave the warm spot they occupied.

Rubbing the sleep from his eyes and feeling like he'd been run over by a particularly vicious truck, Tempest fumbled for his phone. In so doing, he knocked his mug of tea which was still full and quite cold. It spilled on the surface of his desk, but only a small amount before he managed to grab it.

Jabbing the green button on the screen beneath the name 'Sharon Maycroft', he blurted, "Good morning," while using his spare hand to control the spill. He wanted it to stay where it was, not run off onto the floor where it would soak into the carpet. The small lake of cold tea chose not to listen.

"Hello? Tempest?"

"Yup." Tempest ripped off a sock and used it to absorb the liquid. "Sorry, you caught me by surprise. It's early," he pointed out somewhat unnecessarily. "What can I do for you?"

"There's been another attack. I just got a call from my editor. He has a contact in the police, so he found out and wants me to cover it. I assumed you would want to know."

The sound of feet on the floor upstairs let him know Amanda was awake. Likely woken by the same ringing phone that interrupted his sleep, she was up sooner than he would have chosen.

"Um, yeah, thanks," Tempest mumbled, picking up the phone so he could take it with him as he carried the now wet sock to the sink. Rallying his brain, he asked, "Where?"

"In Barming. I'll send you the address. I'm leaving now. Will I see you there?" Tempest froze. Sharon was attractive and single and had made it clear on more than one occasion that she wanted to rekindle their past habit of casual liaisons.

"Um, yes," he tried, hoping there was no way to read anything into his reply.

"Super. I'll be sure to wear my good knickers." She ended the call without another word, but was she teasing or serious?

Unbidden, remembered images of Sharon both in and out of her good knickers swam into Tempest's consciousness.

"Who was that?" asked Amanda, making Tempest jump and squeal in guilty fright.

"Ah, you're up," he said, dropping the sock and heading for the kettle. "Would you like tea or coffee?"

"Neither thanks. I'm going for a run," she said while pulling her ponytail tight.

Now paying attention, Tempest could see she wore running gear. Hair ready, she bent at the waist to stretch off her back, then picked up her right foot to work her quad.

Tempest filled the kettle anyway. He was going out and would take a brew with him in a travel mug. He also needed something to eat.

His phone pinged with an incoming text: the address from Sharon.

"Who was on the phone?" Amanda repeated her earlier question, her voice casual, like she was just making conversation.

Tempest wasn't fooled, but he hadn't done anything wrong despite the images of the half-naked reporter now swirling around his brain and refusing to go away.

Sounding equally nonchalant, he said, "Sharon Maycroft, the journalist."

Amanda stretched off her other quad. "You mean the slutty one who wants to ride you like a fairground and used to do precisely that?"

Knowing he wasn't going to win the conversation no matter what strategy he employed, Tempest said, "Yes, that one. The wizard struck again. Her editor sent her to the scene and she was good enough to pass on the information. I'm heading there as soon as I can get myself ready."

"You want me to walk the dogs?"

"That would be super helpful, yes."

Amanda stopped stretching and faced Tempest, her arms folded across her ample chest.

"You need to watch yourself with her, Tempest."

It wasn't in his nature to display negative emotions in her direction, but he couldn't help feeling Amanda was being unnecessarily hard on him.

"She's just a source."

"Mm-Hmmm. She wants your sauce."

"That's not something I can control, babe, but answer me this – do you think I will jeopardise us to fool around with her."

"That's not how most guys think, Tempest."

"I'm not most guys."

Amanda didn't have an instant reply for once and had to admit, "No, I guess you're not. Sorry. I wasn't trying to suggest you would cheat, but …"

"You've been burned before. I get it. Everyone gets burned at some point." Was now the right time to propose? The ring was upstairs, but they were having a heartfelt conversation about their feelings for each other.

"Look, I'm going to go, okay." Amanda crossed the room to drop a gentle kiss on his lips. "You'll be gone before I get back, so have a good day and I'll see you at the office or back here later."

She was out the door ten seconds later leaving Tempest with the sense of her lips on his. Images of Sharon Maycroft firmly banished from his mind, he closed his eyes, drew in a deep breath, and made a vow to ask the question before the week was done.

Patience

THURSDAY, JANUARY 4TH 0648HRS

Tempest stepped from his car with a travel mug full of tea in one hand and a bacon sandwich in the other. It wasn't exactly the most nutritious breakfast, but it was also something he ate only rarely, and it was warm which was good on such a cold morning.

The gauge in his car recorded the outside air at minus three degrees. Hardly balmy, but at the same time not really that cold when compared to other countries in winter.

Looking about, Tempest peeled back a little more of the foil keeping his sandwich warm and took a bite. Had he not been looking for Sharon and so focused on the scene to his front, he might have noticed the two men in their car.

On the opposite side of the street from the latest victims' house, they hid from the cold in a van displaying a white goods delivery firm on the sides.

"It's the same guy," the driver said to the man in the passenger seat.

"Zephyrus was right."

"Yeah, but he didn't know who it was."

The passenger twitched his eyebrows. "Do we know who it is?"

The driver nodded. "Yeah. That's Tempest Michaels." He pulled out his phone and searched the name to prove he wasn't wrong.

"Is that a problem?"

The driver shrugged. "That's for Zephyrus to decide. Probably not though. He's just another name on the list of people to kill."

Deciding he'd seen enough, the driver slipped the gearbox into first and set off down the street. By the time they passed the man they'd been sent to look out for, he was on the pavement and talking to a smoking hot redhead.

Tempest's concerns that Sharon might continue flirting and making suggestive comments evaporated seconds after joining her on the street outside the victims' house. Professional and businesslike, her only interest in Tempest appeared to be his ability to add to her story.

"It's a serial killer, Tempest. Do you know how rare that is in England?"

"Try not to sound too excited."

Sharon frowned at him. "But it is exciting, Tempest. This is a big story for me. I'm a small-time reporter working for a local newspaper."

"And you have a segment on the local TV news."

"All of which I have worked hard to achieve. This, though ... it's stories like this one that can get me off the local stage and onto the national platforms. I'm not going to celebrate the deaths, but someone has to report what happened here and my work hasn't done your business any harm."

She made a fair point.

Diverting the conversation, Tempest asked, "What can you tell me?"

"The victims are a husband and wife. They were killed in their bed."

"How?"

"Asphyxiated is what I have been told."

"Asphyxiated? Like strangled?"

"Apparently not. It seems they died from lack of oxygen, but they were in their bed. They weren't gagged or bound and there's nothing to indicate their airways were blocked. They just stopped breathing."

"Like magic," Tempest murmured to himself.

"Yes, but you're the leading authority on all things not being what they seem, Tempest. What's your theory? Oh, hold on, don't answer that yet." Sharon fished her phone out and activated the record app.

"I started my investigation less than twenty-four hours ago. I don't have a theory yet beyond confidently saying Zephyrus Frostwind is anything but a wizard. He has some impressive tricks, I can't deny that, but that's all they are. My focus right now is on figuring out who he really is. I think we can assume the name he's using is fake."

"Like a stage name," Sharon added.

Tempest said, "That's right," but his brain had started to fire. Was it a stage name? He'd entered it into a search engine to see if he got any hits. Which he didn't, but that didn't mean anything. The internet is filled with information, but it doesn't contain everything.

A man with a TV camera called to get Sharon's attention. "We're going live in fifteen, okay?"

"I want to interview Tempest."

Tempest didn't want to be interviewed. Not yet when he had no answers, but he need not have worried.

Her producer shook his head. "No, we're going with the chief inspector. He has a statement and is leading the investigation."

Sharon said, "Just one moment," and left Tempest where he was to argue her case.

Left alone, Tempest turned his attention to the house and the police buzzing around it. He wouldn't be able to get inside, which is what he wanted, but as he thought that a familiar face exited the property.

"Patience!" Tempest waved to get her attention and started in her direction. He hadn't expected to see her. In fact, he'd thought she was still off work. When he got stabbed at the conclusion of the Grimm Fairytale's case, she took a crossbow bolt to her chest, just below her left clavicle.

Weirdly, she was wearing a suit and not her uniform. Recently promoted to sergeant, her presence at the scene wasn't that much of a surprise, but why would she be there if she wasn't working?

Patience saw Tempest coming but continued to talk to a colleague. They were on the step outside the house, Patience clearly giving the younger man instructions. With a nod, he set off down the path to the street, leaving Patience alone.

Tempest first met her shortly after becoming acquainted with Amanda. At the time, both women were police constables, but Amanda was already looking for a new career and found it working with Tempest.

She was trimmer than she used to be, Tempest noted, and her hair was less wild and more professionally tamed than he'd ever seen it. The suit went with her heels and coat, the whole ensemble making her look like she ought to be in charge.

"Morning."

"Hey, Tempest. No shock that you are here. This one of your cases?"

"You tell me. Did anyone find a black and white business card with Zephyrus Frostwind on it?"

Patience nodded, her eyes on the skyline. "Yeah. They did. This makes it five dead in just a couple of weeks."

"What's with the suit?" Tempest couldn't resist asking.

Patience looked down at herself and smiled. "You like it? I've had a career shift."

Perplexed for a second, Tempest made the leap soon enough. "CID?"

"Yup. I passed the exam in the summer. They offered me a position in Canterbury almost straight away, but I wanted to stay local. I had to wait this long for a place to become available in Maidstone."

Tempest said, "Congratulations," and he meant it. "So, you're Detective Sergeant Woods now?"

Patience grinned. "Only to the people I don't like. Everyone else calls me Patience. I figure I have at least another promotion before I need to change that."

"Well, I am very pleased for you."

"Thanks."

"When did you start back at work? In fact, scrap that, how are you feeling?"

Patience shrugged. "The mental scarring is worse than the wound. That's almost completely healed. I started back at work yesterday. I needed the distraction. How about you?"

"Oh, I'm okay. I have Amanda to take care of me."

"Yeah, I bet that makes a difference." Patience looked wistful.

Having heard her remark about mental scarring,

Tempest debated asking her whether it was affecting her sleep.

"You know, if you want to talk about it ..."

Patience shook her head. "Not right now. Maybe another time. With vodka."

Tempest accepted her response with a smile of support. Moving on, as that was her request, he said, "Okay then, what can you tell me that I don't already know?"

"That would depend on what you already know, but I'll give you the bullet points."

Two minutes later, Tempest had the names of the victims, their ages, and what they did for a living. He learned the police discovered the first two victims had received calling cards before they were killed, just like Valerie and Richard. Patience ended by giving him details about the most recent attack which included the bedroom door exploding inward.

"The crime scene guys found traces of explosive around the doorframe. Nothing magical about that."

"Nothing magical about any of it," Tempest replied.

"No, but the use of explosives bumps this guy up the list. The anti-terrorist teams are making noises and trying to get involved. They want to know where he got it from."

"No doubt. Anything else I should know?"

"Only that Quinn is running things as usual. CID have the case, but there's no getting away from Quinn's need to be at the front. The higher-ups love him for some reason, so he always gets his way."

"It's because he always makes it look as if the right result came about by his hand alone."

"Did I hear my name being used?" asked Chief Inspector Quinn as he exited the house behind Patience.

"Yes, Ian," Tempest fired back instantly. "I was

compiling a list of life's biggest turd buckets, and you made it in at number one."

Quinn offered him an amused expression. "Lovely. DS Woods, I'm quite certain you have work to be doing and this isn't it. Off you go."

Patience grimaced, her face unseen by the chief inspector.

Tempest said, "I'll catch up with you later."

Turning around, she went back inside the house to leave the two men facing each other.

"What are you doing here, Mr Michaels? I thought your client sacked you?"

"I have another client, Ian."

A muscle in Quinn's jaw twitched. He wasn't happy to see Tempest and never had been despite sending him work several times in the past.

Sharon's producer arrived looking harried. "Are you ready, Chief Inspector? We need to get you into position."

Dismissing Tempest as though he were not even there, Quinn followed the TV producer to a spot on the pavement. Tempest let him go. He had more important things to do.

Phone Calls

THURSDAY, JANUARY 4TH 0823HRS

When he got to the office, Amanda was already there but heading out.

"We got a call about a unicorn," she revealed with a grin. "I put it on the list already."

Tempest would check to see how the standings looked now and needed to add wizard under his own name. The list was started by Jane when she investigated a swamp creature and wanted to record herself as the first of the team to do so. It quickly became a competition with the three detectives scoring themselves against rows labelled werewolf, vampire, goblin, demon, et cetera.

Tempest had the only sewer monster so far but neither of the ladies wanted to tick that box. Now Amanda had a unicorn to investigate and had wasted no time adding it to the list.

"Gotta go." she brushed her lips past his cheek on her way out the back door.

Tempest dumped his things in his office and crossed to

the coffee machine. There hadn't been enough sleep, and he needed caffeine.

"Would you like one, Marjory?"

Marjory looked up from her keyboard. "No, thank you."

He made himself a double expresso in a tiny cup and carried it back to his desk. On the map on the wall, he checked the geography and pushed a pin into the site of the most recent attack. Then he added the names of the victims to the list and stood back, shaking his head.

There was no obvious connection between anyone. Ninety minutes later, he was still trying to find a connection when his stomach rumbled. It was mid-morning, and the bacon sandwich had not sustained him.

The fruit bowl in the corner of his office was empty, save for a rather sad looking banana, so he hooked his coat and took a walk. A small supermarket sat less than a hundred yards down the High Street, so after enquiring if Marjory wanted anything, he set off.

His phone rang before he'd covered five yards. Pulling it from his pocket he saw the name displayed: Richard Cowell.

"Richard, good morning."

"I thought you said this guy wasn't a wizard!"

"That's right. I ..."

"I've just seen him on the internet! And you for that matter. You said it was nothing more than a bunch of tricks and said you could catch him."

"It is just a bunch of tricks, Mr Cowell. There's no such thing as magic."

"Ha! So you say. I've seen my fair share of stage magicians and none of them could do what this guy can. That was magic if ever I saw it."

"I can assure you it was not. I got to see it first hand and up close ..."

"Yes," Richard cut him off again, "He almost barbecued you! You're fired. I'm not paying another penny. I told that big friend of yours to sling his hook, too. I didn't like the way my wife looked at him. Good day, Mr Michaels."

Tempest wasn't used to being hung up on. Nor was he used to losing clients but was down two in twelve hours. It didn't sit well, but there wasn't a whole lot he could do about it. The lack of paying clients meant he could just drop the case and work on something else. He could find out where Amanda was and join her on the unicorn hunt, but his phone rang again and this time the name displayed was that of his mother.

Tempest made a point not to sigh. Even without answering to find out what she wanted, he could already tell it wouldn't be anything good. His mother rarely called for anything good. Occasionally, there would be an invitation for Sunday lunch, but more often than not she wanted to complain. The subject would vary from living in sin with Amanda, to the lack of grandchildren, which seemed to sit in direct contradiction of the living in sin complaint. Or she would feel a need to berate him about missing church because he was working, or that he worked as a paranormal investigator which had to be against God even though she wasn't entirely sure how.

Resigning himself to the imminent earbashing, Tempest thumbed the button to connect the call.

"Hello, Mother."

"I've just seen you on the internet."

Tempest grimaced.

"You were on fire!"

"Only a little bit."

"Mavis at the hairdressers showed me. It's Thursday and you know I get my hair done on a Thursday. It's not fair for you to have things happen to you right before a Thursday, Tempest."

"It wasn't exactly what I had in mind for Wednesday night, mother, but if you've seen the video then you saw my client. I was at her house because a man believed to be responsible for five deaths now was targeting her too."

"Oh, don't give me all that hero nonsense, Tempest Michaels. I get enough of that silliness from your father. You could have been hurt."

Tempest figured it was best not to mention the sear marks on his lower legs or the fifteen separate holes where nails penetrated his skin.

"I'm fine, mother. There's nothing for you to worry about. I will be more careful next time we meet."

"Next time! You can't be serious! He set you on fire, Tempest!"

"The footage makes it look worse than it was."

"The footage makes it look like he's a magician, Tempest. I know you're going to tell me there's no such thing as magic, but you used to believe in it."

"I did?"

"Yes. When you were little, we had magicians come to the house for birthday parties. You and your sister both loved them."

Tempest didn't answer. He'd already turned around and was running back to the office.

"Got to go, mum. Talk later. Bye!"

Naming the Wizard

THURSDAY, JANUARY 4TH 1008HRS

Running back through the door to his office with enough vigour he made Marjory swear in shock, Tempest didn't slow down until he got to the private office at the back. He threw an apology Marjory's way but was too absorbed by the possibility of his new line of thought to check she was okay.

There was no good reason to be as excited as he was, yet a voice in the back of Tempest's brain told him he was onto something.

Obviously, he couldn't talk to the deceased persons, but he had their names and would be able to track down their relatives. Or he could call Patience as she might be able to ask the questions on his behalf, but there was someone he could call straight away.

He just had to hope she would answer.

When she picked up, Tempest was quick to say, "Valerie, I just had a breakthrough in your case. Don't hang up."

"But you're not on my case, Tempest. I let you go, remember."

Brushing it off as unimportant, Tempest asked, "Did you ever have a magician for one of your kids' birthday parties?"

"I'm sorry, what?"

"A magician, Valerie. This could be important. He killed two more people last night."

"Oh, my God! That could have been me!"

"Yes, Valerie, but it wasn't." He chose not to remind her that she survived because he was there to get in the wizard's way. "Magicians, Valerie. Did you ever hire one to entertain your kids?"

"Yeah, once. He was terrible and the kids hated him. I complained and refused to pay him. He got shirty about it, but he left when my husband told him to."

Tempest bit his lip and went for broke. "What was his name, Valerie?"

A tannoy message echoed in the background from her end of the call. "That's last boarding for my flight. I booked a place in the South of France. I've got to go."

"No, wait! I need a name."

"I don't remember, Tempest. It was years ago. It was The Great something-or-other. I've really got to go." The line disconnected to leave Tempest staring at the list of victims and the map. Was he onto something or not?

The people Zephyrus singled out seemed completely random. There was nothing obvious to connect them, but the moment his mother brought up the subject of kids' entertainers, he saw a link that could run between every name on the list. There was no easy way to prove the connection, not without finding more potential victims with the Frostwind business card, but there was another person he could call.

Richard Cowell picked up on the first ring.

"Richard, it's Tempest Michaels, please don't hang up."

"I'm a busy man. Give me a reason why I shouldn't."

"I think I know who the wizard is." He was stretching things to the extreme, but with Richard's help, assuming he was right about the connection, it was entirely possible they might put a name to the mysterious character.

A pause followed, broken when Richard finally said, "Okay, I'll bite. Who is it?"

"We'll get to that," Tempest stalled. "Earlier you said you had seen your share of stage magicians. I didn't pick up on it at the time, but you were talking about people you have hired in the past, weren't you."

"What about it?"

"Did you ever have to fire any of them?"

"A few. Their acts got boring or were too repetitive. Or their assistants left. Everyone knows the punters only turn up because they want to see the sexy magician's assistant wearing virtually nothing."

"Okay, Richard. I need you to cast your mind back to think of one person who might have held a grudge after you let him go. Is there anyone who vowed revenge or …"

"Norman Pickett." Richard provided the name without Tempest needing to finish his sentence. "Went by the stage name The Great Howduzhe. Last I heard he was doing kids parties."

In his office, Tempest punched the air.

Forcing himself to calm, Tempest asked, "I don't suppose you might have an address or a phone number for him, would you?"

Mayhem

THURSDAY, JANUARY 4TH 1026HRS

Richard didn't have a number, but said he might be able to find one if he had his secretary go through his records. Tempest thanked him and asked that he please do so, but expected to find an address long before Richard could call back.

Before he cleared the line the nightclub owner did his best to douse the fire in Tempest's heart. "Norman Pickett can't be the one you want."

"Why not."

"Because he's pathetic. It's the chief reason why I let him go. The punters couldn't warm to him. He wasn't bad as a magician, by which I mean his illusions were better than a lot of the acts I see, but he worked alone, which is always a mistake. You've got to have a sexy assistant. Especially if you look like Norman Pickett. He had a face perfect for radio, if you know what I am saying. His real issue was a total lack of charisma. He was boring. One of the most boring people I've ever met, in fact. I was stuck for an act at the time, and gave him a shot, but he didn't last long. You can't keep a guy on stage if the punters are booing and complaining. So, trust me, this isn't your guy. Norman Pickett doesn't have the gumption to kill anyone."

Tempest acknowledged the advice, but Norman was the only connection so far and had to be explored. Sitting at his desk, it took only a few minutes to find and confirm an address. There was a phone number for the house, but Tempest wasn't going to call it. This required a face-to-face approach.

Itching to get going, he took a slow breath and allowed himself some extra minutes to check the target's social media presence. An up-to-date photograph would eliminate the need to question if he had the right person. It took only seconds to find the right profile.

Norman Pickett wasn't the type to constantly update his social media. In fact, his most recent post was more than a year old, but there were pictures. They showed Norman surrounded by kids at what was obviously a little person's birthday party. He wore a silky black cloak and a top hat over an everyday outfit of jeans and shirt.

Not blessed with looks, Norman's hair had receded away from his forehead, he had a hook nose, a few spots around his chin, despite clearly being in his fifties, and his lanky frame suffered from a pot belly. Regardless, he had, at some point in the past, even if not currently, been a children's entertainer.

Problematically, if asked to describe the man he fought, Tempest would have employed the word 'stocky' or perhaps 'solidly built'. There could be padding inside the cloak to make him look broader than he appeared in the pictures, but when he shoulder-barged him to the ground just as the stun grenade went off, the impression he got was of a man with muscle. Then there was the beard. It could be fake;

that was easy enough to do, but Norman had no facial hair in any of the photographs Tempest found.

Regardless, he had a lead that linked at least two of the calling card recipients and was going to pursue it.

"I'm going out again," he let Marjory know, leaving his office in a hurry. "Not sure when I'll be back." Marjory might have replied, but Tempest was out the door and moving.

Prudence demanded he call the police to alert them to the possible identity of the killer, or that he at least let Big Ben or Amanda know where he was going, but Richard sounded so certain Norman Pickett could not be the wizard, Tempest chose to get a look for himself first.

The address listed under the only N. Pickett in the area was a street in Cobham, a village just off the M2 motorway heading north toward London. At this time of the day with the roads clear of rush hour traffic, it would take less than twenty minutes to get there.

Seventeen minutes after starting his car, he drove past the house. It looked ordinary enough, which is to say there was no ominous black cloud hovering above it, no dead tree in the front garden littered with cawing crows. Maybe a serial killer lived there and maybe Richard Cowell was right. There was one good way to find out.

A quick check of his watch confirmed the time at 1058hrs. Norman ought to be at work, and it was fine if he was. If there was no one home, Tempest would knock at the neighbours until he found someone who could tell him a little more about the man he wanted. If he had a job and was working, Tempest could find him there. The cloak meant he never saw the wizard's face, but he heard the man's voice and would recognise it if he heard it again.

Leaving his car a few yards down the street, Tempest

locked up and paused in front of the house. Dressed in casual office wear and an elegant camel-coloured winter coat, he was anything but dressed for tackling a serial killer. Still, he wasn't really expecting to find Norman at home, and with that in mind he made his way up the garden path to knock on the door.

The house was a small semi-detached with yellow paint and a trim front garden. Whatever else Norman might be, he took care in the appearance of his house. The step outside the front door still showed brush marks where someone swept it recently, and the frosted windows set into the door had been polished.

Tempest pressed a finger to the buzzer and stepped back to wait.

A shadow passed through the light inside the house almost immediately, the frosted panes making it impossible to see who was coming. The sound of a security chain coming out of its guide and dropping to rattle against the door preceded a lock turning. The door swung inward to reveal a man Tempest could easily recognise as Norman Pickett. However, while Norman still looked like Norman from the chin up, everything south was different.

For a start, the pot belly was gone. Norman wore a pair of smart trousers over George boots, and a waistcoat complete with a chain that probably led to a fob watch over a neat white shirt. Tempest noted the ensemble as something he might wear but changing outfits or even wardrobes is relatively easy. All one needs is a little money. Changing one's shape is a lot harder, but that was what Norman had done.

Dieting could explain the absence of the belly, but Norman now had shoulders. The cuffs of his shirt were rolled back to show the bottom half of his forearms where

Tempest could see thick veins over ropey muscle. Norman had bulked up.

Tempest absorbed all that detail while the door was still swinging open. He had a business card in his hand and was about to introduce himself when Norman's eyes flared wide. Still coming forward to fill the door, he reversed direction and threw the door to shut it as he ducked back inside.

There was no need to question the reason for his abrupt reaction. Norman recognised his opponent from the previous evening.

With the door swinging shut, Tempest threw his whole body forward to stop it. Pain shot through his foot where it jammed into the closing gap, but the door bounced back and clanged against the wall a moment later when he powered through it.

Knowing now that he had the right person, Tempest wanted to call the police. There wasn't time for that, though.

Ahead of him, Norman darted to his left, going through a door into another room. Tempest followed running full pelt. The last thing he wanted was to give Norman a chance to be ready, but a two second head start proved to be all the wizard needed.

Hot on his heels, Tempest burst into the kitchen to find Norman waiting. He was moving too fast to make out what he had in his hands, but Tempest instinctively ducked, doing so just as a jet of flame came for his face. He couldn't see what Norman had in his hands, and there was no time to figure it out. Whatever it was, it produced flame and for the second time in less than twenty-four hours Tempest was on fire.

His camel-coloured winter coat, an expensive item he favoured, was alight where the flames licked the material between Tempest's shoulder blades. Had he not been moving so fast and on a direct collision course with Norman, he might have been in real trouble.

His ducking stance allowed him to come in under Norman's arms, driving one shoulder into the wizard's solar plexus. Unaware of the flames licking up his back to singe his hair, Tempest drove Norman into the stove with enough force to jar the device from his hands.

It clattered away behind him, but Tempest hadn't won yet.

He swung a punch into Norman's ribs, landing a solid blow, but the wizard had his back against a solid surface and used it to drive Tempest away. The few inches of room that gave him were enough to free his arms.

Tempest came again, wanting to keep things as close as possible. If he gave Norman room, he would be able to use any weapons he might have secreted about his clothing, but in the five seconds since his coat caught fire the flames had taken hold. Suddenly feeling the heat, both through his clothing and on the back of his head, Tempest had to spin and duck to get into space.

He whipped the coat off, throwing it aside just in time to meet Norman's attack. Kitchens are loaded with weapons, so Tempest was relieved not to see a knife coming his way. Not that a cast iron le Creuset pan was much better.

It cleaved the air in front of his face when Norman swung it. The weight of it ought to have pulled him off balance, but Norman had a second pan in his other hand to counter the effect and he was already aiming it at Tempest's skull.

Instinct dictated he should go backwards to get away, but many years of martial arts training allowed Tempest to view the fight with a calmness few would muster. Instead of moving away, he stepped in, taking the swing early so the meat of Norman's arm collided with his ribs and the pan flew from his hand.

With their chests almost touching, Tempest trapped Norman's left arm under his right and stepped to his left to pull him off balance. Norman continued to fight, his strength a match for the former soldier even if his skills were not.

Struggling as he tried to get Norman down to the carpet, Tempest coughed. The air was smoky and a glance revealed the source: his coat. Except it wasn't just his coat on fire now. It had landed in the gap between the kitchen door and the hallway where it had promptly set fire to the carpet.

And the wall.

Tempest coughed again. One thing about a fight is that you are going to get out of breath. Adrenalin, maximum effort, and using almost every muscle in your body at once places enormous demand on even the fittest.

Norman started to choke. He was trying to say something but heaved and choked instead.

Unable to draw a proper breath, Tempest changed his tactic. It was time to take the fight outside. There were patio doors leading from the open-plan kitchen to the back garden, but still battling Norman there was no option to just open them and walk through. However, as they wrestled to get the upper hand, Norman's foot snagged on a rug. He fell, pulling Tempest with him and the pair crashed through the glass door as one.

Not that the glass smashed. It was toughened and designed to not break. The weaker point was the hinge which snapped under the combination of mass and inertia.

Both men tumbled outside, smacking into the patio where Tempest finally got the better of his opponent.

A hard right cross took the fight out of the wizard. His grip on Tempest faltered which was all he needed. Fire ate at the house, lighting the scene with hellish dancing flames when Tempest scrambled to get behind his opponent. He didn't want to cause injury – claiming to have used minimal force always helps – but he did want Norman unconscious. A sleeper hold would do it and now that he was stunned, it was easy to apply.

Wrapping his right arm around Norman's neck, Tempest applied the pressure he needed to switch off the man's lights. Predictably, Norman had no clue how to break the hold, consequently clawing and scratching at the arm in his bid to get free. Needing no more than a few seconds, Tempest could feel the wizard's fight leaving him when Norman elected to speak.

His words came out more as a rasp than anything else, but there was no mistaking it when he croaked, "My mum's inside."

The Fire

THURSDAY, JANUARY 4TH 1105HRS

Norman lost consciousness before the full impact of his words hit home. Going floppy, his body slumped against Tempest's, partially pinning him until he could manoeuvre his legs and roll. Now free, Tempest stared at the house.

Was Norman's mother really inside? Knowing he was about to lose, it was possible the wizard employed the ruse to make Tempest go back inside the house. He wouldn't be unconscious for long, so maybe it was a last-ditch attempt to escape.

Jumping to his feet, Tempest knew he couldn't risk it.

Out of breath and with his heart banging inside his chest, Tempest ran back to the patio doors. The fire had taken hold, but even though flames were licking across the ceiling both sides of the kitchen door, it was not to the point where he thought the house was beyond saving.

If he had something to fight the fire with. Which he didn't.

Sticking his head through the space left by the broken patio door, he glanced around the smoke-filled kitchen.

There could be a fire extinguisher tucked inside a cupboard ready for the homeowner to deploy, but there wasn't one on display. A garden hose might do the trick, but there wasn't one of those in sight either.

Accepting defeat, Tempest sucked in a deep breath and ran inside. There were two doors leading out of the kitchen. The one where the fire started, which led into the hall, and a second one to the right that went into a dining room.

The dining room led to a living room where Tempest hoped to discover Norman's mother. Finding it empty, he hugged the floor to suck in a fresh lungful of air. It wasn't devoid of smoke, but he could breathe it, unlike the air at head height.

Keeping low, he ran from the living room to the hallway where the flames and heat were almost too fierce to pass. A breeze coming through the still open front door fanned the flames, swirling the smoke. Using his arms to shield his face, Tempest raced to the bottom of the stairs. He wanted to call out, but there was no way to do so without choking.

Pushing himself to get it done before he ran out of air, Tempest took the stairs three at a time. Expecting to find three bedrooms – one at the front and two smaller ones at the back - plus a bathroom, Tempest crashed through the first door.

"Who are you," said a withered old lady sitting on a two-person sofa. There was no bed in the room, just some bookcases, an old record player, and a wall mounted TV opposite the sofa. Norman's mum didn't look anything like him, but had that generic, wrinkly lady in her late eighties appearance. A head framed with curly white hair finished the look. "Here, what's with all that smoke?" she asked, noticing the fog following Tempest into the room.

Speaking as calmly as he could, Tempest said, "I'm

afraid the house is on fire, madam. Please come with me. I need to get you outside."

"Where's my Norman?"

"Already outside." Tempest took hold of the lady's hand. If they dawdled, the fire would reach the bottom of the stairs and that would leave them facing an escape through a window. He would be fine dropping to land on his feet, but estimated that Norman's mother would not fare so well.

However, before he could assist the lady to get to her feet, whereupon he could scoop her into his arms – she looked to weigh about ninety pounds – she hit him with her walking stick. The blow smacked into his right ear and though it didn't contain a lot of force, there really is only one winner in a contest of flesh versus old hunk of wood.

"You're not a firefighter!" she pointed out. "Where's my Norman? Norman!" she shouted. "Norman!"

Wincing from the stingy ear, Tempest grabbed the walking stick before she could land a second hit and did precisely what he should have done in the first place. Taking care, he shoved both arms under her bony legs and picked her up.

"I'll take you to him," he grunted. He'd taken a fresh breath when he burst into her room, but the air was filled with smoke now. His lungs ached, his head pounded with the need to breathe, and his legs were going to start shaking if he didn't replenish the oxygen in his body soon.

Norman's mother fought to get free, but without her walking stick, she didn't have any other weapons she could bring to bear. At least that's what Tempest thought until she sunk her teeth into him.

Halfway down the stairs, he was heading for the door when she bit hold of his left pec. Instant and excruciating pain almost made him drop her and it was only because he smacked her head on the wall when he spasmed in shock that he didn't. The blow to her skull jolted her upper set free, so as she opened her mouth to cry out in pain, her dentures dropped free.

"My geeth! My geeth!"

"Not going back for them!"

Tempest hit the carpet at the base of the stairs and ran through the front door into the blissful cold air outside. There he sucked in a grateful breath.

There were neighbours in the street, horrified faces staring at the burning house. Two women in their fifties came running the moment they saw Norman's mother in Tempest's arms.

"Agatha, are you all right?" one asked.

"Where's Norman?" enquired the second as both women came to the old lady's aid.

"My gat. He needs to go back in for my gat!"

"Gat?" Tempest had no idea what a 'gat' was, but if it was in the house, it could stay there.

"Trixie? Trixie is in the house?" asked one of the women.

"Dat's what I'm daying. My gat is still in there!"

"Her cat!" explained the neighbour. "You have to rescue her cat!"

Certain she must be mad and thinking what he needed to do was check on Norman before he recovered and absconded, Tempest managed to gasp, "Lady, the house is on fire."

"Some hero you are!" she spat and ran to the house herself. Not that she went inside. One look at the inferno raging in the hallway was enough to turn her around.

"Oh, no! Look!" said the second neighbour. She had her

right arm angled up at the house, pointing to the first-floor window where a tabby cat scratched at the window glass unable to get out.

Hating himself, Tempest tapped his right trouser pocket. His trusty multi-tool was tucked beneath the clean, white cotton handkerchief he always carried. He didn't need it very often, but when he did it was priceless.

Going back into the house wasn't an option, but he could see another way to rescue the cat. More neighbours were coming out of their houses, so with a growing audience, he dragged a wheelie bin to the side of the small brick and tile awning above the front door and clambered upward.

The slope of the awning made it hard to balance and then he needed to stretch to reach the window. Holding on by the fingernails of one hand, Tempest took out his multi-tool, folded it out to reveal the pliers, and used them to smash the glass.

At least, he tried to.

Modern glass doesn't break, and the cat, which was meowing at him from the other side with ever increasing urgency, vanished the first time he whacked on the window. Scared, it bolted into the smoke, vanishing from sight.

Tempest whacked the window again, hoping the animal would come to him if he could break the glass and call for it, but jubilant cries from below accompanied the sight of the cat sauntering out from the front of the house a moment later.

Clearly, he could get down now, but in attempting to recover his outstretched position, he discovered his fingertips were at their limit. They lost their fight to keep hold of the wall and he fell, pitching forward to land in the flower bed beneath the living room window. The major problem with that was the abundance of rose bushes growing there. They had been pruned, but that left plenty of old growth with big, spikey thorns.

Untangling himself from the plants that seemed determined not to relinquish their grip on his clothing, Tempest was relieved to hear the fire brigade coming. They turned into the far end of the street, the rumbling engine audible between the whoops and parps of the siren.

Two more of Norman's neighbours came forward to help him escape the roses, but Tempest's attention was on the police car coming from the other direction.

The fire was an accident, and it was tragic, but he'd found Zephyrus Frostwind, and that would justify everything.

The Arrest

THURSDAY, JANUARY 4TH 1129HRS

Tempest thanked those who helped free him from the thorns and made his way to the street to flag down the squad car. Norman was yet to make an appearance, which could mean he was still out cold. Tempest wanted to check on him and would have done so had the cop car not been so close.

If Norman had come around and chosen to leave the area, they could coordinate the search for him. For that matter, if he was still at the property, they could take him into custody, but as the squad car drew near a scream of rage told Tempest the fight was back on.

Norman was not only conscious, he was back on his feet and ready for round two.

Running down his garden path, he yelled, "You burned down my house!" His eyes were mad, his teeth were showing, and he was running straight at Tempest like a man possessed.

Turning to face him, Tempest blocked a punch coming for his head, hooked an arm around Norman's back and swivelled. The wizard might be carrying some muscle, but he had no idea how to use it. Arms windmilling, Norman flew across the bonnet of a Mercedes to land out of control on the other side.

The small crowd of onlookers gasped and wailed to see two grown men fighting in the street. The fire engine pulled to a stop, the men and women on board ready to tackle the fire but distracted by the brawl occurring five yards away.

Tempest followed Norman, going around the car rather than over it, but arriving in the street before Norman could get up.

The squad car's lights strobed and the siren whooped in warning. They were ten yards away and closing fast, but neither man paid them any mind.

Tempest wanted to have the wizard down on the ground and pinned before handing him off, but Norman was on his butt, all his limbs available so there was no easy way through without throwing himself on the ground to start wrestling.

Unhappy about the situation, the firefighter in charge slapped one of his burlier men on the shoulder and ran to stop the fight.

"He set fire to my house!" Norman shouted from the ground.

From the firefighters' perspective, the man on the ground looked like the victim. That he claimed the man stalking toward him was an arsonist or something further strengthened their belief. Especially when the claim wasn't denied.

They moved to intercept.

Tempest didn't want to hurt them, but when they blocked his path, using their combined size to keep Norman safe, he worried they might give him a chance to produce a weapon.

"That's the wizard!" He aimed an accusatory arm. "He's killed five people. He started the fire when he set my coat alight."

Running from their car, the cops came for the one man still being aggressive. The one on the ground looked like he was cowering. The one on his feet was wrestling with a pair of firefighters clearly at the scene to tackle the blazing inferno that was once a house.

"He's Zephyrus Frostwind," shouted Tempest. The cops were shouting for him to get on his knees, but he wasn't about to do so. "I'm Tempest Michaels," he announced, "and this is the killer half the police in the area are trying to catch. Call DS Woods."

Unfortunately, though they heard what he said, they both saw his refusal to get on the ground as resisting arrest. Realising his mistake about a second too late, Tempest eased up on trying to get to Norman and raised his hands. But he did so only half a second before his legs were swept out from under his body.

In the early days of his investigation business, getting arrested became a semi-regular occurrence, but it hadn't happened for months. Most of the cops knew who he was and he always turned out to be in the right. Too late to stop it from happening, he focused not on convincing them to let him go, but in reinforcing their need to arrest Norman too.

"He's mental!" Norman insisted. "Keeps saying I'm that crazy killer on the news. I used to do magic tricks at children's parties. He's got his wires crossed and thinks that makes me the wizard. He burst into my house and attacked me. Then he almost got my mum killed when he set the place on fire!"

The firefighters tackled the blaze, bringing it under control in just a few minutes, but the house was beyond saving. The breeze running in through the front and out via the broken patio door fed the flames like pouring on gasoline. Tempest didn't feel bad about Norman losing his things. He was heading to jail for multiple life sentences anyway, but his mum was a different story. Of course, the fire wasn't his fault, but Norman had spun things to make it sound like Tempest was the one to blame.

The first cops on the scene placed cuffs on both men – it was the only sensible move, and when the next ones arrived, they saw no reason to challenge the decision. Sooner or later someone senior would arrive, so why do something when that would single you out and potentially land you in the doodoo.

Tempest waited impatiently for someone with a brain to show up. Anyone would do. Anyone but Chief Inspector Quinn who was, of course, the one who attended the scene. Swearing under his breath, Tempest had to admit he could have predicted his arrival. The chief inspector was heading the taskforce investigating the wizard and probably got a call moments after he mentioned the case.

Quinn spotted Tempest sitting in the back of a squad car but took his sweet time coming to speak with him. Tempest watched him getting a report from the previous senior person on site, after which he was taken to speak with Norman.

His mother had been taken away in an ambulance; concerns over smoke inhalation enough to make the paramedics nervous when she started coughing. In contrast, Norman had been nowhere near the smoke and was nice and warm in the back of another squad car.

Ten minutes ticked by, each second grating against

Tempest's soul. When Quinn finally deemed it necessary to speak with him, he opened the car's back door and stood in the street, so the cold air swept in to chill the lone occupant.

"You advised my officers that the man you attacked is Zephyrus Frostwind. What makes you think that?"

"Detective work, Ian. He's the link between the victims. Richard Cowell hired and fired him from the Casino Rooms Nightclub in Rochester and Valerie Legg had him as a magician at a birthday party for one of her kids."

"And the other victims? What is his link to Gill Carson? How does he know Diane Meacock?"

"Undetermined. I got as far as the first two and came here to speak with the suspect. He took one look at me and bolted because he recognised me from last night."

"Yes. I asked him about that. He has an alibi for last night. He was at home watching television with his mother, a frail older lady who cannot manage by herself due to several debilitating illnesses. I am quite certain she will confirm his claim."

Tempest thought about getting whacked with her walking stick and wasn't so sure he would list her as frail.

"Ian, he's the one. I'm telling you. When I chased him into his house, he had a device that shot flame at me. It set my coat alight. That's how the fire started. The device is part of a suit he wears beneath his cloak. It's how he produces the fake lights and …"

"I'm going to stop you there, Mr Michaels. At the moment I have a man in custody who forced his way into a private residence, caused a fire, and committed assault. If there was any evidence to corroborate your claims, they went up in smoke. Mr Pickett will be questioned at length, but so far there is nothing tangible to link him to the deaths."

"Are you really that blind?"

"I am a professional law enforcement officer, Mr Michaels. That is what I am. It sets me apart from amateur detectives who think they can do what they want and always end up doing more harm than good. I tire of telling you the same things and of clearing up the messes you make." The chief inspector stepped back from the car and swung the door shut. Tempest heard him say, "Take him away," and moments later one of the first cops on the scene slid behind the steering wheel.

Tempest huffed out a sigh and laid back his head.

The Interview

THURSDAY, JANUARY 4TH 1952HRS

Tempest looked about the interview room trying to figure out how many separate times he'd found himself in it. Five or six was his best guess and only on one of those occasions had he been on the other side of the table.

The door opened and Patience Woods came through it chatting quietly with a male colleague Tempest didn't know. The uniform who escorted him to the interview room stepped out, leaving him with the two detectives.

He waited, feigning patience while inside he continued to boil.

They took their time, acting professionally unhurried as the police so often do. It was a good interview technique Tempest employed himself upon occasion. Bored and frustrated, when the questions finally come the interviewee is only too happy to talk, gabbling answers and spilling the beans.

Tempest felt a little insulted they would try such an amateur-hour tactic. He was also struggling a little with Patience's involvement. They had been friends for a couple of years, but he understood why she was in the room and that it was almost certainly a test designed by Chief Inspector Quinn. He knew of their relationship and was probably trying to prove Patience didn't have what it took to be a detective.

Tempest closed his eyes and waited. When they were finally ready, it was Patience who talked into the recording device to officially log the interview. Formal element complete, she then asked, "Do you know why you are here?"

"Is that an existential question?"

Patience narrowed her eyes and Tempest smiled innocently. He wasn't about to make things easy for her, not when it would do her no favours. The man sitting to her left had been introduced as Detective Inspector Harris which made him her boss. When they were done, he would be able to report that she handled the witness with complete detachment.

Patience tried again. "You were arrested outside the home of Norman Pickett where he lives with his mother Agatha Pickett. You have been charged with assault, affray, and depending on how this interview goes, could also be charged with trespass and destruction of property or possibly arson."

"Have you found the connection between Norman Pickett and the victims yet?"

Patience clearly hadn't been expecting the question. She flicked her eyes over to DI Harris before remembering her training and refocusing them on the interviewee.

"Norman Pickett is being interviewed separately, Tempest."

Tempest relaxed back into his chair and gave the officers sitting opposite his most confident smile. "Then there is little point wasting your time with me. All charges against me will be dropped the moment you identify him at Zephyrus Frostwind. I'm sure the house is unliveable, but I'm also quite certain you can get people inside to search it. The fire didn't rage for long enough to damage it structurally. Unless he is stashing them elsewhere, he will have a whole bunch of those business cards, his Frostwind outfit, and all the clever paraphernalia he wears beneath it to produce his 'magic'. So, while I accept your need to jump through certain hoops, I found the serial killer for you, and you need to focus your efforts on cracking him."

Patience opened her mouth to speak, but DI Harris lifted his hand, cutting her off so he could respond.

"I was warned to expect your lack of cooperation, and that your arrogance would allow you to justify your actions."

"Being right allows me to justify my actions."

DI Harris drew a slow breath through his nose. "Norman Pickett is, as DS Woods explained, being interviewed separately. However, there is nothing so far to indicate his links to your former clients, both of whom were content to reveal they sacked you from their cases, is anything more than coincidence. Mr Pickett worked as a children's entertainer for almost a decade. There must be thousands of families who hired him. You might also like to know his alibi for last night has been corroborated by a third party."

Tempest sat forward in his chair. "What third party?"

"An independent person who made a delivery to the house. At the approximate time you were assaulting a man you claim to be Zephyrus Frostwind at the property of Mrs Valerie Legg, Norman Pickett was answering his door. So, I think we shall dispense with any further discussion regarding your false allegations and focus instead on the very serious charges you face."

Tempest's mind raced. Was he wrong? The DI continued to talk, firing questions across the table, but Tempest made no attempt to answer them. He had no interests in what the police thought or what they were going to do next. He needed to analyse what he knew and check his memory to see if he could have somehow misconstrued Norman's reaction when he opened his front door.

Time passed, the interviewers frustrated by his refusal to respond or even acknowledge they were speaking. He wasn't getting out any time soon, that much was obvious, and to shut them up, Tempest demanded legal counsel, something he'd seen no need for initially. He doubted he really needed it now either, but it served as a way to return to the quiet of his cell where he would be able to think.

Two Places at Once

THURSDAY, JANUARY 4TH 2149HRS

Stephanie Greer checked the street behind her for the third time, a rising sense of paranoia creeping up her spine. There was no one there. Not that she could see, but a distant corner of her brain insisted she hurry home.

Not for the first time since leaving Emily's house, she cursed herself for accepting the glass of wine. Well, the second glass, anyway. She probably could have got away with the first one and still driven the mile and a half back to her house. It was late evening in suburbia; there would be no police patrols around to catch her drunk driving.

Yet she indulged her inner demon and took the second glass because it was tasty, because the first one made her feel relaxed for the first time all week, and because Emily would likely sink the entire bottle by herself if she didn't help to drink it.

Dumped by yet another boyfriend, this time after six months, which was long enough for Emily to think it might be going somewhere, she had called her childhood BFF and pleaded with her to visit. Stephanie just didn't know how to refuse. So she went, drank the wine, and now found herself walking home in the dark.

The streets were safe. That's what she kept telling herself, but then why did she feel so utterly convinced there was someone following her?

Keeping her pace quick but knowing she would have to take her shoes off if she wanted to go any faster, Stephanie wished she'd changed out of her work outfit before heading over to comfort her friend. Her own boyfriend, Neil, was out for a meal and some drinks with an international client. His boss saw such events as part of the job and Neil had long since stopped fighting to avoid them. In truth, Stephanie believed he liked the convenience of the excuse and all the free booze he got to drink at the company's expense.

Regardless, there had been no option to call him to pick her up, and now she questioned why she hadn't called a cab.

Craning her neck to look back down the street, she almost called out to ask, "Is there anyone there?" but the question sounded ridiculous in her head. Telling herself to stop being so stupid, she pointed her head back the way she was going.

And that was when she saw him.

A tall figure in a flowing black cloak hovered a few inches above the pavement no more than five yards ahead of her. He blocked her path, and something told her going around was not an option. Her feet ground to a halt.

A vague blue glow emanated from inside the cowl of his cloak. It cast an eerie light onto his black beard. Terrified, Stephanie looked around. Why wasn't there someone out walking their dog? Or teenagers hanging out on the street corner the way kids that age always do. Should she scream for help?

Stephanie thought all these things in the space between heartbeats, frozen to the spot with indecision. Only when the man raised his arms and blue light began to dance in the air before his hands did her limbs find their ability to move.

"Help! Help me!" she ran back the way she had come, screaming at the top of her lungs. It was late, but not so late that everyone would be asleep in their beds. But if they were awake, then they were watching TV or listening to music, and no matter how loudly she shouted, no one would hear her.

Except someone did. Miriam Hundal had just changed her baby's nappy for the umpteenth time that day and was carrying it outside to the bin when she heard Stephanie's terrified shouts. She wanted nothing more than to get the infant to sleep so she could take a bath, but the panicked cry for help came with the sound of running feet, and when she looked for the woman making all the racket, Stephanie saw her too.

Heart soaring, Stephanie yelled and waved with both arms. "Hey! Call the police! The wizard is after me!" If she could get inside the woman's house, they could shut the door and wait for the police to arrive.

Miriam didn't catch what the woman said. Only the part about calling the police came across clearly. She didn't want to be involved in whatever this was but knew she couldn't run back inside and shut the door either. Then she saw him, a black figure moving through the night. Light from the lampposts made him visible, but truly it was the magic in his hands that caught her eyes.

She beckoned and shouted, "Hurry!"

Stephanie did not need to be told, but rounding the end of the low wall separating the street from the garden, the heel of her right shoe decided it was time to snap. It couldn't take the change in direction. She went down, losing vital seconds, not that she was ever going to outrun the figure behind her.

He'd been toying with her, waiting for there to be a witness, for this time it was more necessary than ever. He allowed her enough time to get to her feet, then released his 'spell'.

Miriam watched in horror. The terrified woman had fallen but was back on her feet. The cloaked figure was too far away to catch her, but it turned out he didn't need to get within touching distance. Looking directly into the woman's eyes, Miriam saw the cloaked figure launch a handful of bright orange tendrils. They crossed the gap from his hands to the woman's body, latching onto her and wrapping around.

She froze instantly, her back arching and her limbs contorted as her whole body seemed to light up from within.

Speaking to the police later, Miriam would recall how she was convinced the wizard would come for her next only to be surprised when he turned around and walked away.

Changing Moods

FRIDAY, JANUARY 5TH 0618HRS

Tempest had been awake for some time when the cop delivered his breakfast on a tray. He was hungry, so he ate it, though it was neither hot nor tasty. The food did what it was supposed to do, which was fill his belly and provide energy. Still in his clothes from the previous day and with shoulders stiff from sleeping on a bed designed to be anything but comfortable, he waited for someone to come.

This was the pattern of events and he'd been in the same position enough times to know there was nothing to be gained by trying to make things move faster. He expected to be given a formal caution at some point in the next hour or so and to be released shortly thereafter. Whether there would then be a court date to follow he could not guess. He still smiled every time he called to mind the incident that landed him with a criminal record, but knew it wouldn't go in his favour when they viewed the charges against him.

Another hour crept by, but when the cell door opened, Tempest was surprised to find Patience outside. She had a coffee in her hand in a to-go cup from a place in Maidstone, and an irked expression on her face.

Tempest greeted her as the old friend she was. "Good morning, Patience."

Patience rolled her eyes. "You are one big pain in my butt all of a sudden."

The remark probably wasn't intended to make him laugh, but Tempest sniggered at her.

"The joys of promotion. Can't go goofing off all the time now."

"No," she whispered. "And it's so boring doing the right thing all the time."

Leaning on the doorframe, Tempest asked, "So what am I looking at?"

"You're going to be released, but it looks like Norman is pressing charges. I mean, his house did get torched."

"He's got worse than that coming, Patience. Give me a day or so and I'll deliver him back here with all the evidence you'll need for a conviction." With a night in a cell to run ideas through his head, Tempest had a loose plan ready to go.

"Um, I hate to break it to you, but Norman Pickett really isn't the wizard. There was another murder last night and it happened while he was still in custody."

Perplexed, Tempest refused to accept that he was wrong and said, "Copycat. Has to be."

"The descriptions match. He left a witness and what she saw was too close to the footage in The Vault for it to be anyone else. He hit his victim with some kind of magical weapon that stopped her heart."

Tempest could think of nothing to say. Ever since his interview the previous evening, he'd fought against a taunting inner voice that wanted him to believe he'd got it all wrong. If he was wrong, he would be charged for attacking Norman and invading his home. That being the case he would go to prison again and for a longer spell this time. What would that do to his relationship with Amanda?

Patience provided the name of the victim and a few more details before handing Tempest over to a constable in uniform who escorted him back to processing. In a daze, he took back his possessions and signed for them, wondering all the time how Norman had done it.

There was no doubt in his mind that Norman was Zephyrus Frostwind. He'd taken one look at the man on his doorstep and bolted. Then he'd used a fire making weapon that fitted to his arm, just like he used outside Valerie's house. None of that was Tempest's imagination, so how could he have an ironclad alibi?

His mind still whirling with questions he couldn't answer, Tempest almost jumped when a horn beeped at him. He was outside the station and focused on nothing outside of his own thoughts when a giant, black SUV pulled to a stop on the opposite side of the road.

Big Ben had come to get him. That meant Amanda hadn't. Was she that upset with him? His phone battery had died during the night, so even though he had it back now, if there were messages from her, he couldn't read them or send one to her.

He waited for a gap in the traffic before jogging across the road. It was cold out and his shirt offered little protection. Thankfully, Big Ben had the heated seats on, and the interior of his car was pleasantly warm.

Big Ben pulled into traffic. "Fun night?"

"Not exactly. I have the right guy, but he's a slippery one and the police are convinced I have it wrong."

"Any chance that you do?" Big Ben flicked his indicator and turned off the main route that would lead them out of Maidstone in the wrong direction. "Hold on. Before you answer that, where am I going? Patience messaged to say I should come get you, but are we collecting your car or do you want to go home first?"

"Car, please." He wanted a shower and some fresh clothes, but there was no need to mess Big Ben around. Once he'd dropped him at the car, he could get on with his day. "Mind if I borrow your phone?"

"Just press the button."

Like any modern car, Big Ben's phone was connected to the media player. Tempest accessed it and scrolled the contacts looking for Amanda. When he found no entry under 'A' for Amanda or 'H' for Harper, he shot a quizzical brow at the driver.

"She's under PC Hotstuff. Remember that's what you used to call her when you first met and didn't know her name?"

Tempest cringed. "And she's been in your phone as that ever since?"

Big Ben shrugged. "Why change it. Besides, your girlfriend is hot stuff."

Tempest scrolled to the 'P' section and pressed the entry.

When she picked up, Amanda said, "What do you want, nuisance?"

Tempest said, "Hey, babe, it's me."

"And more importantly," Big Ben jumped in, "it's also me."

"Oh, you're out already," Amanda ignored Big Ben to speak with Tempest. "I thought you would be a while yet. How come you got Big Ben to come get you?"

Tempest breathed a small sigh of relief. She wasn't mad at him after all.

"Patience called him. He was waiting for me when I got out."

"How are you doing?"

"Mostly just annoyed. He's the right guy," Tempest reaffirmed a stance he wasn't about to relinquish. "He managed to convince someone to give him an alibi, though. Plus, some copycat killed another victim last night. Probably hoping they would get away with murder when the police assume it's the wizard striking again. I've got my work cut out proving Norman Pickett is the guy, but that's the task for today."

"Are you coming to the office? I'm there already. Jane is coming by with Cassie. She wants to talk to us."

"Yeah, I'll be there. I just need to grab my car and get clean. I'll be an hour. Is that okay?"

"Sure. I have a client meeting right before lunch so I'm here for the morning. Maybe we can grab lunch together later."

A broad smile pulled at Tempest's face. This was the opportunity he'd been waiting for.

"That's sounds perfect. I'll book somewhere." He was in the middle of a case that demanded the entirety of his attention, but the world could go hang for an hour so he could propose. He already knew where to go. Sitting on high ground to the west of the High Street, Ormon House overlooked the river, the castle, the cathedral, and the impressive bridge, and if he picked the right table, all could be viewed from a single spot. It was pricey, but that made it all the more alluring.

Promising to get to the office as soon as he could, Tempest ended the call and revelled in the complete U turn his emotions had taken. Sullen and frustrated one minute, ready to dance a jig the next.

"Doing okay?" asked Big Ben. "If you smile any harder your teeth might fall out."

Tempest wanted to explain why he now felt on top of the world, but of all the people on the planet, Big Ben was the last one to share the news with. He would offer his congratulations when the engagement was announced and would attend the wedding as best man. Naturally, the latter was purely to see how many of Amanda's friends he could bed, and to go out of his way to embarrass Tempest with his best man's speech.

It wasn't so much that he didn't believe in marriage, but that he could never understand why a man would shackle himself to just one woman. One hundred women, maybe. In fact, Tempest could recall one episode when Big Ben jokingly claimed to have fallen in love and that he did indeed plan to settle down. It was typical Friday night at-the-pub banter which he ended with a punchline about ruining it by sleeping with the woman's sisters.

And her mum.

Now that he was giving the story some thought, Tempest wondered if it might in fact be an anecdote drawn from his friend's life experience. Choosing not to enquire, he said, "My day started off bad, but looks set to improve. Wouldn't you agree?"

Shortly thereafter they arrived back in Cobham where Tempest's Boxster was exactly where and how he'd left it. He thanked Big Ben, expecting him to take off, but his tall friend said, "I'll see you at the office. I want to hear what Jane has to say. This is about the palace and the royal family, right?"

"That would be my guess."

"Then I want to be involved." Like Tempest, he'd served many years in the army, all of them under the reign of Queen Elizabeth. A new monarch now sat upon the throne, but nothing much had changed. They were patriots and felt no need to explore or explain why they felt the way they did.

Telling Tempest he was going straight to the office, Big Ben took off, his giant SUV thundering down the quiet suburban road until it turned a corner and vanished from sight.

Parents

FRIDAY, JANUARY 5TH 0911HRS

Arriving home eighteen minutes later, Tempest was surprised to find his parents' car parked on the drive. They lived only a few miles away on the other side of the river, but whilst they had a key, they were not known for just turning up.

Their presence was both good and bad. He'd not been able to return for the dogs, but hadn't worried too much because he knew Amanda would manage their needs. They were undoubtedly getting extra attention now, but at the same time Tempest could predict what his mother would have to say when he got through the door.

The dogs barked, but unlike when they were home alone and heard his car arrive, they were not on the other side of the front door waiting to mug him for affection. They were getting that elsewhere.

"Hey," he called into the house, crouching on one knee to fuss first Bull and then Dozer when they ran to greet him. "Everything okay?"

His dad appeared in the kitchen doorway, his eyes wide

in warning. With his hands, he mimed an explosion going off. In his seventies, Michael Michaels was a rogue looking for mischief held barely in check by his wife. His grey hair was going white, and he'd lost some height and some muscle in the last couple of decades, but he was almost always fun to have around.

Brushing it off, Tempest said, "Morning, Dad. Been here long?"

"Nevermind the good mornings," growled his mother, her demeanour predictable. Wearing a pair of purple trousers and a pink top with matching pink knitted cardigan, what she lacked in height she made up for with attitude. Permed grey hair fell in loose curls to her shoulders.

"Let me guess, mother. You feel there is a need to remind me that decent people don't get arrested and believe that I ought to pick a new line of work. One that ensures I stay on the right side of the law."

The essence of her prepared speech stolen, she placed her hands on her hips to say, "Yes! Did you learn nothing during your time in prison? Was it so much fun there that you are in a rush to return?"

"The police got it wrong, Mother. I shall prove that shortly and all the charges against me will be dropped." He made it sound more confident than he felt. "Now, if you don't mind, I would rather like a shower. Have you had breakfast?"

Leaving his mother to fume, Tempest had aimed the question at his father.

"Yes, thank you, son. We ate before we left the house this morning. Amanda said she couldn't get home in time to feed the boys their dinner and asked if we wouldn't mind. We popped in again this morning just to check on them because we didn't know what time you might get home. She left it to this morning to mention that you'd been incarcerated. Again."

Tempest tilted his head to look at his father from an angle. It wasn't like him to jump in on his mother's side.

"I'm just saying it's not something you want to make a habit out of, Son."

"Well, you're right about that, but like I said, the police have got it wrong. The only mistake I made was expecting them to believe me."

To cut the conversation off, he jogged up the stairs to shuck his clothes and get clean, returning freshly shaved and smelling of soap twelve minutes later. A steaming mug of tea sat on the kitchen countertop in his favourite R2D2 mug.

His parents had one each in front of them at the breakfast bar, and a dachshund each sleeping on their laps. On the TV, the morning news played.

Seeing that his mother's ire had waned, as it always did once she got whatever was bothering her off her chest, he kissed her head and enquired about their plans for the coming days.

"I have a nice leg of lamb in the freezer if you fancy coming over for Sunday lunch?" Tempest believed there would be something to celebrate, but didn't want to spoil the surprise.

His father said, "Sounds good to me. We can take a nice countryside walk while it roasts."

"And stop in at the pub on the way back," added his mother.

He asked about dessert and got them to commit to an apple crumble. His mother offered to make one and bring it with her, but Tempest assured her there was no need and promised he wouldn't buy one from a shop, he would make it himself. An enthusiastic cook, his mother had many dishes that could be labelled as showpiece meals. In the eighties and nineties when dinner parties were all the rage, she would be the hostess with the mostess, serving up all manner of decadent dishes from around the world. She could not, however, make an apple crumble. Or rather, she could, but it was best used to repair potholes in the street than for actual consumption.

Tempest finished his tea, dropped the mug into the dishwasher, and with a chunk of his weekend now planned, made it clear he was heading to work.

Mum and dad were on their way to a garden centre, so they all left the house at the same time, their cars heading in different directions when they left the village.

He could have called Ormond House before he left home, but didn't want his parents to overhear his plans and ask questions. They would find out soon enough. Lunch arranged, he sent a message to Amanda stating what time they needed to leave the office, but refrained from telling her where they were going. He wanted it to be a surprise.

Tempest had much on his mind, but what he planned to do upon arrival at the office changed the moment he walked through the door.

Magic House

FRIDAY, JANUARY 5TH 1017HRS

Sitting in the reception area next to the coffee machine was a glum looking man in his late twenties. He looked up when Tempest entered through the back door with the dogs charging ahead.

At her desk just inside the front door, Marjory said, "You have a client waiting when you are ready, Tempest. He's been here thirty minutes already."

A frown creased Tempest's forehead. "Amanda couldn't see him?"

"She has Jane, DI Munroe, and Big Ben in her office. They've been in there since before he arrived and I didn't think it was necessary to disturb them."

Suitably advised, Tempest crossed the room to greet the client.

"Tempest Michaels."

"Evan Longshore." He had a good grip and an earnest face, though it looked a little haunted. A shade under six feet tall, he wore his sandy blonde hair cut short at the back and sides. Dressed in skinny jeans that showed off the muscle in his thighs and calves, his top half was covered in a windbreaker and sweater combination, both bearing designer labels.

"I won't be a moment," Tempest backed away. "Just need to grab my notebook and such. Have you been offered a coffee?"

"Yes, thank you."

Tempest ditched his coat and the dog leads, put his phone onto the charging cradle and collected a notebook and pen from his desk.

Returning to the chairs in reception, he asked, "What is it you think we can help with, Evan?"

Evan exhaled through his nose, pulled a face that made Tempest think he was figuring out where to start, and let his shoulders slump.

"You know, I've been trying to work out how to explain this for hours. Since last night when she vanished actually, but every way I try to explain it sounds crazier than the one before."

"Evan, we specialise in crazy. What you think weird will just be regular for us. Let's start at the beginning. Tell me who it is that went missing." Tempest genuinely expected Evan to reveal his cat had wandered off or that one of his goldfish had absconded. Now that he was talking, it was painfully obvious Evan was far from the sharpest tool in the shed.

"My girlfriend, Winter. She just disappeared and the worst thing is I think I know what happened to her."

"Go on."

"Well, I know this is going to sound ridiculous, but I live in a magic house."

Tempest didn't react. He wanted to say, 'There's no such thing as magic,' simply because it was such a topical subject. Yet he refrained, choosing instead to ask the question, "Why do you think that?"

"Because it just is. There's no other explanation for all the crazy stuff that happens. I'm talking about unexplainable phenomenon."

Amanda's door opened, conversation spilling out as the people inside moved into the main office space.

Tempest kept his attention on the client, keen to hear more precise details.

"Please give me an example."

Evan chewed his bottom lip for a thoughtful second before saying. "The coffee table. That's where it started."

Not following, Tempest echoed, "The coffee table?"

Amanda and the others were drifting in his direction.

"Sorry, can we get to the coffee machine?" Amanda went around the back of the chairs while talking to Tempest. "Apologies for interrupting. Is this a new client?"

"Possibly. I have only just sat down with him. This is Evan and he has a rather unusual problem. His girlfriend has vanished, and he believes he lives in a magical house."

Attention turned to the client, but Big Ben leaned in close to Tempest's head to whisper in his ear, "You're going to want to hear what I just heard."

Tempest nodded to acknowledge the comment, but kept his attention on Evan.

"So there's this coffee table in the house, right. I bought it second hand a couple of years ago. It doesn't look like anything special. It's just an old wooden coffee table, but it must have belonged to a witch or something. Or maybe a sorcerer spilled a potion on it one time. I dunno, but if you put things on it, they vanish."

Amanda took her turn to frown. "They vanish?"

"Well, sort of. What I mean is they go to where they live.

Plates and cups find their way back to the cupboard. Rubbish like empty pizza boxes go out to the bins. Beer cans magically take themselves to the recycling."

Amanda looked at Jane. "He's joking, right?"

"I swear," Evan protested. "I wouldn't make this up. The coffee table is only the start of it though. The same sort of thing happens in the bedroom. If I leave my clothes screwed up and dirty on the floor, when I return they are back in the drawer or the wardrobe, clean, ironed and put away. It's a little scary, if I'm honest."

Amanda agreed. "This is a little scary. You think your house cleans up after you?"

"What else could it be? The fridge magically restocks itself. If I put a dirty plate in the sink it reappears in the cupboard the next day and don't get me started on the dishwasher. I come home sometimes to find the dishwasher running all by itself. I can see you are finding this hard to believe. Trust me, I was too to start with, so about a month ago I started to really challenge the magic. Instead of just leaving a small mess on the coffee table or on the bedroom floor, I would have my mates over to watch the match. We would leave the place looking like an absolute tip and do you know what I discovered?"

"I'm sure the answer is going to stun us all," muttered Marjory from her chair.

"The magic wasn't limited to the coffee table like I thought it was. If the mess spilled onto the carpet, that would clean itself as well." Evan looked around at the faces watching his in stark disbelief, and remembering why he came in turned glum again. "So, yeah, I live in a magical house, but Winter disappeared, and I'm worried the house did something with her."

Amanda took a seat next to Tempest. "Let me guess, all her things went at the same time."

Evan's eyes popped out on stalks. "Oh, you guys really are good at this stuff. Yeah, I checked her wardrobe and it was empty. The house took her and all her things. I mean, I thought maybe she sat on the coffee table and found herself in the dishwasher or something, but I couldn't find her anywhere and wherever she is now, I guess there's no phone signal because she's not answering."

Tempest asked, "In the days before she went missing, did she say anything to you about the house? Specifically, I'm asking if she brought up the subject of the mess you like to leave."

Evan's face showed the awe he felt. "How did you know, man? Oh, my god! Can you guys all read minds?"

Amanda borrowed the notepad and pen from Tempest's unresisting hands. "I'm going to need your girlfriend's full name and her phone number. She deserves to hear this story."

Evan looked from Tempest to Amanda and back, not following what was being discussed. "So, do you think you can help me?"

The detectives all looked at each other and Tempest said, "Anyone want to volunteer?"

Amanda said, "I'll tell him."

Tempest stopped her with a gentle hand to her arm. "I think perhaps a gentler approach would work better."

Big Ben chuckled, "I've got it. Poor guy will need some cheering up afterwards. I'll load him with some top tips for how to get over his loss."

"Loss!" Evan repeated the word. "You think Winter is dead?"

Marjory barged her way into the midst of the group.

"Get out of it the lot of you. This will stem back to his mother. I've met men like this before. It's not even really his fault, although most men aren't actually quite this stupid."

Evan blinked, certain he was being talked about, but not sure why.

Marjory nudged Tempest out of the way and settled in the chair opposite Evan. When no one moved, she angled death eyes at them. "Go on then. Clear off."

They drifted away, back to the private offices at the other end of the room while straining to hear what Marjory was saying at the same time.

Big Ben tapped Tempest's elbow. "Come on, you need to hear about the palace."

A Royal Problem

FRIDAY, JANUARY 5TH 1031HRS

With the door closed and everyone crammed into his office, Tempest listened as Detective Inspector Cassie Munroe spoke.

"The royal wedding between Prince Marcus and Nora Morley is in less than three weeks. There have been twenty-three deaths in the extended royal family over the last nine months. That's a four thousand percent increase over any period in the last two hundred years. Someone is behind it, and I have a fairly good idea who. Unfortunately, no one else sees things the way I do."

"Except us," said Jane. Born James Butterworth, Jane was gender fluid but more commonly identified as a woman. She wore wigs until a few months ago when her hair grew long enough to replace them, and rarely picked clothes from the 'boy' side of her wardrobe these days. Originally hired by Tempest as a receptionist, she soon proved her worth as an investigator and was able to lend a unique insight into many cases due to her former life in a cult of vampire wannabes. "I think Cassie is onto something, but she is very much on her own in trying to prove it."

Frowning, Tempest asked, "Your bosses don't believe the evidence?"

"That's just it," said Cassie. "I don't have any evidence. What I have is conflicting circumstances and a deep-rooted belief that the taskforce created to quietly investigate is getting nowhere because they are looking in the wrong direction."

"You think the person behind it is Lord Edward Chamberlain," Tempest knew this from conversations with Jane.

"That's right. He's thirteenth in line to the throne, which is too far down the line of succession to ever be crowned under normal circumstances. Too many would have to die for him to ascend, and all the deaths so far have been from members of the family further down the pecking order."

"So what makes you so sure he's behind it?"

Cassie held up her right hand, extending her fingers to count. Folding down the first, she said, "The first victim was his older brother, a person he would have to get out of the way if he wanted to become king. As you know, Nugent died inside a fire-breathing flying suit, but the suit was shot full of holes by the palace guards and he was not. That tells me the body was planted, and I found further evidence at the scene. Unfortunately, I wasn't swift enough to secure the site where the flying suit crashed, and my boss arrived and took over. Before I could do anything about it, the footprints we found near the body were trampled and unusable. Since then, I have been keeping a close eye on Lord Edward, but he is on to me. I was able to recruit his girlfriend to help me spy on him, but he is wily and wary enough to ensure he gave nothing away. I think you know the girl in fact."

"It's Mindy at the wedding place around the corner," Jane supplied. "But she's out now. She helped Cassie once, but just like everyone else she doesn't believe her boyfriend is behind the deaths."

Picking up again, Cassie said, "Most recently, he spoke with my boss, and I have been ordered to desist any investigation into Lord Edward's movements. If I get caught again, I will be sacked."

"Which is where we come in," said Jane. "Cassie can get us access to the wedding and to the palace beforehand, but she can't be seen associating with us. If she gets caught, we will lose the chance to figure out what he plans to do."

Tempest gave a slow shake of his head. "It's hard to believe people are being so blind. Why won't your boss entertain the idea that Lord Edward might be a threat? Don't they have to investigate every tangible concern in the build up to such a public event?"

"History," said Cassie, looking a little ashamed. "I have history with my boss and I'm on thin ice. He wants me to go over his head so he will have grounds to sack me and get me out of his life for good. What you are witness to is a deliberate tactic. If I go over his head and I'm wrong, he will have what he wants. If I do nothing, and I am right, he will blame me for whatever tragedy occurs. If I go over his head and I'm right, he will claim I subverted the chain of command in a bid to make him look foolish. He'll make me look like a loose cannon and I'll end up fired anyway. Basically, I'm getting fired, but my last act will be stopping Lord Edward and to do that I have to catch him in the act."

"The only question," said Jane, "is whether we are willing to drop everything here to help out at the palace."

Tempest looked around the room at his friends. "It seems to me this is a decision everyone needs to make for themselves. It also seems as though each of you has already made it. For me, there really is no question beyond when you need us to start?"

Cassie sagged a little, relief washing over her to hear she had the whole team. It wasn't much, not compared with what she ought to have at her disposal, and she was asking them to investigate a case that had no supernatural connection whatsoever. Nevertheless, they were patriots, they had a record for solving unusual cases, and they were volunteers. If anyone could save the day, and the royal family, it was the team from the Blue Moon Investigation Agency.

Mostly Naked

FRIDAY, JANUARY 5TH 1113HRS

Cassie outlined the royal wedding itself and talked about her need to bring them into the palace as soon as possible. She could deal with their clearance and assign them roles. There were so many extra people being brought in for the wedding that she believed they would go unnoticed. Not least since she was the one in charge of police matters at the palace.

They set a date for the following week and Cassie departed with Jane. They had more groundwork to cover.

Amanda met with her client, and Big Ben left in search of brunch. Left alone, Tempest returned to the wizard case. Knowing the real identity of Zephyrus Frostwind and proving it were two very different things. However, he had leads to explore and believed his task would be easier because he wasn't trying to figure out the 'who' of the case for once.

Placing a call to Sharon Maycroft featured high on his list of things to do. She'd messaged the previous evening while he was locked up, stating that she needed to see him and had information to report. Tempest assumed that meant responses to her press coverage of the case. She had promised to show the wizard's calling card and request anyone holding one contact her newspaper.

He hoped she had an abundance of names, because it would increase the likelihood of figuring out the 'why' of the case, but at the same time he didn't want there to be dozens of potential targets. Like everyone else, the poor woman from last night appeared to have no direct link to the previous victims. However, Tempest believed her death came at the hand of a copycat. Unless ...

A worrying thought entered Tempest's head, reminding him of the plague of evil Klowns he fought two years ago. They came from nowhere, their presence and crimes unexplained until he figured out they were motivated by a single individual operating as the leader of their twisted gang. What if this was like that and Norman wasn't alone? Could he have disciples?

It was a question for Frank, which was okay because he needed to speak with him anyway. In Tempest's brain resided a madcap plan most would consider lunacy, yet if it came to it, he knew it would probably work. To draw out the wizard at least. However, it wasn't something he could enact in an instant. It required planning.

Also on his list of things to do was look deeper into the first five victims. Operating under the assumption they each had a link to Norman, he wanted to examine their social media profiles. People posted pictures of their kids' birthday parties. If The Great Howduzhe performed at some point in the past, the photographs showing him would be there. It would all be additional evidence for when he caught Zephyrus and unmasked him. Tempest couldn't see a better way out of his current situation than to show the world the man inside the cloak and the clever devices employed to produce his 'magic'.

Ready to get started on the list of victims, he elected to grab a cup of coffee first, but turning around to leave his office found Sharon standing in the doorway.

"Oh, hey. I was going to call you shortly," he said.

Sharon was dressed for work again, her fitted dress accentuating her figure while making her look elegant, tall, and sophisticated. Her red hair looked to be salon fresh and cascaded over her right shoulder. Her heels added four inches to her height, making her eye level with Tempest, who was doing his best not to notice how good she looked.

"Were you, Tempest? Were you going to call me?"

"Of course," he replied, turning away to focus on his whiteboard of case notes. He wasn't interested in Sharon. Truly he wasn't. Yes, she was an attractive woman and they had slept together in the past even if it was almost two years ago. He was in love with Amanda and had an engagement ring in his pocket that he planned to slip on her finger in the next couple of hours. "I got your message. Were you successful in getting people with the Frostwind calling card to come forward?"

"I was," she said, placing her handbag on the floor and closing the office door. "That's why I came here. It's sensitive information we should protect from being overheard."

Wondering whose name might be on the list if she felt the need to shut the door, Tempest put the whiteboard marker back in its pot and made it clear he was paying attention.

"Did you get many responses?"

"Yes, but let's park that for a moment. I want to talk about something else first."

"Oh?"

"I've seen the way you look at me, Tempest."

Tempest felt heat rising on his cheeks. It was true. He never intended it and would never act on it. Short of fitting himself with blinkers like a horse he wasn't sure how exactly he could stop himself from noticing other women.

"I'm with Amanda," he replied, his eyes cast down at the carpet. "I'm planning to propose." Almost no one knew, but telling Sharon felt like self-defence.

"Then I shall have to take drastic measures. I want you, Tempest. I should have acted on it sooner, but since it's not too late …"

Inside his head, a maelstrom of responses swirled like they were caught between multiple tornadoes. He had to admit he knew she was interested, but failed to anticipate that she would announce it in such an open manner. But that was how Sharon worked and why she was successful in her career. She was forward and gregarious. They got together the first time because she pursued him. He was always too expecting of rejection to make the first move. But what was he supposed to do now? He needed to kick her out and make it completely clear he wasn't interested. That would be easy enough because he wasn't. Genuinely and with no need for caveats. Yet, she was a useful tool, she was bringing him work right now, and they had history. So how to word his rejection in a manner that wouldn't leave her wanting to dump a bucket of water over his head?

His rapid musings halted in an instant when he heard a series of press studs popping in the manner one might associate with a garment being ripped open. It was followed by the almost not-there sound of the same garment dropping to the floor.

Lifting his head, even though he knew he shouldn't, Tempest's wide eyes gawped at the Weald World reporter. Her dress was lying in a crumpled heap on the carpet to leave her exposed in panties and a bra so sheer he could swallow them both without needing a glass of water.

He swore. A single word containing four letters and a meaning he ought to have considered before uttering it.

Sharon smiled sexily, her eyes betraying a hunger that went straight to Tempest's trousers.

"I was thinking the same thing," she murmured, her voice suddenly husky. "On the desk?" she enquired. Crossing to place her palms on it, she looked over one shoulder and winked.

Tempest hadn't moved from the spot, his limbs seemingly frozen, and that might have worked out better, but terrified Marjory might walk in and misconstrue what she was seeing, he grabbed Sharon's dress and begged her to put it on.

Holding it out with one hand, he wasn't expecting the mostly naked woman to loop her arms around his neck.

Of course, that was the absolute worst moment for the door to open and therefore precisely why it did.

"Temp, I'm heading out, but I should be back for our lunch app ..." Amanda stopped talking.

Sharon said, "Oops," in a tone that let Tempest know she didn't mean it.

Amanda didn't even look at him. Her eyes remained fixed on Sharon the whole time. She closed the door and could be heard speaking to someone outside a moment later.

Rushing, Tempest ripped the door open to find Amanda speaking with a middle-aged woman who was clearly her client.

"Out this way, please. We'll take my car."

"Amanda, you have to know that was not what it looked like."

"I'm with a client, Tempest. I won't be back for lunch."

She hadn't bothered to turn to look at him and was heading out through the back door to get to the carpark.

"Amanda, don't blow off lunch. It was going to be special." He really didn't know what he was supposed to say. He wanted to grab her arm and make her listen, but the wave of ice emanating outward from her core told him attempting to touch her would be a mistake.

"Was going to be, Tempest. Past tense. A bit like us."

"Come on, Amanda," he followed her out to the carpark where she finally had to turn around and face him, if only so she could get into her car. "You don't mean that. I thought she had information for me."

"She certainly had something for you."

"Something I don't want."

"Tempest," Amanda glared at him over the top of her car door. "You're still holding her dress."

He glanced down guiltily at his hands and in that moment she closed her door and fired up the engine. Moving to pursue when she reversed from her parking spot, he stopped. There was no point chasing her down the street protesting his innocence. She needed the opportunity to calm down and assess what she'd seen. Given a little time, Amanda would realise her actions were overly harsh and would recognise he'd been ambushed.

Annoyed, disappointed, and very much frustrated, Tempest made his way back to his office. Sharon was still there, still mostly naked, and sitting on the edge of his desk. From the doorway he threw the dress in her general direction, spat, "Get dressed," and shut the door with her inside and him very much not.

Facing back into the office, he spotted Big Ben coming through the door. He had a tray of cream cakes balanced on his right hand.

"Chocolate eclair?" he wafted the box under Marjory's nose. "Or are you more of a raspberry slice kind of gal?"

Marjory took a dim view of Big Ben but wasn't above being bribed with confectionary.

Holding the lid for her to make a selection, he then turned the box toward Tempest. And saw his face.

"Someone flush your goldfish?"

"Not exactly. I was taking Amanda out for lunch."

"Okay."

"You know. For *the* lunch."

"She turned you down?"

"It's not lunchtime yet, but I suspect the event has been postponed at the very least."

Big Ben sighed. "What did you do this time?"

His office door opened and Sharon came out. She wasn't naked, but she was still doing up the final poppers on the front of her dress.

Big Ben's eyes flared a little. "Nice one. She caught you though, right? I can teach you how to get away with this stuff."

Tempest looked around for something heavy he could use as a bludgeon.

Sharon's expression was hard to read, though it was distinctly 'not positive'. Stuffing first one arm and then the other into her coat, she fluffed her hair to make it fall over the collar and levelled an even stare.

"I can't say I'm not disappointed, Tempest, and I know I didn't misread your eyes, so the ball is very much in your court. You know what I want."

At his very core, Tempest knew his character. He

detested letting people down or creating ill-feeling unless it was genuinely deserved. In Sharon's case it clearly wasn't. He didn't feel that he'd misled her, but wasn't prepared to deny all guilt when he knew there was a smattering of truth to her claim.

"Sharon, what I want is to marry Amanda. I was planning to propose to her at lunchtime today." He removed the ring from his pocket to accentuate the point. He could have remarked that her unexpected nakedness had undoubtedly scrubbed that plan, but she was astute enough to know it already. "I hope we can continue working together, but our relationship has to stay professional."

Sharon took a tablet from her handbag, and focussing on that for a moment, jabbed at the screen with an impatient index finger. Stuffing it back into her handbag, she looked up to meet Tempest's eyes.

"I just sent you a list of all those who contacted the station to claim they were in possession of a Zephyrus Frostwind business card. How many were making it up I cannot say, but the list provides addresses and phone numbers too, so you will be able to contact them." She started walking for the door, pausing in front of Big Ben. "Are you also so deeply in love with someone that you don't fancy me?"

Big Ben's wolf's smile would have touched the walls if it grew any wider.

"No, angel, I am not only free, but completely available and unbelievably talented."

Sharon hooked her arm through his. "Super. Let's go." Walking across the office arm in arm with Big Ben, she turned her head to provide a parting comment. "You're too interesting to alienate, Tempest. I still want an exclusive when you catch this guy, okay."

Watching her go, Tempest said, "Understood."

She exited the premises with her arm looped through Big Ben's, turned right, and vanished from view a few moments later.

Silence ruled, but only for a beat. Marjory, proving she heard and saw everything that went on in the office, had a question.

"You're planning to propose to Amanda?"

"I am."

"Might want to give it a while until she calms down, eh?"

Tempest huffed out a deep sigh.

"And maybe send some flowers."

Professional Moping

FRIDAY, JANUARY 5TH 1200HRS

Moping wasn't a skill he wanted to perfect, but in the hour following Sharon's departure, Tempest gave it a jolly good go. The list of people claiming to hold a Zephyrus Frostwind business card was open on his computer, but concentrating on it proved impossible.

He'd been an hour or so away from getting down on one knee. An hour or so. How far away was he now? Amanda would calm down; of that he was certain.

Well, fairly sure, at least.

It wasn't as though he was also naked when she walked in. If she'd caught him in a hotel room with another woman, or discovered he was sending secret messages, there would be justification for her anger, and he would have accepted the consequences. However, none of those things transpired or even came close. He was entirely innocent, and she would see that soon enough.

If not soon enough, then eventually. He hoped.

His stomach grumbled its emptiness, the otherworldly gurgles like the mournful moans of a spirit attempting to contact the living. It would take no more than a few moments to find sustenance at one of the many outlets available on Rochester High Street, yet believing Amanda might reappear at any moment, he ignored his hunger.

Groaning at the hand fate chose to play him, he called the Ormond House to cancel lunch, then forced himself to focus on the case. They had all agreed to clear their workload so they could work with Cassie. By the following week, just a few days away, they were all going to Buckingham Palace and from there would find themselves embroiled in royal wedding preparations. They were going undercover, which in Tempest's case meant adopting a disguise. His face had been in the papers and on television too many times for him to think no one would recognise it, but shaving his usual face fuzz off might be all the situation required.

To that end, he wanted to put his all into catching Norman Pickett. That started with compiling a watertight case that would disprove the man's alibis. That led Tempest back to wondering if he had accomplices. His mother claimed he was at home with her last night. Or perhaps she simply knew better than to argue when he made the claim to have been with her. Either way, Agatha Pickett wasn't someone he was going to cross-examine.

Refreshing his screen to bring up the list of names provided by Sharon, he started at the top.

Two hours later, his stomach's rumblings had increased in both volume and regularity, so they now reminded him of a flatulent opera singer warming up from the wrong end. Amanda wasn't coming back, and if she did it wasn't going to be so they could go for lunch, so with a heavy heart, he donned his coat.

"I'm going to grab a bite to eat," he announced, heading for the door. "Can I get you anything?"

Marjory shook her head. "No, thank you. I've already eaten."

Still annoyed with how his day was going, not least because he spent the night in jail and hoped to turn things around so it would become a day he would remember for other reasons, Tempest settled into a booth at the coffee shop across the street.

A tuna melt, the cheese from which oozed out onto his plate, plus a blueberry muffin, and a hot chocolate provided more calories than he needed, but balancing his carbs, proteins, and fats was the furthest thing from his mind.

Taking a bite from the still-too-warm sandwich, he did his best to think about the case, but thoughts of Amanda pestered his mind. Should he call her? Should he text? What would he say if he did send her a message? Was it best to leave her to cool down? What would happen the next time Sharon turned up somewhere wanting an interview?

Unable to fashion worthwhile answers to any of them, he took out his notebook and began to jot notes. Not about his relationship dramas, but regarding Zephyrus and Norman Pickett.

Of the almost thirty names he got from Sharon, seventeen answered their phones when he called. None of them knew who Zephyrus Frostwind was or why he deemed them worthy to receive a business card. Most were good enough to answer his questions about employment, relationship status, education, and more, but a few refused.

Like the victims already recorded, plus Valerie and Simon, the clients who got away, they appeared to have nothing in common. They all lived in different parts of the area, they were different ages, worked in different places ... but more than half of them had hired a magician to attend a kid's party or were able to report having an altercation/aggressive conversation with a magician when they took their kids to a party. It linked them, but it was those he spoke to who had never heard of The Great Howduzhe that gave him the biggest clue.

Having more or less tripped over the 'who' of the equation, Tempest remained fuzzy about the 'why'. Okay, so Richard Cowell sacked him from his gig at the nightclub, and Valerie refused to pay him, but neither incident seemed sufficient justification for murder. At least, that's what he thought until he learned a little more.

One of the people on the list was Chris Street. A gardener by trade, Chris knew Gill Carlson and the pair of them went to school with Norman Pickett. Chris reported hearing about Gill's murder, but failed to connect the dots until Tempest called him. At school, Norman was the dweeby, skinny loner and Chris admitted bullying him. He defended himself by claiming it was never physical, but Tempest knew how harmful words can be, especially when they come as a constant barrage of abuse.

Tempest sought to confirm Gill was equally guilty of the bullying, but Chris surprised him. It turned out Gill married the girl Norman spent his school years fawning after. Elaine Prescott was too pretty for him by a long way, but she had a soft spot for the skinny loner and defended him all the time.

The marriage lasted a few years, but Gill turned out to be a serial cheat and a man willing to physically abuse his wife. Elaine finally ran away, finding refuge in a women's shelter. Chris didn't know what happened to her after that.

Gill was killed not because of anything to do with Norman's work as a magician, but because he married the woman Norman loved and then treated her like dirt. It made the spree of murders all about vengeance and nothing else. Once the clues lined up, it seemed obvious, but until he saw it Tempest had been looking for financial gain as the motive behind the wizard's crimes.

Realising it was nothing more than a gut full of revenge came as a relief. But knowing the 'why' didn't answer the 'how'. How was Norman producing such brilliant magical effects? The flame thrower thing was easy enough to figure out, not least because Norman tried to use one in his house. But the sparkles that follow his hands, shooting lances of glowing light from his fingers, firing nails from nowhere ... these tricks and more remained unexplained. Partially unexplained, anyway.

Unable to sleep the night after his fight with the wizard, Tempest's middle-of-the-night research was his first foray into the world of illusions. He learned about the props required to produce effects those watching could not explain, and that gave him ideas about some of the tricks Norman employed. However, if he was to beat Norman the next time they met, the subject required greater exploration.

Tempest picked at his blueberry muffin, enjoying the flavour but conscious he'd bought it only because it was Amanda's favourite. Lunch eaten, and head still conflicted, he left the coffee shop, but he didn't return to the office.

Turning right, he walked in the direction of the bridge. Passing The Vault, scene of Gill Carlson's murder just two nights earlier, he continued to a florist. It was almost directly opposite the wedding boutique owned and run by Felicity Philips. Aware it was she who landed the prestigious contract to run the imminent royal wedding, Tempest mentally noted an intention to drop by her place of business in the coming days.

A gentle beep sounded when he pushed the door open to enter the flower shop and again when he let it close behind him. Assailing his nose, the mingling scents from thousands of blooms filled the air with a cloying fragrance. There were worse things to smell, but in the confined space it was almost strong enough to make his eyes water.

Behind the counter, two women in their late thirties assembled bouquets with practiced, efficient ease.

"Be right with you," said one.

It wasn't his first time in the shop, but he wasn't frequent enough to know the ladies by name. The thought made him question if he'd been remiss in buying flowers. He bought them, and not just on birthdays, valentines, and other special occasions, but how often was often enough?

Looking around, he tried to name some of the stems so he could instruct the florists on what he wanted rather than ask for something pretty. Amanda was a fan of gerberas which the shop had in a variety of colours. They would need to have their stems wired, he knew that much, otherwise they went floppy after just a couple of days in a vase.

Seeing the lady who spoke to him move her bouquet to one side, Tempest turned his attention to the counter. The door beeped, announcing another customer entering the shop, though Tempest saw no reason to turn around to see who it was.

"Now what can I get for you?" asked the florist.

"Two dozen of the deep pink gerberas, please," Tempest instructed confidently.

"Would you like them made up into a bouquet? We can put them in a water balloon to stay fresh and present them in a box."

Tempest knew to expect the up-sale and wasn't going to fight it.

"That would be lovely. Thank you."

"And what are they for?" the lady enquired.

From behind him a voice said, "A shag."

The florist choked on a laugh.

Tempest frowned and turned to face Big Ben.

"Is there a better reason for buying flowers?" Big Ben asked, his tone innocent.

Still laughing, the florist said, "We get lots of men buying flowers as an apology."

"And that would be this one's reason, but I am not most men." Big Ben drew in a slow breath that inflated his chest a few more inches to make him look even bigger than normal.

The florist still working on a bouquet behind the counter mumbled, "No, you are not."

Big Ben went around Tempest. Aiming smouldering eyes at the poor woman, he asked, "Ever screamed a man's name while lying on a bed of rose petals in the royal suite of the Savoy Hotel?"

Her jaw dropped open and Tempest wondered if a little dribble might spill out.

Attempting to break the spell, for at that moment it could be argued that magic really did exist, Tempest said, "The gerberas?"

The other florist, unable to take her eyes from Big Ben, fumbled for the vase of gerbera stems and almost dropped it before finding the effort required to focus on her job.

"Right, yes. Gerberas in a water balloon," she murmured, struggling to concentrate. "What is it you need to apologise for?"

"Nothing, thank you."

Big Ben chose to answer the question as well. "She walked in on him holding another woman's dress in his hands. She had been wearing it."

Both women stopped what they were doing and scowled.

"And you think you can fix that with some flowers?" snapped the one serving him.

"Men," said the other lady, using an expletive either side of the word.

"It was a misunderstanding," Tempest defended himself. "The woman took her dress off. I was trying to give it back to her so she would put it back on."

"A likely story. I think you should get your flowers elsewhere." The florist folded her arms for good measure.

Not for the first time in his life, or even in recent weeks, Tempest questioned if it would be a service to the world if he took a blunt object and used it to beat Big Ben to death. Instead, he tipped his head toward the ceiling and gave it a 'why me' shake.

Big Ben burst out laughing. "I'm sorry, I can't do it to the man. Ladies," he addressed the florists. "He is completely innocent and deserves your sympathy. The lady in question is something of a fiery temptress as I have recently discovered. Not his lady, but the one who elected to remove her dress in his office. His lady is something else and quite how he manages to keep her from straying I have no idea. You want to show them the ring?" he encouraged.

Tempest fished it out.

The nearest florist said, "Wow? Is that a whole carat?"

The other florist hastened to get a look.

"No," said Tempest. "It's three."

"Three carats," the ladies breathed the words with reverential awe.

Five minutes later he left the shop with an extra-large bouquet the florists insisted he wasn't to pay for. They wished him luck and sent him on his way. When the door closed behind him and Big Ben did not appear to be following, Tempest looked around to see a lady's hand turning the sign around to show 'closed'.

It was the middle of the afternoon, but apparently they now had something better to do. And it involved Big Ben. And the shop being closed.

Building Site

FRIDAY, JANUARY 5TH 1514HRS

A light drizzle began to fall on his walk back to the office. Holding the flowers to his chest, Tempest moved to the side of the street where the buildings offered some protection, but it wasn't far to go to get back to the office.

"Those are nice," Marjory remarked as he came past her desk.

"Gerberas are her favourite."

He carried them to his office and set them on the windowsill at the back. Amanda still hadn't messaged him, and he couldn't decide if that was because he was yet to message her. If they were to be married, did he really want to set a precedent for their relationship by being the one to run after her? He genuinely hadn't done anything wrong, yet he was the one buying flowers and fretting over what action she might take in revenge.

Determined to do nothing more and discuss the matter calmly when they were home together later, he went back to the case.

It was time to explore the 'how'.

Norman dressed the part and looked the part and a quick check revealed the video of their fight, if it was okay to call Tempest getting his butt kicked 'a fight', now had six million views. Six million people had seen Norman produce sparkling lights with his fingers and eject fireballs with his hands. The threads remained the same and he was still getting hundreds of abusive 'You tried' memes in his inbox. Others still argued the magic was real, but both sides made Tempest even more determined to 'pull back the curtain'.

Settling into his chair, his hunger satiated, Tempest delved into the world of magic. But only for about a minute.

When he visited the house of Walter and Vanessa Freeman, Patience told him the victims died from asphyxiation. Sparkly lights were one thing, but starving a person of oxygen couldn't be achieved with the same sleight of hand. Nor could impaling a person with iron bars.

Tempest opened a new tab to start a fresh search. He could come back to the magic trick stuff but had to figure out a few other things first. Certain he'd seen a picture or report listing the building firm working the site where the iron bars were stored, Tempest found their name a few minutes later.

Reeves & Son Builders appeared to be a small family firm operating out of the Luton end of Chatham. He phoned the landline number hoping he would reach an office.

"Hello?" answered a woman in a voice that suggested he had the wrong number.

"I'm looking for Reeves & Son."

"Oh, yeah, right. He usually uses his mobile for work

stuff. No one bothers with the landline. Don't know why he even lists it."

Seeing nothing to be gained by entering a conversation, Tempest ended the call and dialled the mobile instead.

"Hello?" the same response in the same tone of voice, but this time the person at the other end was a man.

"I'm looking for Reeves & Son. Have I come through to the right person?"

"Yes. I'm Sid Reeves. Here to solve all your building needs. From roofs to paving, we cover the lot. How can I help you?"

Tempest started with an introduction and followed by explaining his reason for calling.

Instantly defensive, Mr Reeves said, "I'll tell you what I told the police. The iron bars weren't ours. We don't use anything like that. The closest we ever get is a grid we put into larger slabs sometimes."

This was information he'd not found anywhere else. "But the bars are a standard building product, yes?"

"Yes, but not one we would ever use," he repeated his point.

"I've no doubt you are busy, Mr Reeves, but is there any chance you or someone from your firm can meet me at the site? I need to figure out how he was able to fling them across the street."

"Ordinarily I would say no, but today's your lucky day. The police kicked us off the site when the accident happened, so we started a different job. We got back to the place in Luton today."

"You're there now?" Tempest began to rise from his chair.

"That's what I said."

It took seventeen minutes to get from Rochester to Chatham and through it to the Luton arches on the far side of the business district, a distance of less than three miles. The bumper-to-bumper traffic and constant, unavoidable lights on the one-way system meant he probably could have walked it as quickly, but the rain continued, and he was pleased to stay dry inside his car.

The building site occupied an empty plot where a house had clearly once stood. Galvanised steel fence panels, the kind that come as a modular system and are popular on building sites, separated the construction area from the street. Behind the fence, half a dozen men in clunky boots, thick coats, and hard hats, went about their business oblivious to the traffic going by and the man now trying to get their attention.

A big concrete slab covered a third of the available ground area and they were building up from that. Concrete mixers, chaps with trowels and piles of bricks, plus chaps running mini diggers and dumpers to a skip parked at the far end of the site, all made too much noise for conversation to be possible. But they noticed when Tempest let himself through the fence.

Three of the workers stopped what they were doing to intercept the interloper.

Tempest identified the gaffer and pointed to draw the workers' attention his way. The man he took to be Sid Reeves had a large building plan in his hands. The rain had left off and he appeared to be consulting it, no doubt confirming they were doing things right. He had his back to Tempest but turned when one of his guys waved to get his attention.

Tempest waited at the edge of the site next to the fence.

He didn't want to be too precious about the mud and muck but wasn't dressed to negotiate puddles.

"Tempest Michaels?" he stuck out his hand to shake.

"Yes. Sid Reeves?"

Introductions complete, Tempest asked about the iron bars.

"They were inside a pipe, which is another strange thing because we don't use that kind of pipe either. It was concrete and would be used in heavy duty sewer work. That's not something we do, so like I said to the police, someone planted them here."

"That would be my guess too. Can I see where they were?"

Sid led Tempest across the building site, ignoring the puddles and mud which he splashed through with oblivious abandon. Tempest accepted his fate and followed, soaking his socks almost immediately.

Lined up against the far edge of the site where the building next door ended in a brick wall, pallets of brick ready for use were stacked neatly in piles two high.

"When we got here, the pipe and a few of the iron bars were sitting right here on top of these. Like I said to the police, we didn't put them there."

"The police removed them?"

"They certainly did. I had to answer a whole bunch of questions, let me tell you. That's not a day I'm going to forget in a hurry. They thought it must have been negligence on my part, but we take every precaution. Those iron bars were planted."

Tempest didn't doubt it. Turning to face away from the bricks, he looked out of the site to the road and the cars going by. Diane Meacock died on a Sunday in the middle of the afternoon. She was on the opposite side of the street when the iron bars impaled her. Today that feat would be all but impossible, yet at that time on a Sunday, there wouldn't have been much traffic around.

"There was nothing else here?" Tempest asked.

"No, but it's funny you should ask because it looked like there was."

Tempest had Sid show him what he meant. It couldn't be seen now. Wind and rain had eroded the marks, but when they were called to the site the day of the 'accident' Sid's son found scuffs in the dirt behind the concrete pipe and a mark where it looked like a cable might have rested.

"Any idea what the scuff came from?"

Sid gave an exaggerated shrug. "No idea, but if you want my guess it had to be some kind of powerful electromagnet. I've had some time to think about what happened and whatever was used to make the iron bars move, it had to have some juice behind it. The body was gone by the time we got here, but the police showed me the iron bars and some of them were impaled in the brickwork on the other side of the arches."

Tempest looked where Sid pointed. "That's forty yards away," he remarked. "What do the bars weigh?"

"About fifty pounds each. They're six foot long. Sharpen one end and it would be like throwing a javelin."

"Were they sharpened?"

"Didn't need to be. That much steel moving fast enough to lodge itself in brickwork forty yards away ... it would go right through anything that got in its way."

Tempest looked around some more, crossed the road to inspect the holes and take some pictures, and satisfied himself that he'd seen all there was to see. Norman wasn't relying on tricks alone to perpetrate his murders. The use of an electromagnet yet again suggested a level of sophistication that would require planning and preparation. He would have to know his victim would be walking in front of the building site, but also know what time, that the site would be empty so he could set the weapon up, and must have tested it to be certain it would work.

"Any idea where a person might hire an industrial size electromagnet around here?"

Merriweather's

FRIDAY, JANUARY 5TH 1530HRS

Tempest muttered it as a joke while jotting down his need to find out, but Sid surprised him.

"Only one place I know of that would have that kind of thing: Merriweather's in Dartford. They're a big electrical firm. One of the last independent ones around. If they haven't got one, no one will."

Thankful for the help and advice, Tempest shook Sid's hand and let him get back to work.

On his walk back to the car, parked just around the corner, the rain restarted, this time with some intention behind it. Fat drops soaked the ground in less than a minute and spurred Tempest to hurry.

Safe inside his car, he started the engine and used his phone to look up Merriweather's. Dartford wasn't far to go, and experience dictated he was more likely to get answers if he went in person, but he also wanted to visit the coroner's office and there were only so many hours in a day.

Accepting that he couldn't do both, he tapped on the hyperlinked phone number and let it connect.

"Merriweather's," said a man, his voice rhythmic and upbeat as though he was having a great day and loved his job.

"Good afternoon." Tempest explained who he was and why he was calling, but not that the electromagnet might have been employed to carry out a murder.

The sound of fingers on a keyboard filtered down the line, the man at the other end humming a pop tune while he looked.

"Yes, we did rent one out last month. That's a fairly rare item. Can't say I recall ever renting it out to anyone myself."

Almost holding his breath, Tempest asked, "What dates did it go out and come back, please?"

More key tapping followed by, "It was hired on December 12th and off-hired on Monday 18th."

The dates were bang on for Diane Meacock's murder. Norman killed her on Sunday 17th and returned the electromagnet the following day.

Daring to hope, Tempest asked the big one, "What is the name on the agreement, please? Who hired it?"

"Oh, um, sorry. I can't give out personal information. GDPR and all that."

Sucking some air through his teeth as he thought, Tempest questioned how he would get the information. Breaking in was always an option, but he'd only got out of custody a few hours ago. Thinking perhaps Patience might be able to help, another idea hit on him.

"Yes, of course," he said. "Perhaps, though, you can tell me if I get the name right? Just a yes or no will do. Is the name of the hirer N. Pickett?"

"Um, no. Sorry. That's not the name I have."

Tempest clenched his fists and bared his teeth. It was not what he'd expected to hear, and the news messed with his theories. Now he really needed to see the name. Assuming he wasn't wrong about the electromagnet being used to fling the iron bars, either Norman used an alias, or he had an accomplice. The latter strengthened his concern there might be more than just Zephyrus to deal with but also explained his alibi. If he'd driven to Dartford, slipping the man on the phone a couple of notes to grease his palm would be possible. The option to go was still there, but the round trip would take a couple of hours with rush hour traffic clogging the main artery running north to south. On a different day, that might not matter, but his desire to resolve the issue with Amanda made him want to be home at a sensible time. Being out for hours hunting down clues to solve a case would make it look like he didn't care and nothing could be further from the truth.

Sensing an opportunity, Tempest took the man's name, thanked him, and ended the call. Next, he composed a message to Amanda.

'Babe, I'm working the wizard case and might be late home. We need to talk about what happened at the office today, so I hope you will be there to sit down with me. If you let me know what you are in the mood for, I can bring something nice for dinner.'

He read it twice, rewrote it six times, and finally sent it.

Ordinarily, getting home late wouldn't concern him one little bit. In fact, his aim to be home around 1700hrs was to do with the dachshunds and nothing else. The more he thought about Amanda's reaction, the more it irked him. Why would she assume the worst? He'd never given her any reason to suspect he might cheat on her.

Firing the engine to life, he scrolled through his list of contacts to find the local coroner's office and dialled the number. He was heading to Dartford to get the name which meant he didn't have time to visit the coroner in person. However, he was on first name terms with one of the team.

"Good afternoon," he said when the receptionist picked up the call. "This is Tempest Michaels. Is Dr Raffety in?" If not he had his mobile number and could call him directly.

Patched through, a few moments later Dr Gerald Raffety was on the phone, his Irish accent always a joy to hear. He was one of those permanently upbeat people whose enthusiasm infected all those he came into contact with.

"Tempest!" He trumpeted the name. "What devilish drama are you involved in this time?"

They first met six months ago when Tempest investigated reports of a phantom figure at a pub in East Malling. Gerald was called to the scene when Tempest found the body of the landlord, and they cracked the case together when the autopsy revealed a ghostly handprint on the man's back had been made with liquid nitrogen. When the arrest was made – the bar manager did it – he was sleeping with the landlady and wanted to take over the pub – they ended up staying in the bar for a few drinks and discovered they had not only both served in the Army but were in the same patch of desert in Iraq at the same time in 2003.

"Gerrie, I'm interested in the wizard case. Two victims came in last night. Walter and Vanessa Freeman. Can you tell me anything about them? Specifically, how they came to die?"

Tempest tried not to guess how Norman might have achieved the double murder, but the 'how' of it could be important.

"Ah, well, you're in luck, my boy. I attended the Freemans myself. However, I had to dig to find the cause, finally discovering it in their lungs."

"Their lungs?"

"That's what I said. At first I thought they had been asphyxiated but couldn't figure out how until I opened them up. They were both poisoned with an aerosol. It's still being analysed but my best guess is that someone used a concentrated bug spray on them. Now, you're probably struggling to understand how a bug spray can be that deadly, but most of them contain hydrogen cyanide. Sprayed right into their faces, if they got a lungful of the stuff, it would kill them. Cyanide inhibits the body's ability to draw breath by blocking the chemical reaction in the lungs. I only figured it out because I found Isopropyl Myristate and Aminomethyl Propanol in their lungs. Hydrogen cyanide breaks down almost immediately, but those two and other trace chemicals get left behind. Whoever this wizard fellow is, he's a clever one."

"What else can you tell me?"

"Only that death was instant and the killer clearly has something vaguely resembling a conscience because he opened the window to make sure the gas would be gone before anyone else came in the room."

"He was specific about his target."

"He was. There were two kids across the hall, and he left them alone."

It hardly made Norman a better man, and it didn't qualify as a redeeming quality, but it was something.

Tempest thanked Gerald for his help and suggested they should grab lunch sometime soon. Having a friend in the coroner's office was never going to be a bad thing.

Traffic on the A2 dual carriageway leading north to Dartford flowed for once, his journey taking less than half the time he'd mentally allotted. The sun had all but given up for the day when he set off and was well over the horizon by the time he parked his car outside Merriweather's.

The name of the man he spoke to less than forty minutes ago was Alan. Pushing his way through the entrance door to the service desk, he looked about to see how many staff there might be to pick from. With less than an hour to go until closing time, it was unlikely Alan would be on a break; an assumption that proved accurate when Tempest heard him speak.

Tempest expected an older man, someone in his fifties perhaps, but Alan had to be seventy-five if he was a day. He wore his white hair cut short at the back and sides, and must have once been a body builder for his shape wasn't far from the tailored 'Vee' dedicated gym goers achieve through many years of lifting. Unlike the twenty-something man to his right, Alan's biceps filled the sleeves of the firm's polo shirt.

Tempest waited in line behind a man hiring a ride-on rotavator, but a female staff member became available.

"I can help you over here," she called. The badge on her uniform identified her as Wendy.

The question was whether he was better waiting to speak with Alan or starting afresh with someone else. The woman waited for him; her eyes expectant. She was in her twenties and made Tempest wish he had Big Ben with him. Sending him in to bat would guarantee a result. Stuck doing it himself, Tempest flashed her a smile – an engaging one that could not be confused as flirtatious.

"Hi." He stopped in front of her and took out his wallet. Lowering his voice, he said, "My name in Tempest Michaels, I'm a ..."

"Oh, my God. I know you. You're that ghost hunter."

The man serving a customer to her left twitched his eyes in Tempest's direction. Tempest smiled nervously.

"Yes, that's right. I'm rather hoping you will be able to furnish me with a name." He kept his voice low and leaned closer in a conspiratorial manner. "It's part of an investigation."

"Into a ghost?" Wendy asked, her voice a whisper.

Sensing he was onto a winner, he leaned just a little bit closer so he could almost whisper into her ear. "Not this time. It's a wizard."

Wendy gasped, her eyes alive with excitement.

Two minutes later, Tempest slid back into his car. No doubt Wendy had broken the firm's GDPR rules to provide the name, but she assured him no one really cared about that nonsense, promised she wasn't going to tell anyone just in case, and said that if the person was a criminal they didn't deserve the privacy protection anyway.

Inclined to agree, Tempest put the name into his phone and searched. It wasn't just a name though. Wendy had turned her screen so he could snap a photograph of the hire docket. It showed the name, phone number, and home address.

Unfortunately, searching the internet for Alex Mullen returned hundreds of hits. Refining his search to find the right one would take a little time, but was doable, yet Tempest could see a simpler solution. He was going to knock on his door.

Accomplice

FRIDAY, JANUARY 5TH 1643HRS

The address for Alex Mullen took Tempest to Northfleet, a town bordering the Thames on its south bank. The dirty urban sprawl exemplified the worst features of life in a concrete jungle. Graffiti clung to every surface, public spaces had been vandalised, litter clogged the branches of plants that were already barely clinging to life, and there was nothing to see in any direction except more of the same. It made Tempest glad to live in the countryside where the views were of trees and vineyards.

He cruised past the house, going slow to be sure he had the right one before parking his car almost fifty yards down the street when he finally found a space. The houses were terraced, each one a narrow rectangle sandwiched between those on either side. They would once have been uniform, with period stone features above the doors and windows and chequerboard tiles leading through manicured yards to the front door. They were all different now, the decades of life and generations of inhabitants changing or neglecting what once made the street attractive.

The front wall outside Alex's house had collapsed inward, and not recently. Weeds grew where dirt carried on the rain, gathered in the nooks and crannies to give the plants a toehold. The gate sat to one side, leaning against the wall between his house and the neighbour to the right. Rust streaks ran from it to stain the concrete.

Nudging a pile of free newspapers to one side, Tempest rang the doorbell and knocked for good measure. With cars bumper to bumper at the kerb, there was no way to know which one might belong to the house. In truth, he figured Alex was more likely to be at work than at home, but the sound of movement inside the house suggested he was going to get to speak to someone.

A chain rattled and a lock turned before the door swung inward and a scruffy man peered around it. He didn't want to open the door far enough to show the inside, probably because it was as dirty and run down as the outside, Tempest guessed.

"Alex Mullen?" he enquired. Alex was somewhere in his early forties, going bald, filling out around his midriff, and very much on the short side at maybe five feet six inches.

"Whatever it is, I haven't got any money to buy it, and if you're wanting to talk to me about politics or religion, you can sling your hook." He started to close the door, but Tempest was too quick for him.

Wedging his foot in the door, he said, "Actually, I wanted to speak to you about the electromagnet you hired from Merriweather's." The announcement caught Alex by surprise, his head snapping up from glaring at Tempest's foot to meet his unwavering gaze with one of fear. "You know, the one Norman Pickett used to kill Diane Meacock."

He held up his phone to show the photograph of the hire docket on the screen.

All the colour left Alex's face.

"Perhaps you should let me in so we can talk," Tempest suggested. "This is just one piece of evidence. I have plenty more," he lied.

"I ... I don't know what you are talking about. I don't know anyone called Norman Pickett. You need to leave."

"Or what?" Tempest gripped the edge of the door threateningly, "You'll call the police." He watched Alex swallow hard. "Didn't think so." There was no doubt he could overpower the smaller man, but the night in a cell made him hesitate. Alex was guilty, but Tempest didn't know what of. He'd hired a piece of machinery, but did he know in advance what it would be used for?

Stepping back a bit so he wasn't right in the homeowner's face, Tempest offered a more relaxed approach.

"Okay, Alex, let's say I believe you are a small cog in Norman's machine."

"I told you I don't know who Norman Pickett is."

"And I don't believe you, so stop wasting my time with pointless lies. Norman Pickett is Zephyrus Frostwind and he is using props and tricks to murder a bunch of people. I haven't figured out why, yet, though I believe he is working down a list of people who have, at some point in his life, done him wrong. In his eyes, at least. He is going to get caught soon, and when that happens all those who have helped him will find themselves in police custody answering some very uncomfortable questions. You will be one of them. That I can promise." Tempest paused to see if Alex wanted to say anything.

He looked nervous, his eyes flitting left and right and down, but never up to look at the man on his doorstep.

Continuing, Tempest said, "You can get ahead of it all, Alex. You can be the one who escapes prosecution if you volunteer what you know. Admit your part now, freely and wholly, or confess it later in a police interview room. Which would you prefer?" The ball firmly in Alex's court, Tempest stopped talking and waited.

It took a few seconds, but Alex finally lifted his face to meet Tempest's eyes. Unfortunately, where he expected to see resigned defeat, defiance had found a home.

"You think it's all just props and tricks? He set fire to you the first time you met. What? Didn't think I would have seen it. That video is everywhere, man. I don't think I need to admit anything. The police arrested Norman and let him go. There's no evidence against him thanks to you and there never will be. Don't worry about trying to catch him though, soon enough he'll come for you. No one can stand against him, and next time you meet you won't live to tell the tale." Triumph sparkled in Alex's eyes and a smile teased his mouth.

Tempest punched him in the teeth.

He didn't put a full allotment of energy into it but swung his right arm with enough juice to knock Alex back into the hallway. The door clanged against the wall and bounced back only to be stopped by Tempest as he stepped over the threshold.

His face now showing shock, Alex scrambled back across the carpet to get away. Tempest stalked after him.

"At least we now know where we stand. The police will have the evidence showing your part in Diane Meacock's murder in the next few minutes. Go on the run, wait here to be arrested, race back to the hive, it will make no difference in the end. Please let Norman know I look forward to seeing him again."

Message delivered, Tempest left the house, his phone in

his hands as he sent the hire docket to Patience. He followed it with a call.

"Tempest. What's that thing you just sent me?"

"It's proof the wizard isn't working alone. The name of the alibi who came forward to place Norman Pickett somewhere else last night, was that Alex Mullen by any chance?"

Patience consulted her memory. "No, that's not the name I have."

"Then he has more than one accomplice." He explained what the electromagnet had been used for, told her about his encounter with Alex, and even admitted assaulting him.

"Don't go giving Quinn more ammunition," Patience warned. "If you go back to jail so soon after being released, especially if it's for another crime involving violence, you won't be out a few weeks later like you were last time."

"Would you believe that I am restraining myself for precisely that reason?"

"You need to work harder at it. Let me look into this electromagnet thing and I'll get back to you."

Catching her before she could clear the line, Tempest said, "Did you read the coroner's report on the Freemans?"

"Yeah. They inhaled hydrogen cyanide."

"Which means one of Norman's other friends works with chemicals or is a chemistry teacher or has access to industrial strength bug spray or something like that. All in all we have not one serial killer, but a team of them. Maybe you want to take a closer look at the person who alibied Norman for last night's fight at Valerie Legg's house."

With a thank you for his help, Patience said she was going to delve deeper into the case, this time viewing it from his perspective. Norman wasn't considered to be a suspect and no one was watching him.

"Keep it that way if you can?"

"Are you kidding?" Patience questioned. "If I can prove he's behind it, I have to make the arrest. You know that."

"Yes, I know that, and if you have an airtight case I fully endorse you bringing him in. But I'm not convinced you're going to have enough to put him away. He needs to be caught in the act."

"And how exactly are we supposed to do that?"

"Ah, well, you're not. I am."

"Didn't he set you on fire last time?"

"Only a little bit."

"A little bit on fire? Oh, well, that's all right then. Don't go doing anything stupid."

Before he ended the call, Tempest confirmed the police had the list of calling card recipients collated by The Weald Word. Naturally, they got it long before he did and were speaking with all the potential victims to find what linked them, but Norman still wasn't in the picture.

"That's a mistake," he assured her.

"So you keep saying."

He explained about Gill Carson and Elaine Prescott and from whom he'd learned about the connection. "I believe you will find people on the list who have no connection to Norman Pickett."

"We already are."

"That's because he is targeting them on behalf of his followers or accomplices, whatever you want to call them. This murder spree is bigger than one man's desire for revenge."

"That's quite a stretch, Tempest. Do you have any proof? Any proof at all?"

"Other than equipment hire dockets and a feeling in my water? No."

"Didn't think so."

"Just do yourself a favour and explore the possibility that I'm right."

"Only because it's you and you usually are."

Tempest ended the call with a promise that she would be the first person he called when he had Norman in custody. Then he gunned his engine and pointed it south. It was time to return to the office.

Round Two

FRIDAY, JANUARY 5TH 1712HRS

Halfway back to Rochester, a text from Amanda pinged onto his phone. Knowing he shouldn't look while driving, Tempest read it anyway.

'*We can talk when you get home, just know that I am not mad at you. Sorry, I didn't message earlier, but I had to leave or I would have slapped that woman all over your office. She has been after you for months, I just never imagined she would try something so blatant. If you need to work late to crack the wizard case, don't worry about me. I'm at home with the dogs already. They've been fed and are on the sofa with me while I do some research. Love you.*'

Feeling much relieved, Tempest returned his attention to the road and had to slam on the brakes because he was going significantly faster than the other vehicles around him. Traffic was slowing, the unavoidable result of a million people all leaving work at the same time. He crawled alongside the other cars, vans, and trucks all the way to the slip road leading off the motorway and into Strood. There he was able to speed up, but not for long.

Thankfully, though it was slow, the rest of the journey

through the towns wasn't far and he pulled into his parking space behind the office at 1742hrs.

Tempest knew without needing to go inside that the lights would be off. Marjory liked to keep to the clock, which meant she was never late, but was putting on her coat two seconds after five o'clock rolled around. Entering through the back door, he fumbled his way in the dark and settled into his office. He didn't turn the main office lights on, he didn't need them, opting to use a standard lamp in the corner behind his desk to provide illumination.

Back on the case, Tempest was going to look at more of the business card recipients – those who hadn't answered their phones the first time he rang them were going to get a second call, but first on his list to investigate was Norman Pickett.

Was Alex Mullen one of his known associates? Would he show up on his social media feed? Finding out wouldn't take long and in scrolling through Tempest could note any other names that occurred semi-regularly.

Opening a fresh tab to start the search, movement caught his eye. It came from outside the glass front façade of the office. Squinting at the softly lit street outside, he saw nothing. Dismissing it, he was turning back to his keyboard when it happened again. A delicate flickering of green light. He was seeing it through the frosted glass, but there could be no mistaking what it was.

It came again, flickering like lightning at waist height, a glowing lime green ball of light made indistinct through the film over the glass.

Coming out from behind his desk, his body drawn to confirm what he already knew, Tempest stood up and in so doing lifted his head above the level of the frosting. Outside a figure in a black cloak grinned.

Inside, Tempest growled, "Norman." Exploding into action, he ran to get outside. Cursing as he ran past Marjory's desk, he reversed course to grab the spare key from her drawer and snatched up a four-hole punch for good measure. In terms of weaponry it lacked in almost every department except heft, but there was nothing else to hand.

The cloaked figure turned away from the window, crossing the street to the other side where he paused in the darkness of a narrow alley between two of the city's ancient buildings. Vehicles rarely enter the High Street, it's a pedestrianised area set up that way so tourists can meander and explore, staring at the ancient architecture without fear of being run down. So how was Norman creating magical sparks in the air without being seen?

Tempest found out when he wrenched the door open.

The rain fell in sheets. It coated the ground with a half inch of water and each fat drop sent a splash upward to a height of half a foot. The people caught out in it hunkered under umbrellas, their eyes cast down and their pace fast. They were too preoccupied to notice the strangely dressed man lurking in the mouth of an alleyway.

Tempest's coat was on his desk but even wearing it he would be soaked in no time at all. Would the rain nullify Norman's ability to throw fire? Or poison gas? That he was being led into a trap seemed obvious, but he knew the ground and wasn't about to let the fake wizard escape for a second time just because he felt some trepidation.

Trepidation? Tempest's pulse jackhammered with the fear he felt. Maybe Norman wouldn't be able to set fire to him this time around, but that gave him no comfort. In the back of his head, he had an outline plan for how he might even the odds, but it required preparation, and he was yet to even start the process. He wasn't ready for this fight, but going after Norman was non-negotiable.

Norman let the lime green lightning play between his hands again, drawing his fingers apart so the threads running between them stretched and sizzled. Then he turned and stepped into the shadow cast by the buildings and promptly vanished.

Jaw clenched, both against the chill of the cold rain soaking instantly through his cotton shirt, and to gird his loins for the fight to come, Tempest ran into the storm. The sensible move would be to call the police, but he didn't have his phone on him and wasn't about to go back for it.

His vision instantly clouded by rain which soaked his face and everything else, Tempest collided with a couple in suits hurrying through the storm.

"Hey!" yelled the man.

Tempest ignored him, racing to catch his quarry.

The woman asked, "Did you see what he was holding?" but her words were lost in the drumming of the rain.

Once he was in the alley the rain diminished. It continued to fall, but slicing through the air at an angle, far less made it into the gap high above Tempest's head.

Oblivious, Tempest charged forward. The alley led to a service yard behind the shops. It could be accessed by the alley and through a steel mesh vehicle gate to the rear. He splashed through puddles keeping the cloaked figure in his sights.

He lost sight of him briefly when Norman rounded the rear of the building, but two seconds later Tempest caught sight of him again. He was facing back the way he had just come and walking backwards to draw Tempest in. The vehicle gate was locked, not that scaling it would prove too difficult if Norman wanted to keep going, but he stopped in the centre of the loading yard.

Certain Norman had a plan, Tempest regretted not going back for his phone. Knowing help was on its way would be a big comfort. Were there steel bars and an electromagnet in one of the yard's corners? Was the fake wizard about to unleash some other clever trick?

Hefting the four-hole punch, Tempest figured speed was his friend. Maybe if he sprinted, Norman wouldn't have time to do whatever he had planned. Had he looked around instead, he might have seen the attack coming.

Ambush

FRIDAY, JANUARY 5TH 1724HRS

Something hard struck the back of his head just behind his right ear. Stunned, Tempest dropped the four-hole punch and pitched forward, instinctively moving away from the source of pain. His brain supplied a message, telling him it was a bottle because it exploded on contact and there was glass in the air.

The cloaked figure was directly in front of him and that could only mean one thing: he wasn't alone.

Staggering, Tempest tried to put distance between himself and whoever was there, but the second man was too savvy and followed his glass missile with a melee attack. He swung haymaker punches, driving Tempest back and forcing him to defend as blow after blow came at him.

Dressed in a black cloak just like Norman's, the rain-soaked cloth clung to the man's frame. He was taller than Tempest, but skinny, his frame gangly more than anything else. The cloak covered his face, but not to such an extent that he couldn't see.

In contrast, from the direction he faced, the driving rain hit Tempest's eyes, fogging his vision once more, and though he didn't think he was concussed, the blow to his head had rattled his brain and he felt uncoordinated. He could tell the man he was fighting was neither trained nor proficient – had he been Tempest would have been on the ground and in serious trouble, but just when he thought about trying to catch the next punch, he was hit from behind.

This time the attack came in the form of a flying kick that threw Tempest into the first attacker. Crying out in pain, he nevertheless grabbed the first man. Mostly this was to arrest his fall so he wouldn't find himself on the ground. That's where most fights end up, but Tempest knew if he went down while they were still up it would all be over.

Now that he had hold of the first man's cloak, Tempest let his momentum carry him through the spot where he'd been standing. That took the man off balance while in turn helping Tempest to regain his. A quick check over his shoulder confirmed the second attacker was following and that was all the invitation he needed.

Kicking out, he used the first man as a point from which he could pivot and swept his right foot in a high arc to nail the second man in the face. He ran straight into it, the stupid cowl of his cloak blocking enough of his peripheral vision that he never saw it coming. As his right foot continued around, Tempest brought it down, planted it hard and used a combination of weight and inertia to throw the lighter man in his grip.

Directly at his colleague.

It was precisely then that the third man got involved. The one Tempest saw through the office window and assumed to be Norman hadn't been able to get close enough to throw a punch. Until Tempest got the upper hand, that is. When the first attacker careened into the second, the third sent a hard right cross right through Tempest's jaw.

It had juice behind it.

Brain rattling inside his skull, still dazed from the blow to the back of his head, Tempest went down. He could do nothing to prevent it, his body wouldn't respond to his commands. Everything in his head was sludgy, his thoughts weighed down as though they had to wade through thick mud to get anywhere. He knew they were coming and that not getting up spelled serious trouble, but they were on him before there was any chance to rally.

A kick to the ribs shunted him across the soaking wet tarmac, a second hit the meat of his arm as he tucked to protect himself. Deep inside the fog, he registered the need to sweep his limbs out and around. Catching a leg in exchange for opening himself to another kick was the only way out of his situation, but lacking coordination, he took a foot to the gut the moment he exposed it.

"The cops!" shouted one of the men.

Another kick landed, this one a glancing blow to his face when he twisted to look. Flashing red and blue filled the alleyway. The cops really were here and for once Tempest was pleased to have them around.

"Do we leave him?"

"Yeah. Let's go!" They were speaking quietly so as not to be heard by the cops.

"But I've got a knife. I can finish him!"

"No! We only needed to distract him. Now move!"

From his position on the ground, Tempest heard their feet moving away and the sound of the vehicle gates rattling when they went over them to escape. He rolled onto his back and groaned. It wasn't the first time he'd lost a fight, but taking a beating never gets any easier. That it was his own fault just made it harder. Underestimating an enemy. It was a classic rookie error.

A voice echoed down the alleyway, "I'm going to check down here."

Tempest saw torchlight illuminating the narrow space between the buildings and was getting gingerly to his feet when the cop holding it appeared. Bright light burned his eyes when the cop aimed the beam directly at his face and he lifted an arm to block it.

The cop was on his radio in seconds while simultaneously calling to his colleague. Tempest managed to just about get himself upright by the time the police officer crossed the remaining yards.

"Are you badly hurt?" he demanded, holding the lapel radio with one hand while using the torch to check Tempest over.

With light playing over him, Tempest could see the blood on his shirt. It stained his right shoulder. There wasn't a huge amount of it, certainly not enough to be a concern, but it came from where the bottle hit his head. Probing with careful fingers, he winced when he found the wound.

The officer used an arm to guide Tempest back toward the street. His partner arrived, running back to join up with them from wherever he'd gone.

"This is the guy?" he asked.

The first cop said, "Haven't got that far yet."

Tempest asked, "What guy?"

"There were reports of an armed man chasing someone. Are you armed?"

Tempest looked down at himself. His clothes were plastered to his skin and his hands were empty. Where did they think he was managing to conceal a weapon? Clicking, he realised what they meant.

"I had a four-hole punch in my hand. It was the only thing I could grab."

"Why did you need a weapon at all? Who were you chasing?" This from the second cop who was clearly the more senior of the two. They were both men in their twenties with short hair and trim figures like they'd been cast in the same die and painted to not quite match.

Feeling the cold creeping into his bones, Tempest said, "Look, can we get back to my office. It's just over there and it's warm and dry inside." He indicated the way with a nod of his head.

The cops had no desire to stay outside either. They had an ambulance coming, and didn't cancel it when Tempest assured them it wasn't necessary. In the area when the call came in, they were dispatched to check out the report. Now they needed to figure out what was what and cop number two, who identified himself as PC Mailer, was gravely concerned Tempest had left a body somewhere.

Crossing Rochester High Street to get to the office, he persisted with his questions.

"What happened to the guy you were chasing?" Then to PC Holland, his partner, "I think we might need to get additional units down here to check the area. There could be someone injured in that yard where you found him."

"Don't bother," Tempest replied and was about to explain how the fight went when he pushed open the office door and froze.

It looked like a tornado had been through it.

Cursing, Tempest raged, "Aaah! That's what he meant." The cops came in behind him, their eyes taking in the destruction. "One of them wanted to stick me with his knife and another said their job was to distract me." He explained as he hurried to his private office at the back of the building.

The main office had been trashed, but his desk and everything around it had suffered far worse. The computer was destroyed, his laptop was missing, taken by whoever Norman sent.

The cops hovered in his doorway.

"What happened here?" asked Holland, the friendlier of the two.

Despite how wet he was, Tempest slumped into his office chair. He bluffed Alex Mullen about having evidence, so the wizard and his followers reacted to remove it. If they examined his devices, they would soon figure out he had almost no evidence at all.

Sighing, Tempest said, "Norman Pickett is Zephyrus Frostwind. He's killed six people now if you include Stephanie Greer and will kill again because Chief Inspector Quinn refuses to listen. I was building a case and had evidence linking him to the murder of Diane Meacock, a death that was listed as an accident until yesterday." Okay, so the evidence was tenuous at best and mostly existed in Tempest's head, but if he needed further proof he was on the right track, this was it.

PC Mailer was more interested in the report that brought them to Tempest in the first place.

"What about the person you chased?" he persisted, his hand poised on his radio to call for assistance.

"It wasn't one guy, it was three. The one I was seen chasing lured me into an ambush. I got my butt kicked, so don't worry about there being anyone you need to go save. Chances are I would be on my way to hospital right now if you two hadn't showed up when you did.

PC Holland made a happy face like a puppy wagging its tail when praised for being a good dog. PC Mailer's expression remained dubious.

Their radios crackled and the voice from dispatch advised they should remain at the scene and keep their 'suspect' under observation. Units were on route.

Quinn

FRIDAY, JANUARY 5TH 1803HRS

Tempest fetched a hand towel from the toilet under the watchful gaze of PC Mailer. He used that to dry himself as best as possible. From a drawer in his office, he dug out an old t-shirt that had been there for months. It was crumpled and creased but it was dry and that was the only thing he cared about. PC Mailer argued when Tempest said he wanted to go out to his car but relented when Tempest pushed him to justify his concerns. Inviting both cops to follow him, he collected his ready bag from the boot and changed his trousers too. Forced to go commando, not that it mattered, he emerged from the toilet wearing a pair of the black rip-stop cargo trousers (he owned more than one pair), the crinkled t-shirt, and nothing else. Not even on his feet.

Paramedics arrived ahead of the additional officers, but the cut to the back of his head had stopped bleeding by then. They put a dressing over it and checked his bruised ribs, confirming his opinion that none were broken. They hurt and he would be sore for a week or more, but he knew it could have been much worse. His face hurt where the punch rattled his jaw, but he couldn't find any loose teeth.

The paramedics were all but finished when Chief Inspector Quinn came through the office main door. Following him in were a duo of sergeants and a young female constable, all in uniform.

Tempest drew in a deep breath that hurt his ribs and contained nothing but a premonition of impending aggravation.

"As I understand it, Mr Michaels, you are once again at the centre of an event that requires the involvement of multiple officers."

Convinced he was wasting his breath, Tempest said, "It was Norman's people. They were dressed in full-length black cloaks and one of them produced sparks from his fingers to make me think he was Zephyrus Frostwind."

"Still trying to blame a man with multiple alibis, Mr Michaels?"

"I'm still trying to catch a serial killer before he can strike again. What are you doing?"

Flanking Tempest on either side, PC's Mailer and Holland stayed quiet.

Never taking his eyes off Tempest, Quinn aimed his attention their way, "Get back outside and secure the area where you found Mr Michaels. Then conduct a search. Forensics are on their way along with CID. The rain will make things harder, but if you find blood I want to know about it."

"We're done here," announced the lead paramedic as Holland and Mailer hustled to get back outside.

Quinn said, "If you are not immediately needed elsewhere, I would like you to hang around. Mr Michaels has a habit of injuring people. There may be a victim in need of your skills."

"There isn't," said Tempest, "and the only blood they will find is mine."

"We shall see."

Determined to stretch things out, the chief inspector kept Tempest at the office while the forensics team and six officers combed the yard and the surrounding area looking for any indication Tempest might not be giving an accurate recounting of the event.

Despite his aching body and pounding head, both of which calmed with some painkillers he popped from a blister packet in his desk drawer, Tempest started to tidy.

"What do you think you are doing?" demanded Quinn.

Tempest narrowed his eyes. "I'm putting my office back together, Ian. I need to work here."

"Oh, I don't think so. According to you this office was ransacked by the accomplices of a dangerous serial killer. We need to check for prints, hair, and fibre. They will have to take photographs and catalogue what was taken. I'm sure you want these miscreants caught, don't you, Mr Michaels?"

Tempest folded his arms and waited. It was a trap, and he had no patience for the chief inspector's ridiculous games.

"Unless you would rather come clean and admit you trashed your own office in a bid to perpetuate the stupid lies you told yesterday. You think that by muddying the water sufficiently, you will be able to make it seem as though you had some justification for burning down an innocent old lady's house."

Letting a grin tug at his mouth, Tempest said, "You're

going to look pretty stupid when I catch Norman Pickett and expose the truth."

Quinn matched Tempest's smile. "How are you going to do that from a cell, Mr Michaels? You are a convicted criminal, a man of violence. I am duty bound to take you off the streets and see you locked away where you can do no more harm. You admit to chasing a man this evening. What did you do to him, Mr Michaels? Where is he now?"

"You're an idiot, Ian. So you go ahead and waste everyone's time. The team you have working outside in the rain won't find anything because there is nothing for them to find."

Only one of the sergeants remained in the Blue Moon office, and though he said nothing, it was clear from his face he didn't like what his boss was doing. No one believed Tempest chose to destroy his own office, just like none of them expected to find an injured victim Tempest left stuffed in a wheelie bin somewhere. Not even Quinn, though he would never admit it.

The chief inspector was wielding his power, messing Tempest around just because he could. Yet Tempest knew the slightest hint of a chargeable offense would be enough for Quinn to place him under arrest. He didn't want to spend a second night in a cell, so kept his mouth shut and played along.

Four hours later, when the forensics guys had gone through the office with a fine-toothed comb, he was finally allowed to tidy up.

Pausing in the doorway like Columbo, Quinn shot a final remark, "Do try to stay out of trouble, Mr Michaels. I fear you bring all these problems upon yourself. Perhaps if you left police work to the police you would not suffer as you do."

Inside his head, Tempest used both hands to throttle the irritating idiot.

Amanda had messaged several times throughout the evening, checking in to see why he wasn't home yet and questioning if he was still at the office. He'd expressed a desire to talk and then failed to show up. He let her know why he was still at work but left out the fight and his injured state and omitted to reveal the destruction wrought by Norman's minions.

While in theory he'd left his office door open and anyone could have wandered in, it had to be Norman or persons he sent. The whiteboard of notes was now just white, any files he had on his office computer or laptop were gone. Amanda's computer was trash, so too Marjory's so while he knew the information was backed up onto the cloud, he held next to no hope whoever had his laptop hadn't accessed and erased it all.

Sure, he had passwords and such, but a tech savvy person could get around them.

Working until 2300hrs, Tempest tidied as best he could. They were going to need new computers, but other than that the damage was minimal. He could sort that over the weekend and have the office ready for business on Monday morning.

Tired, in need of a bath and a meal, he took his still wet clothes and headed for home.

Norman Pickett was going down and the crazy plan itching away inside Tempest's head was about to come to life.

Breakfast

SATURDAY, JANUARY 6TH 0711HRS

"I know I say that you can achieve anything, Tempest, and that I am constantly amazed at the things you just go ahead and do that I would never even consider attempting, but this is fairly nuts."

Amanda sat across the dining table from him, her now empty breakfast bowl of fruit and yoghurt pushed to one side. In her hands, she held a cup of tea, the steam rising to make a few stray wisps of her blonde hair move about.

By the time Tempest got home the previous evening, she had gone to bed, but was still awake reading when he came in. He updated her on the evening's drama while she checked his wounds and made him a sandwich. She also ran him a bath and tried to get the blood out of his shirt. That it was white made it worse, but left for hours it probably wouldn't have mattered what colour it was. It went in the bin.

"I think it just *sounds* nuts. Honestly, I think this is the right way to go."

"But you're going to be careful, right?"

"And I promise to take Big Ben with me."

Amanda rolled her eyes. "Yeah, like that's going to reassure me. That giant doofus would start a fight with a bear and leave you to deal with the mess it made."

"Only if it was a boy bear," Tempest grinned. "If it was a girl bear he would ..."

Amanda flapped a hand in the air, begging him to stop talking. "That's not a mental image I need in my head. Look I can rearrange my plans so I'm there with you."

"No need. You've made arrangements with a client. My case isn't bringing in any money, and neither is Jane's. At least one of us ought to be paying the bills."

They both knew the bills were just fine. The business overheads amounted to a fraction of what the three detectives brought in and there was a fat wedge of money in the accounts.

"Seriously, though, if half of what you say is accurate, you are going to be outnumbered. Big Ben might be tough, but he's not indestructible. You need more people."

He was about to argue when he saw a new opportunity. "I think you're right." He picked up his phone. "It's about time I called in reinforcements." When the Blue Moon business first started getting busy, he would regularly involve his friends from the pub. Over time, as their lives took them in new directions – Basic turned out to be an entrepreneurial genius, Hilary quit his job to help develop Basic's business, and Jagjit settled into life as a married man – doing crazy stuff as a team happened less and less. They worked together on the Brothers Grimm fairytale case, but prior to that months had passed since he last had them out at night.

While Tempest's fingers flashed across his phone, Amanda drained her cup and took it to the dishwasher along with her breakfast bowl. Kissing Tempest on the head, she let him know she was heading upstairs to get showered and dressed.

On a different day he might have seen that as a subtle invitation to join her, but his ribs were too sore to contemplate that kind of activity. The engagement ring was back in the little drawer of his bedside table where it weighed heavy on his mind. They were supposed to have talked about Sharon and her near nakedness in his office when he got home, but the subject never came up. It was as though they both saw it for what it was and silently agreed to just put it behind them.

Yet he still needed to ask her *the* question. More and more it preyed on his mind that he was trying to engineer the perfect time or the perfect scenario, but maybe he just needed to get on and do it. He could be waiting on one knee when she came back downstairs ... He could be, but it didn't feel right. He was only going to do it once and there had to be something special about it.

Group message sent, Tempest finished his own mug of tea and set about getting ready for the day.

Using the League

SATURDAY, JANUARY 6TH 0942HRS

Frank sucked some air between his teeth. "You're sure about this, Tempest?"

Tempest nodded. "Yup."

Frank scratched his jaw. "I don't know. If word gets out …"

"How would it? Look, either I'm right or I'm wrong. If I'm wrong the League gets the chance to recruit a powerful mage. You said that's what they want to do."

"He would be a serious asset if we can turn his talents toward the fight against the encroaching forces of darkness."

"I'm sure." Tempest worked hard to keep his tone free from any hint of sarcasm. "But if I'm right, you can save the League a lot of wasted effort and expose a charlatan."

Frank said, "When you put it like that … but hey, do you really want to put this much money down?"

"Sure. He's never going to get his hands on it, is he?"

"He will if you are wrong and I'm almost one hundred percent certain you are."

"Then you'll be wanting to come along to see him turn me into a frog, won't you."

Frank's frown was epic. "Transmogrification isn't real, Tempest. Mass cannot be cancelled out for a start, so even if magic could change the form of a thing into something else, you would wind up with a Tempest sized frog."

Standing next to Frank, Poison's face crinkled. "Ewww!"

Frank looked at Tempest, clearly expecting him to do something and Tempest looked right back at him.

After a few seconds, Frank said, "You're waiting for me to do it now, aren't you?"

Tempest shrugged. "Now would be good."

Shrugging brought a twinge from the small wound on the back of his head. The paramedics closed it with a couple of steri-strips, but there was bruising beneath the skin. Overall, he didn't feel too bad, though taking a deep breath brought more pain than he was willing to endure. Painkillers took the edge off, but too many of those would dull his reflexes.

Grumbling and muttering, Frank fetched a laptop from under the counter. It was an old thing Frank swore by because it was built by the Russians during the Cold War and would withstand not only the EMP from a nuclear strike, but dragon fire, Elven steel, and probably being sat on by a troll. He'd paid someone to adapt the inner gubbins so it would do internet and stuff.

Tempest started to go around the counter so he could see what Frank was writing.

Frank picked up the laptop and hugged it to his body.

"No, you stay that side. It's bad enough you know how the League communicates. I'm not going to risk you seeing what is being written or the names of those writing it."

Raising his hands in surrender, Tempest moved back to his side of the counter.

There were customers in the shop, a trio of boys who looked to be about thirteen. They were leafing through comic books while side-eyeing Poison. Looking at some of the meatier tomes against the far wall of the shop was a man in his fifties. Heavyset with curly blonde hair that was probably cute when he was a baby, but had been left to grow long and bushy, he made his choice and moved to the counter.

Frank took the laptop and reversed through the door into the offices beyond.

Tempest waited, but sensing he was encroaching on the customer's personal space, he drifted a yard to the left where a display of *Chucky* figurines in various stabby poses could be purchased for eyewatering amounts.

Frank reappeared just as Poison wished the customer a pleasant day, addressed him by name, and hoped she would see him again soon.

"Right, that's done. I still think you're mad, but I'll be there. Maybe when he commands the air in your lungs to freeze, I will be able to come forward to represent the League and explain it was a test."

"That's the spirit, Frank."

Cheerful and optimistic, Tempest bade them a good day and went shopping. He wasn't grocery shopping through. Oh, no, this was much more interesting. The type of shop he wanted wasn't one you could find any old place; it was kind of special. Frank would have known exactly where to find what Tempest needed, but asking the bookshop owner would have revealed his plan and Tempest wanted it to be a surprise.

The journey took almost two hours, mostly because he

had to negotiate the M25 and the giant four lane ring road circling the nation's capital could be relied upon to be choked with traffic regardless of day or even hour.

When he left a little more than an hour later to make the return journey, the Porsche was stuffed to the gills with all he believed he would need and his wallet was lighter to the tune of more than a thousand pounds. It was a hefty chunk of cash for a case he wasn't getting paid to solve, but vindication was going to feel oh so good.

By the time he left the motorway at the top of Blue Bell Hill, the sun was already plummeting for the horizon. Long shadows cast by the trees looked like evil fingers scratching at the road. He blasted through them, heading back to the village where the guys were waiting for him in the pub.

Battle Planning

SATURDAY, JANUARY 6TH 1528HRS

Having alcohol before going up against the wizard was a poor plan, but they all agreed one wouldn't hurt. In fact, since they were going to have something to eat before setting off, two would be okay.

Picking up his third pint, Hilary asked, "How sure are you that this guy can't actually control the elements?"

Tempest didn't need to think about his response. "One hundred percent. I saw one of his flame thrower thingies when I went to his house. The fire didn't magically burst forth from his fingertips. Like all good stage magicians, he has made clever props to deceive the eye."

Jagjit frowned. "But you said he got sacked because he wasn't a good magician and that he then started doing kids parties and was even worse."

"That's right." With hours to kill in the car, Tempest once again called as many of the Frostwind business card holders as he could. This time it included the families of the victims. Just as before, the results were problematic. Of the six victims, only two had hired Norman Pickett, but two of those who hadn't did reveal issues with different magicians they'd hired for their kid's parties.

"You think it's a league of them?" Big Ben sought to confirm.

"Something like that. Norman might not even be the ringleader, but I think he probably is. If we view the others as his minions or disciples, we can see how he has alibis and why he wasn't the one who hired the electromagnet. He's clever and he's sneaky, and he's dangerous, but most importantly for us, he isn't expecting opposition."

"Ok, but how are we going to beat him?" asked Hilary.

"We're going to out magic him." Tempest's answer made everyone look his way. "I have a few things in the car to show you. When we've done here, which we probably ought to be quite soon, we'll head back to mine so I can show you what I mean."

"Is it just us?" asked Big Ben. As the designated driver, he was on diet coke and itching to get on with some head cracking. "Or are Amanda and Jane coming too. This feels like an 'all hands on deck' type of situation."

Tempest shook his head. "Jane's still with Cassie and Amanda has a unicorn to investigate."

Jagjit snorted his beer. "A unicorn? You mean some fool is paying your firm to investigate a mythical creature that's going to turn out to be a horse."

Basic spoke for the first time in half an hour. "You don't believe in unicorns?"

The table all turned to look at him. James 'Basic' Burham, so called because God only loaded him with the most basic programming, was not known for asking questions. In fact, he was better known for the exact opposite.

Jagjit said, "No, Basic. That's because unicorns are not real."

"Course they are."

"They're really not," said Tempest.

Basic tried to hook one of his eyebrows in a quizzical fashion but couldn't get the muscles to obey his commands. In the end he used a stubby sausage of an index finger to lift it.

"You fink a brontosaurus leopard moose on stilts is real, but a unicorn isn't?"

Duly challenged, the first time Basic had ever offered a response with such depth and clarity, Tempest looked around the table for help.

Jagjit said, "A what now?"

"Brontosaurus leopard moose on stilts," Basic repeated sounding disappointed no one knew what he was talking about. "You know, guys, a giraffe. If a creature that ridiculous is real, a unicorn has to be."

Hilary picked up his pint. "He's got you there."

Twenty minutes later, their drinks finished, the crew arrived at Tempest's house. Each of them had a set of the black ripstop trousers and Kevlar vest, items Tempest furnished them with shortly after the first time they all came together to work on a case. Big Ben's were size XXL to fit around his chest and arms whereas Hilary, as a man who hadn't been inside a gym since he left school, wore a medium. And it was loose.

They all owned matching fingerless gloves with Kevlar knuckles, but they weren't wearing them tonight. Tempest supplied them with an alternative bought specifically for the case. He also provided underwear which came as a shock to the guys.

"We need to wear this?" questioned Jagjit.

Once Tempest explained its purpose the guys couldn't get it on fast enough.

First to be dressed, Big Ben scooped his fingers through a tin of black stuff and passed it to Tempest. Tempest scooped some and passed it to Hilary.

"What's this?" Hilary asked.

Big Ben smeared it across his face in fat diagonal lines. "Camouflage Cream," he replied.

Tempest said, "We need to be invisible until we are ready to show ourselves. Surprise will be our ally, and this will take the shine off our faces."

The guys didn't bother to argue, except Jagjit, who pointed out his skin was already brown and therefore wouldn't reflect the moon the same way. It was not an argument he won.

"Now you understand the plan?" Tempest had been through it twice. His question was aimed more at Hilary and Jagjit than Big Ben. There was no point seeking confirmation from Basic – it was given that he didn't and would make things up according to the situation.

Jagjit looked at Hilary when he said, "It seems simple enough."

"I think so too," Tempest agreed.

Big Ben scratched his head. "I'm still a bit iffy on the numbers. There's five of us, but we don't know if we are up against two or fifty."

"That's right, we don't. I believe the number will be higher than five, but much lower than fifty and I'll tell you why. If I have figured this out correctly, Norman Pickett is on a path of revenge that once he started became impossible to stop. Someone or something tipped him over the edge, and he set about creating the Zephyrus Frostwind persona. Along the way, he recruited disciples, but I cannot see how he would attract a small army of them. Not everyone who gets stepped on in life turns into a murderous sociopath. Three of his helpers turned up in Rochester last night and at least another one ransacked my office while the first three were giving me a beating. Add Norman to that list, who was slick enough to ensure he was elsewhere yet again, and we have at least five. We need to assume they are all capable of murder. One of them killed Stephanie Greer while he was being questioned by the police."

Jagjit interrupted. "Are we sure that wasn't some crazy copycat?"

"We cannot be certain, but I would lay money on it being one of Norman's followers creating the perfect alibi. I cannot be sure Norman will turn up tonight, but I believe he will, so we need to get into position and be ready."

He looked around the loose circle they had formed, meeting the eyes of each of his friends. There were mixed emotions showing. Big Ben wanted nothing more than to get to it, Jagit and Hilary displayed trepidation, though they did not articulate their worries, and Basic … well, there could have been anything going on in Basic's head including a reverberating echo from the dawn of time.

Getting into Big Ben's utility vehicle, Tempest remembered a point he was yet to raise. "Oh, Frank is probably going to show up, too."

"And Poison?" asked Big Ben, waggling his eyebrows and snorting like a bull. Known for being able to bed just about any woman, he was yet to get anywhere near Frank's attractive assistant. For a long time he kept his distance out of respect for Tempest since Poison was clearly interested in him, but that barrier had long since evaporated.

Tempest sighed. "Yes, I think she might turn up as well, but can we leave the heavy flirting until after we defeat Norman and his disciples?"

"Roger. Fight first, shag after."

Punching the start button with a thick index finger, the engine roared to life and they set off, their destination a Neolithic monument believed, much like Stonehenge, to have mystical properties. The location was Frank's suggestion, both for its remoteness and because the Kent League of Demonologists used it on occasion for meetings and ceremonies.

Just one of a number of such sites spread across the region, Kit's Coty occupied high ground close to the top of Blue Bell Hill. Big Ben parked half a mile away, the team undertaking the rest of the journey on foot.

"What if we have to make a fast getaway?" Hilary asked. He was the worrier of the group, but also an important voice to have around lest Tempest forget something vital.

"We will be approaching from the direction of the car and will keep us between it and Norman. If we have to bug out," Tempest used the military term for a tactical withdrawal, "we can hot-foot it back to the car. They won't catch us even if they follow and there is always the option of going through the woods to get home if we get split up. Aim your body downhill and try to avoid low branches. The first place you will come to is the village. We'll rendezvous back at the pub." Turning to address everyone, Tempest asked, "Is everyone clear on that?"

They were.

The area around Kit's Coty was dark. There were no houses so there were no lampposts, but that worked in their favour. They would see and hear cars approaching from a long way off and were getting into place early enough that their eyes would be well adjusted to the dark by the time anyone else arrived.

The stone tomb or, to use the correct term, 'Long

Barrow' was in an exposed area where the moon shone down to illuminate it. Forming a rough circle approximately forty yards across, a small visitor's centre with information about the site sat to the west. To the north, Blue Bell Hill dominated the skyline and to the south the lights of Maidstone reflected down from the thin clouds covering it.

The visitor's centre closed at 1700hrs, and now sat dark and silent, an alien blob on the otherwise natural landscape.

Wrapped up warm, with layers they could easily shed when the time came, Tempest and his friends looked at the low ground to the east where the only road in and out would announce arrivals more than a minute before they reached the site.

Jagjit nudged Tempest's arm and pointed. Two sets of headlights had just turned off the main road.

Confusion

SATURDAY, JANUARY 6TH 1827HRS

Big Ben questioned, "What time did you say they were supposed to get here?"

"1900hrs."

Big Ben drew a deep breath through his nose, assessing their early arrival. "They wanted to be here before the League. They are bright enough to think strategically."

Tempest shrugged, the motion unnoticed in the dark. "Makes no difference. When they close their doors and the lights go out, we attack, just as planned. If possible we take out everyone but Norman."

"If they are all wearing cloaks, it's going to be tough to figure out which one he is."

"Accepted, but ideally there will be a point where I get to face off against him."

"Which is where I come in," said Hilary.

The cars were coming closer, approaching without any sense of stealth or caution. Once off the dual carriageway the road was a straight shot through the trees until it drew almost level with the site, then it swung around in a 'U' turn to enter the carpark. For what Tempest had planned, the location could not have been more perfect. It was remote and the trees would shield the imminent light show from unsuspecting eyes. Unlike his previous fight, there would be no kids around to livestream it onto the internet.

"Guys, into the treeline." Big Ben ushered Basic, Hilary, and Jagjit backward. "And keep your eyes closed like we discussed. Your night vision is going to be a powerful weapon."

They merged with the trunks of larger trees, their black clothes and blacked out faces making them invisible. Even a person looking for them wouldn't be able to pick them out among the shadows.

In the almost silence of the woodland, disturbed only by the occasional sounds of an owl hooting or an unseen creature scurrying through the undergrowth, it was easy to judge how far away the cars were. They heard them ease to a stop and waited for the drivers to turn off their headlights.

Through his eyelids, the thick blanket of utter darkness returned and Tempest opened his eyes. There had been too little practice for what he was about to attempt, but that was okay. He wasn't trying to fool anyone. The object, beyond stopping Norman Pickett's reign of terror and bringing him to justice, was to erode the damage done by the video of their first encounter. Tempest took his business seriously, so the negative comments and general laughter as he flailed and hid and got set on fire, were the kind of publicity he could do without. If he got things right tonight, any negative impact would be eradicated.

Whispering, he said, "Okay, chaps. I hope you're all wearing your best fighting trousers. It's time to go to work."

The two cars had stopped thirty yards away on the other side of the carpark, not far from where the road came in. Parked so they faced each other at a distance of perhaps eight or nine yards, which looked odd, the interiors were completely dark and whoever was inside was making no attempt to get out.

In a line, his team advanced like ghosts. They were all armed, not with traditional weapons, but with something far, far more suited to the occasion.

The leftmost car flashed its headlights, the sudden brightness sending a knife of searing pain into Tempest's eyes. He hadn't expected it and the impact on his night vision was instant. Were they clever enough to have done it deliberately? To his left, Hilary winced and rubbed his eyes, trying to rid them of the same halo now messing with Tempest's vision.

To his far left, Big Ben hissed, "More cars!"

Indeed, there were two more cars pulling off the main road and clearly heading for the carpark. The road didn't go anywhere else.

When the cars reached the end of the road and swung around, their headlights would illuminate the five men now halfway across it. They would be caught in the open and dressed as they were there could be no question they were not members of the League Norman had come to meet.

"Quick, back to the trees!" Tempest turned and ran, keeping low and making as little noise as possible. Getting noticed now would change everything, they had to remain in stealth mode.

They made it back to their start points just as the next two cars entered the carpark. Strangely, they didn't join the first two cars, but drove past them, splitting off to park well away from each other and those already there. Frowning with confusion, for it had to be a deliberate tactic, but one which Tempest could make no sense of, he watched. Just as before, they extinguished their headlights, plunging the whole area back into darkness.

His night vision shot in his left eye, his right eye, which he'd closed and kept that way, was recovering. The occupants remained in their cars. Just like the first two, these cars had reversed into their parking spots so they faced inward and toward the other cars.

Apart from the gentle metallic pinging of engines cooling, there was almost no sound at all, until the car that flashed its lights earlier did so again. This time in a pattern.

The car that arrived with it responded by activating its four-way warning indicators. They flashed twice and went out. The car to their left, the last one to arrive, wound down the rear left passenger window.

Ever more perplexed, Tempest watched in rapt fascination. Now was the time to move, but the outlined plan for their ambush was based on the cars being all in one spot. Coming from the dark they would attack at speed, windmilling through the cloaked idiots before they knew what hit them. Spread out as they were, that was now impossible.

Yet withdrawing was a worse option. They were going to have to split in two, deal with one pair of cars and move to the secondary targets as swiftly as they could. In all likelihood, Norman or someone, depending how many had tricks up their sleeves, would have time to retaliate. That was going to make things tricky, but Tempest and his gang were prepared for that eventuality. In fact, they were counting on it.

Just about to step out of the wood line for the second time, Tempest glanced to the right. There was another car coming.

Big Ben appeared next to him, his passage through the

trees making no noise at all. He wasn't alone, for Hilary and Jagjit were by his side.

"That's five cars now, Temp," Jagjit pointed out. "I know you said we would probably be outnumbered, but this is getting silly."

They didn't know how many people were in each car, when they turned off their engines, the interior lights had not automatically illuminated the occupants – another indication that Norman and his followers were more strategically aware than he'd given them credit for. His voice from the previous night echoed in his head, cursing him once again for underestimating his opponent.

Was he walking his friends into a trap? Did Norman somehow know to expect trouble? He was here to meet with representatives of the Kent League of Demonologists. Was it the money he offered that tipped Norman off? Or was it simply natural for him to be suspicious?

The fifth car turned into the carpark, dimming its headlights instantly to then cruise across the tarmac. The driver angled to a spot well away from the other cars, but very much closer to Tempest and his friends. Reversing until the back bumper almost touched the plants, it stopped less than two yards from where they stood.

Crouching, Tempest could see there were two people inside. It looked to be a man and a woman. The woman was behind the wheel.

Hilary asked, his voice a careful whisper, "What the heck is going on?"

Just like before, there were headlight flashes, this time originating from the latest arrival. They were 'answered' with indicators, windows going up and down, and finally a door opening.

To Tempest it read like some kind of strange code, almost like a language known only to those inside the cars.

A figure emerged from the open door; a short, rotund man with a bald head that reflected the moonlight. He scurried from his car to the one next to it. The backdoor opened before he could get to it and he slipped inside, closing it gently.

Straining his eyes and crouching so he was able to look through the glass, Tempest still struggled to make out what was going on inside.

Until Big Ben sniggered.

Consenting Adults

SATURDAY, JANUARY 6TH 1843HRS

Like a beam of light hitting his skull, Tempest understood what he was seeing.

The man and woman in the car nearest to them both got out. The dark made it hard to see their features with any clarity, but he estimated their ages to be somewhere around mid-forties.

Jagjit, having reached the same conclusion said, "This is a dogging site. Isn't it?"

Letting his head hang down so his chin touched his chest, Tempest sighed, "Yes. And now we have to convince them to go somewhere else."

Reaching into his pocket, Tempest took out a torch. They all had one, packed for when the fight was over and the police would come. Stepping out of the trees, he raised his voice, "Hey."

Having left their car, the couple in their forties were making their way across the carpark but hadn't got very far. Startled by the unexpected voice, they spun around. Their faces bore surprised expressions which turned to ones of abject horror when they saw the five black-clad and face-painted men coming their way.

The man screamed. The woman slapped his arm. "Get a hold of yourself, Nancy."

In the torchlight, they were more visible, which is how Tempest could see 'Nancy', which he suspected not to be the man's real name, was wearing a tight red dress and black ankle boots with fishnet tights.

"My apologies for startling you," Tempest attempted to reassure them. "There is no cause for alarm."

"We're not doing anything wrong," the woman insisted, her stance defensive and aggressive. "We're not hurting anyone. You have no right to push your ideals onto us."

"I assure you that is not my intention." Tempest wanted to move them on; Norman could arrive at any moment and when he did there was going to be a battle. Assuming the presence of so many cars and people didn't spook him. It wasn't safe for the doggers, if that was the correct term, to stay where they were.

From the other cars, those inside were emerging, getting out to see what might have caused Nancy's scream.

"What's going on?" asked a man in his sixties. His voice possessed an air of pompous authority that made Tempest think convincing them to move on was going to be distinctly harder than he'd hoped.

Over her shoulder the woman said, "These guys just came out of the woods." Narrowing her eyes, she looked along the line of black-clad men. "You're all religious nuts, aren't you? They've come to save us from our life of sin, Ron," she said to the pompous man.

"Sounds like it, Gail," Ron agreed.

There being nothing to gain by answering her question, Tempest got straight to the point. "Listen, it's not safe for you here tonight. None of us care what you get up to. You're all consenting adults, but something is about to happen here, and you need to be somewhere else when it does."

"Oh, something is about to happen here, young man," said Ron, a throaty rumble of anticipation in his voice. "It involves that Volvo over there, a young couple, a bottle of ...."

Tempest covered his ears and sang, "La, la, la, la, la, la, laaaaaa." He didn't think himself to be a prude, but he really didn't want to wake in the middle of the night to find his brain filled with uninvited images conjured by the older man's description of his intended liaison.

When the man's lips stopped moving, Tempest removed his hands to find Big Ben talking.

"I've got to hand it to you. That does sound like fun."

The woman shot him a wolfish smile. "You can join in anytime you like, sexy."

Nancy grumbled, "I'm standing right here, you know."

She kept her eyes locked on Big Ben when she snapped, "Shut up, Nancy."

The occupants of the other cars were all getting out. Most of them were in a state of undress and one man, reversing out of a back seat, had his bottom on display, the moon catching the white of his cheeks.

Tempest exhaled hard and fought to stay calm. "Look at us, I beg you. Why do you think we are dressed like this?"

It was supposed to be a leading question, but Nancy said, "It's a fetish thing," before Tempest could complete what he wanted to say.

"No! No, look, you really need to go somewhere else." He didn't want to reveal who they expected to arrive in the next few minutes for fear it would cause them to stay.

Encouraging them to move on was not, however, working. If anything, they were digging their feet in even harder.

Bolstered by their numbers as more of the dogging group came to join Nancy and his female companion/wife/owner, they voiced their rights to 'dog' in ever increasing volumes.

Lambasted by the onslaught of angry doggers, Tempest was desperately trying to devise a new strategy to get them moving, when new headlights appeared on the slip road.

Moving suddenly, he grabbed Nancy's dress. "Is this all of you?"

"Huh?"

"Are you expecting anyone else?"

Leaning away and pulling at his dress, Nancy said, "Hard to say. Different people come and go as they want."

The pompous man in his sixties said, "It's not like we have a club charter and membership fees, young man."

Out of patience, Tempest growled, "Get them into the woods!" Dragging Nancy, he snagged the arm of the woman who came with him.

Big Ben reacted first, but the rest of the guys quickly followed Tempest's lead.

"Seriously," Tempest battered down the protests before they could arise. "We are not here for you. Get into the treeline and keep quiet. Just for a minute. I'm literally trying to save your lives."

As though finally sensing how serious he was, the group of doggers stopped fighting. Tempest and his friends got them into the shadows a metre or so into the woods where they all waited silently.

There were two cars approaching, but the second turned out to be a mid-sized panel van. That alone made Tempest believe they were not seeing fresh doggers arriving.

Now conscious of his breath fogging in clouds above his head, Tempest kept still and whispered for everyone else to do the same. Largely aimed at the doggers, the instruction went for everyone.

The car, a ten-year-old Ford Focus, stopped in the middle of the carpark, the driver invisible inside the dark interior. The panel van pulled up behind it. Their behaviour was already markedly different from the doggers when they arrived.

In the trees, no one spoke. The only sound beyond the running engines was a faint stirring of the trees where a light breeze blew.

Nothing happened for nearly a minute. Watching the car and van for any sign of movement, Tempest imagined the occupants scoping out the cars, wondering who might be inside. If Norman was in the car, was he expecting members of the Kent League of Demonologists to emerge now that he'd arrived? Whoever the new arrivals were, they showed no desire to exit their vehicles.

Telling himself that to show himself could very well trigger Norman to choose flight instead of fight, Tempest continued to wait and was rewarded when the driver's door of the old Ford finally opened. The interior light came on, bathing those inside in dim light that seemed bright in the abject darkness.

Tempest grinned. "Gotcha."

Big Ben whispered, "What's the plan?"

This was not how they rehearsed it. Not even close. But the two former soldiers had been in enough war zones and tense situations to know plans rarely survived the first encounter with the enemy.

"Give me a minute," he replied, stepping forward to the edge of the treeline. Another step and he would become visible. They wouldn't know what they were seeing, not at first with his all-black outfit, but the moment he opened his mouth Norman would know it was a trap.

Turning to face his team, Tempest said, "I'm going to draw them out. They will think I'm alone. You guys circle around to come at them from the sides and behind. When Norman confronts me, all eyes will be aimed in my direction."

Big Ben nodded, liking the hastily concocted tactic. "All eyes will be on you. We'll go through half of them before they even know we are there." He made it sound easy, not because it necessarily would be, but to give Hilary and Jagjit added confidence. "Ready guys? Let's move."

Tempest stepped onto the tarmac, making himself visible. His arms hung by his sides, his hands open and clearly empty.

"Good evening, Norman."

Battle

SATURDAY, JANUARY 6TH 1902HRS

A broad-shouldered man in a full-length black cloak had just exited the Ford Focus, his attention on the other cars parked in a loose circle around the perimeter of the carpark. He wasn't looking Tempest's way at all until he spoke. Now aiming his face squarely at the black blob set against the even blacker murk of the woods, he squinted to make out what he could see.

Tempest walked forward confidently, closing the distance and making sure to keep attention focused on him. He couldn't tell if the man he addressed was actually Norman Pickett, that was just an educated guess, but when the man lifted his head and the familiar bushy black beard caught the moonlight, he knew he'd got it right.

"What is this?" Norman asked. "Where are the League?"

Tempest had multiple responses from which to choose. He was tempted to laugh and belittle the fake wizard. Equally, he was tempted to reveal Norman had walked willingly into his trap, but to give his friends more time, he said,

"They are here, Norman. They are watching. They want to know if you are the real thing. I know the League guys quite well, you see. I told them you are nothing more than an idiot with some fancy tricks. That's the truth after all, so they are holding back to see which of us is right."

Norman squared off against his opponent. Flinging his arms outward to make his cloak open and billow, his feet visibly lifted from the ground. Then, bringing his palms together and drawing them apart he produced crackling dark blue lightning that jumped between his fingers.

"Neat," said Tempest, sounding bored. "What are you going to do with that?"

The doors to the panel van opened, more figures in black cloaks exiting from the front and sides to join Norman and his driver. Tempest counted twelve of them. This was going to be easy.

"Here, Zephyrus," said one of the cloaked men fanning out from the panel van. "I think there are people in that car." He pointed to a Peugeot. "On the back seats." He squinted and moved around a bit to get a better look. "Actually, I think they are having sex."

"They probably *are* having sex," said Ron, stepping out from the trees. "This is our place, and I want all of you to go somewhere else."

"Yeah," said Gail, also leaving the woods and bringing Nancy with her. "I'm getting cold out here. I'm not supposed to be getting cold. I'm supposed to be getting fu …"

"No one needs the details," Tempest cut her off. It was fighting time. He had Norman and his followers exactly where he wanted them. They could take them all out and defeat Zephyrus Frostwind right now. The cops would come, his name would be cleared, and the damage done by the video of their first fight would be completely undone. But none of that was possible with civilians in the line of fire.

Norman stared incredulously. "What the heck is this now?"

Struggling for an explanation, Tempest tried, "Unfortunate timing?"

Striding past him, Ron said, "Right you lot. I've had enough of this. I'm Lord Ronald Bagshire, The Right Honourable Chancellor of the High Court. If you're not here to participate in tonight's activities, you can all just sling your hooks."

Light still playing between his fingers, Norman flicked his right arm out like a lance. Thin lines of the same deep blue shot from it. They crackled with energy, zipping through the air to hit Ron square in the chest.

Tempest couldn't move fast enough to stop it from happening, Ron was just too far ahead of him. He cursed himself for not predicting Norman's attack.

Ron spasmed, arcs of the deep blue lightning shooting across his body, down his legs and into the ground where it earthed.

From the doggers behind him, someone squealed in shock. Nancy screamed with fear.

Gail said, "Oh, get a grip, Nancy!"

Tempest sucked in some air and yelled, "Attack!"

Big Ben burst from the trees. From stationary to a full sprint in just a few yards, he had Hilary just behind him. From the trees on the other side of the carpark, Basic exploded. Bellowing like a moose with anger management issues, he hefted a chunky branch like *Captain Caveman*. Hot on his heels, Jagjit was doing the same thing. Or trying to. He weighed half as much, didn't sound dangerous, and the chunk of tree he carried was more stick than club.

Yet he was a dark shape coming out of the shadows and that made all the difference.

The cloaks turned as one, twisting to face the noise which meant none of them saw Big Ben whose approach had been silent. Six feet seven inches of muscle and trained rage ran through the first three of Norman's men as though they were not there.

For Tempest, revelling in Norman's confused panic, it was like watching a car mow through a crowd. However, when Big Ben got to the next in line, the cloaked figure ducked his swing. Big Ben's scything arm carved a path through empty air and when the figure popped up a moment later, he attacked Big Ben's exposed back.

Tempest couldn't see what he hit him with, but Big Ben dropped like a stone.

Just reaching the line of cloaks, Hilary's charge petered out. He was brave enough to be there, brave enough to follow Big Ben into a fight, but facing multiple opponents alone when they had just put down a man he'd never seen beaten was a test of courage he failed.

On the other side, Basic had his club held high and was moments from bonking heads when a flash-bang went off. Tempest knew to expect them and the guys had all donned ear protection in the moments before their attack, but the effect, while less than it had been for Tempest two nights ago, stopped Basic and Jagjit all the same.

Hilary swooped on Big Ben. He was getting to his feet, the cloaked figures all backing up and tightening their formation around the panel van as they reacted to the unexpected attack.

Groaning and uncoordinated, Big Ben let Hilary pull

him back. They stumbled, never turning their backs on the enemy as they sought to gain a little breathing space.

Norman turned to face Tempest once more. "Did that go according to plan?" he asked, his voice loaded with amusement.

From the ground to his left, Gail wailed, "Ron's dead! You killed him."

The news pushed Tempest over the edge. He left home tonight with one simple aim: to end the wizard's reign of terror. He would achieve that aim, he was quite certain, but letting Zephyrus claim another victim wasn't part of the plan.

"Gentlemen," Tempest spoke to his friends. "It's time for plan B."

"Plan B?" questioned Jagjit. "I thought we were already on plan B."

Sighing, Tempest said, "Okay then. Let's call it plan C."

"Can it be plan 'magic'?" asked Hilary. "That sounds cooler."

Tempest muttered several expletives and walked forward until he stood about five yards from Norman. Standing in front of the Ford Focus with the driver a couple of feet behind and to the right, Norman held his ground and once again pressed his palms together. Drawing them apart the dark blue lightning reappeared.

Tempest flung his arms out to either side and with a flourish brought them back together in front of his face. When he drew them apart blood red lightning crackled between them. Then he rose to a height of six inches above the ground.

He looked at Norman, a wide grin glued to his face.

Magic Battle

SATURDAY, JANUARY 6TH 1909HRS

The shock on Norman's face was a dream come true, but his dumbfounded expression didn't last long. Repeating his attack on Ron the Right Honourable Chancellor of the High Court, Norman threw out his right arm, aiming it like a spear.

Thin lines of dark blue shot across the carpark to strike Tempest in the chest. He opened his arms to get them out of the way and let Norman's throw hit its mark. He looked down at the lines of crackling light. They were stuck in the material of his Kevlar vest where more of the blue light sparked and arced outward.

"A modified taser and some fibre optics," he observed. "I figured it would be something like this, so we are all wearing conductive suits under our outer layers. They earth directly into the ground, so your sideshow parlour trick won't work on us." Reaching up with his right hand, he wrapped the thin lines in his palm and yanked.

Pulled off his feet, Norman stumbled, releasing the weapon from his hand so it clattered onto the ground.

No Such Thing as Magic

Now holding the optic fibres up to the moon so he could better examine them, Tempest casually asked, "How do you get them to snap out and go rigid like that?"

"Zephyrus, they know!" said the man next to him.

Regaining his composure, Norman opened first his right palm and then his left, each revealing a ball of flame that seemed to sit in his hands. "You will die now, Tempest Michaels. Your lack of humility before great power will be the last thing you will ever know."

Moving fast, Tempest reached behind his back. This was either going to work or he was in a lot of trouble.

The first fireball left Norman's right hand and he was already rotating his body to throw the second one when Tempest pressed the button on the device he held. Of all the items he purchased specifically for this fight, the shield was the most expensive. By a long way.

In front of his body a wide, round sheet of Perspex opened out. Lit from within to display Celtic runes around the circumference, it formed a barrier between his body and the same ball of fire that set fire to his trousers.

His world exploded in bright fiery orange light, the jelly-like liquid in the flaming balls sticking to the shield.

Casting it aside, its usefulness all but spent, Tempest asked, "What else have you got?"

Zephyrus laughed, but there was an unmistakable edge of nervousness to it. "An army, Mr Michaels, I have an army."

Tempest looked around him to the figures not quite huddling next to the panel van. They were surrounded by Big Ben and Hilary on one side and by Basic and Jagjit on the other. Three of them were poised, waiting for Tempest's signal. The third, Hilary, had been given a different task and was doing what he could to get it right.

"I'm not sure those sorry-looking saps count as an army, Norman."

This time when Norman laughed, it sounded genuine. "Ah, yes. I'm afraid this is where you discover how badly you underestimated me, Mr Michaels. The men you can see are nothing more than my personal protection detail. I sent the army ahead to wait in the woods." Raising his voice, he shouted over his shoulder. "Show yourselves!"

Big Ben spun around, gritting his teeth as he prepared to defend against whoever came out of the darkness. On the other side of the panel van, Jagjit grabbed Basic's shoulders to get him looking the right way.

Nothing happened for a few seconds, but the faint sound of people moving through the woodland soon reached their ears. They were trying to make as little noise as possible, but there was no mistaking that Tempest and his friends were about to be distinctly outnumbered.

The doggers, who for the last minute or so hadn't moved, decided to make a break for their cars. Mistaking their panicked stampede for an attack, some of Norman's disciples moved to intercept them. Poor Ronald the Right Honourable lay on the cold ground, abandoned by those who were going to make his evening more interesting.

Big Ben didn't know quite where to look. This was a full skirmish and about to become a rout with them on the losing end if he didn't change things up really soon. Forming fists, he was about to swing around to close quarters with the wizards at the panel van when a diminutive figure stepped out from the trees.

It was closely followed by another and then two more, each of them carrying a sheathed katana.

Finally, Frank stepped onto the tarmac. "Wotcha, chaps.

Sorry we're late. We ran into a bunch of these guys in the woods." He nodded at the cloaks. "They appeared to be waiting for something."

To his left and right, clad head to toe in figure-hugging black that extended over their heads to leave just their eyes showing, were Poison, Mistress Mushy, Bob, and Hatchett. Tempest could identify them without needing to see their faces.

"Did you leave any of them alive?" he asked.

Frank shook his head in disbelief. "We don't kill humans, Tempest. Only monsters."

Looking uncertain for the first time since he arrived, Norman moved his hands in a concentric circle motion.

Following suit, Tempest matched the fake wizard when he produced sparking light once more and around the perimeter of the carpark, Big Ben, Jagjit, and Basic all did the same.

Hilary gasped, "This is so cooool."

Still thrown by the loss of his 'army', Norman spluttered, "How are you doing that!"

Tempest shrugged. "They sell this stuff over the counter, Norman. I will say it took a fair amount of practice to make it look convincing, but I think doing it at night when visibility is lower and light effects show up better really helps. The floating thing is cool, too, and had me stumped until I found the extending leg braces."

He lifted one trouser leg to reveal a device strapped above his ankle. It extended up to his knee and was fitted with a machined rod activated by a solenoid. He had one on each leg.

"I figured out how you managed to kill your victims, too. Not that you killed them all yourself, did you Norman?

The question right now, is how many of your followers are going to jail for murder and how many will be wise enough to surrender before this gets any worse for them?"

Enraged, Norman shouted, "You won't be around to find out!" Dropping the sparkling magic, produced by a similar set of gloves to the ones Tempest and his friends wore, Norman reached inside his cloak to produce two obsidian blades.

Swishing them through the air, they lit from within, purple light inside the swords creating a blur in the air. Grimacing menacingly, he came forward, the swords still moving as he advanced with one intention: to kill Tempest Michaels.

Tempest raised his right arm, his empty palm out to face the advancing wizard.

"I even figured out how you made those steel bars fly across the street. It was magnets, Norman." Tempest took aim. "Like this one."

A piece of steel the size of a shot glass sprang from his arm when he reached up to activate the magnet. Norman never saw it coming. It smacked into his forehead from a distance of less than two yards, bowling him over backward like he'd been hit in the face with a baseball bat.

He crashed to the ground, hitting it with his neck and flipping over like a freshly tossed caber to land on his front.

The man who drove the Ford Focus hadn't moved. His feet were glued to the spot and his mouth hung open.

Tempest wasted no time getting to Norman, but just in case the nearest of his followers thought about doing something foolish, he barked, "On the ground! Now!"

Big Ben dropped the sparkly light show, his booming voice filling the night to make the rest of the cloaked figures surrender.

Jagjit and Basic did the same from their side and Hilary filmed the whole thing.

Frank ambled over to where Tempest knelt on Norman's back. One knee in the middle of his spine, he used a thick, plastic zip-tie to secure his hands behind his back. The fake wizard was out cold and might very well be concussed given the size of the egg protruding from his forehead. Rolling him over, Tempest checked his pulse again and content the man wasn't about to die on his watch, gave his bushy black beard a tug. It didn't budge, but when he rolled Norman's head to one side, he found an edge. Using a fingernail, he peeled it away.

"I've got one like that over here," said Big Ben upon seeing Tempest stand up holding his prize. Not worried about how roughly he handled the man in question, he yanked the beard free to an accompanying cry of pain.

"Me too," said Jagjit.

It transpired that more than half the men wore them beneath their cloaks.

"Arrrrggh!" screamed one of them. "That's attached!"

Big Ben gave it another tug just to be certain.

Hilary continued to film. "Boy, are you guys going to regret your choices," he remarked, zooming in close on the line of exposed faces.

Big Ben said, "You want to talk about regret? If I had a pound for every time I have done something I regret, I would have ..." his eyes rolled up as he performed mental arithmetic, "three quid."

"Three quid?" questioned Jagjit. "From your entire life you have three things you regret?"

Big Ben smiled. "Yeah, it's not easy being this amazing."

Content the cloaked figures were secure, Tempest aimed an expectant expression at Frank.

Frank sighed and stared up at the moon, his hands thrust deep into his pockets.

"You were right, Tempest. Again."

Aftermath

SATURDAY, JANUARY 6TH 1922HRS

The doggers were scattered around the carpark. Only Nancy and Gail had been able to get to their car, but Gail couldn't find her keys, so they'd hidden behind it where they were joined by another couple.

When Tempest hit Norman with the hunk of steel and the fight ended, they ventured out but made no attempt to leave. He didn't ask, but Tempest suspected they were hoping everyone would go now so they could resume their activities. This despite Ron's body still lying in the open.

The doggers gathered around him, all looking down at the large, older man.

Gail said, "Someone should say something," looking around at her fellow nighttime carpark tryst enthusiasts for a volunteer. When none came, she nudged Nancy with an elbow.

"Oh, um ..." Nancy mumbled, no doubt trying to think of something eloquent to say.

Ronald sat up.

Nancy screamed.

Gail rolled her eyes. "Oh, for heaven's sake, Nancy. Do shut up."

"What happened?" Ron asked.

By the time the first police cars arrived, led by Patience because that was who Tempest called first, the video of the fight with the wizards was going viral. Tagged to the first video, which now had more than ten million views, Hilary made no attempt to cut or edit the raw footage.

"It needs to be raw like this," he explained. "If we doctor it, people will question whether what they are seeing has been messed with to add the effects. This way, even though it's a little long and I haven't always got the camera pointing in the right direction, no one will doubt its authenticity."

"It's a lot like *Blair Witch*," remarked Jagjit, likening it to the famous 'found footage' film.

Agreeing, Tempest turned his attention to the arriving police cars. It was fifteen minutes since he knocked out Norman Pickett, the time since utilised to get the wizards off the ground and sitting on logs along one side of the carpark where Basic wielded his club and watched for anyone who might be foolish enough to make a run for it.

Poison and the ninjas had gone back into the woods to fetch the 'army' they encountered. It turned out to be another dozen men, all in the same black cloaks. Their hoods were down to reveal black eyes and bruised faces and more than half of them winced when they walked. The ninjas led them back to the carpark where they were instructed to sit with the rest of Norman's followers.

The next time Tempest looked, the ninjas were gone, but Frank remained at the site. The police take a dim view to people walking around with deadly weapons such as katanas, so even though they dealt with more than a dozen of Norman's followers, it was best the ninjas were elsewhere when the authorities arrived.

Patience shook Tempest's hand. "Are you trying to get me promoted to chief constable?"

Tempest smirked. "Not exactly, but someone has to process this lot. I can't do it."

"Yes, but you sent me everything I needed to solve the case. Over the last few hours, I've worked with some of Chief Inspector Quinn's team to follow the lead from the hire docket and make the connection between Alex Mullen and Norman Pickett. The case is basically closed already. Alex Mullen used to date Stephanie Greer, the victim from the night Norman was in custody. She dumped him for another guy who, surprise surprise, also got a Zephyrus Frostwind business card through his letterbox the week before Christmas. We sent a team to arrest Alex, but he's not home."

Tempest pointed. "That's because he's over there." He waved and called, "Hi, Alex."

Patience lifted her radio to cancel the arrest warrant. When she was done with that, she said, "The team are still figuring out who else might be involved, but now we have these guys in custody," she glared at the sorry-looking figures on the logs, "connecting the dots will be a whole lot easier. Have we got a Shane Hawkes here?"

Multiple heads swung inward to look at a man who looked about as guilty as can be.

Patience said, "That's the guy who provided the alibi for the night you fought Norman outside Valerie Legg's house. How about Angelo Mutini?"

Their eyes were drawn to a head that snapped up in startlement.

"That guy works at The Vault," Patience explained. "I

guess that's going to be how Norman got in without being seen the other night. One way or another, these fools are all responsible for six murders." Patience shook her head and laughed. "And you got them all in one go. How exactly did you pull that off?"

Tempest tapped the side of his nose. "A magician never reveals his tricks."

The Big Question

SUNDAY, JANUARY 7TH 1249HRS

With the wizard case closed and the thing at the palace about to fill their days, Tempest found himself with no ongoing cases for the first time in months. The business of paranormal investigation had been busier than he could ever have imagined right from the day the local paper ran his advert incorrectly. Having nothing to do was a rare treat.

Finally escaping the cold at Kit's Coty, he arrived home to find the dogs wagging their tails in excitement. He knew via text messages that Amanda was still out. She'd solved her case easily enough, finding the unicorn at a neighbour's house. It was a horse, obviously, but at the same time her client could be forgiven for her confusion. The horse was being used as a prop for a film and to stop the creature from going cross-eyed and freaking out when they led it onto set having just stuck the horn on, they were leaving it in place so it could get used to it.

Amanda would be home soon enough, but that gave him time to tidy himself up. He'd done precisely that but fell asleep on the couch with the dogs on his lap before finishing his first rum and coke.

In the morning, they fooled around and when they were up they ate a leisurely breakfast. Tempest had but one plan for the day, to finally pop the damned question. Slyly suggesting they take the dogs for a countryside walk and perhaps stop somewhere for a drink, he made sure the ring was secure in his coat pocket, safe inside its little box.

The dogs scampered, sniffing here and there and racing each other to the next enticing smell while behind them the humans held hands and chatted about everything and nothing. Their route took them along the canal path leading from the River Angel pub toward Maidstone town centre.

Tempest had a destination in mind, a particular spot from their past that held particular significance. It was the spot they first met. Like it was yesterday, he could recall how he felt when he first saw the blonde vision bedecked in her police uniform.

Coming toward it, the dogs took off, barking and haring away. They had probably seen a rabbit and were unlikely to go too far, yet caution dictated he go after them just in case. Letting Amanda's hand go, he saw them stop, their attention drawn to a new smell.

He smiled and reached into his pocket. It was time.

Turning around, he found nothing but empty air where Amanda had stood only a moment before. She wasn't there now because she was on the ground. Or, more accurately, down on one knee.

Reaching up with both hands, which held and cupped a ring box containing a thick band of white gold, Amanda smiled and asked, "Will you marry me?"

Afterword

Hello, Dear Reader,

Thank you for reading all the way to the end and beyond. This book took me longer than anticipated to write. In fact, it has been almost a month since I started it. Except that claim isn't entirely accurate because I wrote the plot for the book almost two years ago.

Known for never plotting, it was a step change from my usual process, but necessary as I planned for the story to be turned into a graphic novel. I thought it would be a fun collector's piece and wanted to see Big Ben and others from the cast brought to life in a visual manner, rather than just in people's heads.

That the graphic novel never came to pass was a mix of poor timing, the wrong people, and the author being distracted by other projects. However, with the story fleshed out, I knew I had to write it and fooled myself into thinking it would be easy to pen since the whole thing was plotted. That proved not to be the case.

My brain doesn't work like that, so as soon as I started

to write, I found myself wanting to change the plot. That is very much how my brain works; finding better ideas once the story begins to take shape.

I am often asked how many Blue Moon books I will write and if I will end the series. The answer to both is that I am undecided. This is the only Blue Moon book I will write this year and will not yet commit to writing one next year. I have so many other projects that excite me, I need to clear some of the older, established series out of the way, so I can focus my efforts on them.

A few things to explain about the story:

Kit's Coty is a real place. In fact, most of the places I describe in my books are real. I adapt the geography sometimes because a story demands it, and invented Tempest's home village of Finchampstead because when writing the first book I described my own home and village in such detail that it was like giving a route map for fans to find me. The megalithic rocks at Kit's Coty are walking distance from my house. I went there first in the 70's on a school day trip.

Dogging is not a subject I knew anything about prior to writing this book. Other than what it was, I suppose. I shall make no comments regarding the 'hobby' if that term can be used to describe it, but as I was writing the final scenes and wanted something fun to throw Tempest and everyone else off balance, the remote carpark location presented itself as an obvious location at which practitioners might meet.

One of the points of this book, and certainly why I had to write it now, was the need to link it with the royal wedding storyline. What happens next for the Blue Moon crew will not feature in a book that sits in their series, but in the final book in a series about a high-end wedding planner called Felicity Philips.

If you have arrived at the author notes by reading from the start to the finish, you might now be thinking Felicity Philips might appear in a future Blue Moon book and you would be correct to make that assumption.

You do not have to read my Felicity Philips series if 'Agatha Christie on acid with a side order of talking pets creating havoc' isn't your thing, but you will be missing out if you do not. Tempest and pals have already appeared in one of her stories and she has popped up in another of my series already.

Regardless, the next Blue Moon book will pick up not long after the events described here, so you can avoid the royal wedding story without ruining the next book in this series.

When I started writing this series in 2011, I had two miniature dachshunds for company. I was a captain in the British Army and in the winter dressed them in black coats onto which I stuck the rank of a second lieutenant. They were my subalterns.

Inevitably, they got old, and we finally lost the second one a few months ago. They were called Tank and Ranger, named after characters in a series of books my wife and I both read. We discussed the subject of replacement dogs at length over the course of the last few years, never able to decide whether to or not, and what breed to get if we did.

The day after finishing this book, I found myself looking idly at puppies for sale and the next thing I knew we had two of them. We have miniature dachshunds again, this time called Bull and Dozer. Right now they are weeks old and full of puppy enthusiasm, but they will grow and mature and inspire more Blue Moon adventures, I'm sure.

How many more Blue Moon books will there be? Well, I'm not sure. This is where I started, so Tempest, Amanda, Big Ben, and the other characters hold a special place in my heart. I will be sorry to see an end to their adventures, but at the same time if I stretch things out for too long the books will become stale. I have seen this with other series and refuse to fall foul of the temptation to keep going when really I should stop.

That said, I can see me writing several more books and have not only titles but vaguely fleshed out plots for some of them. The next adventure might involve a phantom executioner roaming the streets of Rochester at night.

Ultimately, I expect to reach thirty books, but if I can find a tangible way to end it there, I will probably do so.

In the meantime, if you have not yet done so, you should explore the spin-off series set in America and Australia. They have proven popular and are all written under licence by established urban fantasy authors. Tempest, Big Ben, Frank, Patience, and more appear in them.

Take care.

Steve Higgs

More by Steve Higgs

vinci-books.com/porkpie-pandemonium

A retired detective with a nose for trouble wanders into a town hiding a deadly secret ...

Melton Mowbray is world famous for its pork pies, but beneath the façade lies an undercurrent of lies and deceit, and Albert Smith just saw something that made him curious. The operation hiding in plain sight is worth a lot of money. The kind of money people will kill to protect and now they need to make him vanish.

Good luck with that. Albert spent decades taking down criminals and his mind is as sharp as it ever was.

Turn the page for a free preview...

Pork Pie Pandemonium: Chapter One

EXTRA PORTION OF MEAT

The scream cut through the air at such a volume that Albert could have heard it if he was in the next county. By his side, his assistance dog, Rex Harrison, reacted, taking his eyes off the diced pork for the first time since they came in.

The screamer was a woman in her late twenties called Claire. Albert knew her name because everyone in the class had been given a large white sticker to write their names on. She was here with her boyfriend, a tall, skinny lad called Kevin, who looked to be younger than her, but not by much. Her eyes were as wide as any person's he had ever seen, and she was staring at the counter in front of her in an accusatory manner.

Then, she turned around and threw up.

Albert took that in his stride; he had never been affected by people vomiting. With his wife he raised three children, and it had always been he that dealt with their sickness. She dealt with the poop.

As everyone else backed away, Albert found himself curious and walking around to Claire's side of the table before he thought about what he was doing. He didn't have to go far, his eyesight, providing he wasn't trying to look at something up close, was pretty good. Arriving on her side of the table, he spotted what had affected her so. There was a thumb resting on top of her pile of pork.

Teaching the class, where attendees got to raise their own handmade pork pie, was a short woman in her fifties called Belinda. 'It's someone's thumb,' she observed, rather unnecessarily, since everyone could already see what it was. Belinda wore a navy-blue apron on which the firm's logo and name were emblazoned. Agnew's Perfect Pork Pie Emporium stretched across her chest above a picture of a tasty looking pork pie. Like everyone else in the room, her blond hair was encased in a net to stop it falling into the food. The net struck Albert as a little unkind in his case since he only had about eighteen hairs left on his scalp. The whole concept of bothering with them was, quite frankly, ridiculous since they let him bring his German shepherd assistance dog, Rex Harrison, into the class with him. The dog wore a hair net on his head too - Albert's silent dig at the pointless adherence to rules. Rex didn't look happy about the net.

When Belinda moved in with a bowl, clearly intending to remove the thumb, Albert raised his voice, 'Don't touch that, please.'

Belinda's head snapped around along with everyone else's. Suddenly on the spot now that all eyes in the room were looking his way, Albert gave them his serious expression. 'I'm a retired detective superintendent from Kent. I'm afraid we need to treat this as a crime scene and bring in the local police.'

'But I have another class in an hour,' Belinda protested.

Pursing his lips and shrugging, Albert said, 'I'm afraid

that is unlikely to proceed. Do you want to call the police yourself?'

A teenage girl burst into the room, flinging the door open in her haste. She looked to be sixteen or seventeen and was also wearing one of the firm's aprons. 'What was that scream?' she asked, concern etched on her face.

'You need a hair net to be in here,' snapped Belinda.

Albert expected the young woman to be cowed and apologise, but she narrowed her eyes instead. 'Oh, be quiet, Belinda. You have a dog in here for goodness sake.'

Rex Harrison sniffed the air, thinking to himself, not for the first time, that humans liked to mess around with their food before they ate it. He could never see the need for all the fuss. He licked his lips - there was a pile of pork just inches from his nose and no one was paying any attention to it.

'Don't even think about it,' said Albert, leaning down to make eye contact and be sure Rex knew the comment was aimed at him.

Rex thought something impolite in response and put his head down in a display of obedience. He didn't take his eyes off the pile of pork though.

The teenage girl could see the cluster of people forming a ring around the thumb so came into the room just as Albert spoke up. 'There's a human thumb in your meat mix. You need to call the police so they can identify who it belongs to. Is the meat brought in from somewhere?'

'Goodness, no!' exclaimed Belinda. 'It is all diced by hand on the premises.'

Kevin, the boyfriend of the young woman who found the thumb sniggered. 'Diced by hand. Nice one.'

The unnamed girl in the firm's livery was now staring at the thumb as it sat atop the small mound of meat at Claire's station. Albert wondered who she was since she was very young to be in a position of authority. She had brown hair pulled into a ponytail that hung down her back to a point between her shoulder blades. Her brown eyes were bright and lively, sitting above high cheekbones. She was an attractive young woman, Albert observed idly. She reminded him a bit of his Petunia when they first met. The girl was five feet eight inches tall and a hundred twenty pounds. Years of being a cop made the assessment of descriptive features second nature. While Albert noted what she looked like, she bit her lip as if trying to reach a decision. After a second or so she nodded her head before turning back to Belinda at the head of the table. 'Belinda can you call the police, please?'

Belinda gave a frustrated sigh. 'Just pick it out, Donna. I've another class in an hour.'

Albert thought he might have to step in or call the police himself, but Donna wasn't to be swayed by her older coworker. 'Now, please, Belinda.'

'You're not the boss here, Donna,' snapped Belinda, tearing at the bow to undo her apron. 'I'll not be given orders by a child. See how long you've got a job when your mum finds out her best cook walked out.' Then she threw her apron on the floor, followed it with the hairnet and stormed out. The door slammed behind her.

Donna made eye contact with the people around her, all of them paying customers. 'I'm very sorry, everyone. This class is over. If you come out to the front counter, I will give everyone a full refund and a coupon to rebook at half price.'

'But we are only visiting Melton Mowbray today,' complained a woman to her left. It prompted other complaints and Albert thought the poor girl was going to have a fight to get them to leave until another man spoke up. He was in his late sixties, grey hair going white above dark brown eyebrows and next to him, a woman of similar age standing close enough that they had to be husband and wife.

'It's not the poor girl's fault,' he remarked, stilling the torrent of complaints. 'There is a thumb in the meat. I for one do not wish to make a pork pie to take home that may have other parts of the same person in it.' He turned his attention to Donna. 'Thank you for the offer of a refund. Good luck with the police.' With that, he went to the door, the rest of the class following though many continued to mutter.

At the door, the woman who complained first nudged her husband. 'There's another place across the street. I bet they don't have thumbs in their meat. Let's go there. Look everyone, they have a class on at two o'clock.'

The door shut as the last person went out, leaving Donna in the room with Albert and Rex Harrison. The young woman reached into the back pocket of her jeans to produce a phone. 'I guess I'll call the police then,' she mumbled, still staring at the thumb.

'I'll do it,' volunteered Albert, reaching into his trouser pocket for his own phone and patting his other pockets to locate his reading glasses.

They're on your head, thought Rex Harrison, wondering how it was that the man misplaced them ten times a day.

Donna shook her head. 'No, it should be me. It's my family's shop.'

Smiling in a bid to help the woman relax, Albert dialled three nines anyway. 'It doesn't matter who calls them. The customers cannot leave though, they will need to give statements.'

Donna pulled a face, looking at the crowd waiting for their refunds. 'I don't think that is going to go down very well.' She heard his call connect as she opened the door to leave the classroom, the voice at the other end asked which service Albert required. She didn't want to deal with the restless customers, some of whom would be going straight across the road to the opposition, Simmons Perfect Pork Pie Palace, an outfit whose sole aim seemed to be to put her family's shop out of business. She didn't want to be in charge either, but mum had her appendix out in a rush yesterday which left her as the only Agnew standing. Like or not, it was her shop to run until her mum was well-enough to return to work.

Pork Pie Pandemonium: Chapter Two

SABOTAGE

The police were coming, which was duty done so far as Albert was concerned. He needed to hang around and give his statement, but he had nothing helpful to tell them. Outside the classroom, the small crowd were still bickering and moaning about not being given their refund, Donna using the tactic to keep them in place until the police arrived. Albert chose to stay where he was, spying a stool in the corner he could rest on. His knees were already beginning to ache.

Not getting to make and eat the porkpie was annoying, he had to admit. The pilgrimage to Melton Mowbray from his house in West Malling was the first leg of an intended tour of Britain. For fifty-two years his wife moaned at him for his inability to cook. It was good-natured mostly, she was happy to cook all the meals and he was only too happy to let her, but when she passed exactly twelve months ago yesterday, he had to fend for himself for the first time in his life. Born of that struggle came a bucket-list plan to learn to cook some of his favourite dishes. The British Isles had so many famous meals: Lancashire hotpot, Eton mess, Eccles cakes, Cumberland sausages ... the list was long and extensive. For no better reason than he couldn't think of a reason why he shouldn't, he packed a small suitcase and a backpack, clipped Rex to his lead, and set off.

Three years ago, when aged seventy-five, he gave up driving. He no longer felt that his reactions and eyesight were sufficient to be behind the wheel, but rail, bus, and the power of his own two legs would get him to all the destinations he wanted to visit. People described him as sprightly now. It used to be strong or athletic, but those days were far behind him. His muscles were strong enough to support him, but weak now by comparison with his glory days, and they hung from his frame in a disappointing way. At a shade over six feet, he had been considered tall in his youth. Age had shrunk him, so he stood just over five feet ten inches tall now, but while his body withered, and despite a spotty memory, he felt his mind was still sharp.

At his side was Rex Harrison, an assistance dog who was no such thing. Three years ago, his wife, Petunia, muttered and moaned about Albert needing an assistance dog because his hearing was going and because he was getting forgetful. He didn't think they would give him one and never bothered to apply to any of the charities who supply them because he expected the assessment process would be demeaning. However, he loved his wife and together they had enjoyed owning dogs in the past, so he cooked up a cunning plan. It required a little subterfuge, a purchase via an online shop, and a phone call to an old friend. It also relied on human nature to prevent people questioning what they were being presented with.

In retrospect, his plan hadn't been all that clever at all because he was stuck now with a large dog who was the only canine in the history of the Metropolitan police to have been fired for having a bad attitude. The phone call he made was to another retired cop who he knew to have children and grandchildren still serving. He could have called his own children - they were all police officers, but he didn't want them to know what he was up to. The call led to the team who trained the police dogs where, Albert assumed, he would be able to pick up a young dog who had failed the initial training. They tricked him though, seeing the chance to offload a dog who had been returned to them for rehoming just that week. Albert didn't find out about the attitude thing until weeks later when he questioned why his dog kept playing tricks on him. The purchase he made online was a harness and jacket with assistance dog down each side.

No one ever questioned it. Not once. And he got to take him everywhere, including into a pork pie making class which was his first attempt at learning to make a traditional British dish. However, his quest to become a capable cook was not going very well so far.

The jingle of a door opening heralded the arrival of two uniformed police officers. Agnew's shop was located at one end of Melton Mowbray's High Street and the cops were most likely on a routine patrol nearby which explained their fast response time.

Albert got up from his stool, his knees protesting with a click from each as he straightened. He was going to join the others outside now so the uniforms could do their job, but as he passed the thumb, still resting on top of the pile of glistening pork, he noticed something.

Leaning closer and pulling his reading glasses down off his head, he said, 'Here, Rex, what do you make of this?'

Albert made a habit of talking to the dog as if he

expected a response, and it annoyed Rex that the human never listened to any of his replies. He moved in closer and jumped up to place his front paws on the table so he could get a better sniff.

Albert had spotted a tattoo on the thumb, that was what drew his attention, but as he peered at it, he felt the familiar pull of a mystery. It was hardly the first time this had happened since he retired; his detective's brain refused to switch off. His children, and indeed his wife, most usually accused him of meddling. Well, none of them were here now. He moved around to get a better look at the thumb from different angles.

The thumb was severed just behind the second knuckle, but it wasn't a clean cut. It looked a little mangled, as if it had been crushed, and the skin was ragged as if torn. He needed to pick it up to get a better look, but wouldn't allow his curiosity to overcome his desire to preserve the scene for the serving police officers. The tattoo was of a woman, though part of it was missing, still attached to the victim's hand. However, what he could see had a lot of detail for such a small drawing, and though he had never been a fan of tattoos, he had to admire the skill involved. Around the woman's feet were small goldfish and she was posed as if treading water.

Rex sniffed deeply. He couldn't see the tattoo from his angle, but it wouldn't have meant anything to him if he could have. His nose was giving him all the information he needed. The severed digit stank of old engine oil and gasoline, two scents he associated with mechanics or places where mechanics worked on cars. Behind those smells he could detect the powder that came from WorkSafe gloves, a brand of glove favoured by mechanics.

'Can you step this way, please, sir?' The question wasn't

really a question; it was a polite way for the police officer, now halfway through the door, to order Albert to remove himself. Albert knew the door had opened because the volume of chatter increased dramatically a moment before the cop spoke.

He straightened up, with a small groan as his back protested, and smiled at the young man in uniform. 'Yes, of course. Come along, Rex.'

Rex turned his head to look up at Albert, not that Albert was paying any attention. 'What about the meat?' he asked. The old man responded to the dog's odd chuffing noises by ruffling the fur on his head. Rex did not, however, get an answer.

In the shop's reception, just beyond the door, the customers were getting restless. They wanted their refund and they wanted to leave. The cop waiting for Albert to leave the classroom, gave up holding the door because he was getting accosted by a woman who insisted she be allowed to record her statement first because she had better things to do than, 'Stand around here all day'. Her insistence led to an argument as other customers demanded the same.

No longer being observed, Albert quickly took out his phone and got a shot of the thumb, taking a few pics at different angles so he caught the tattoo in as much detail as possible. He had no particular reason to do so other than the familiarity of recording evidence. Knowing it was time to leave, he started toward the door. 'Come along, Rex. We really ought to go now.' Then he paused – Rex was suspiciously quiet. Narrowing his eyes to squint at the disobedient canine, Albert found Rex innocently looking back at him.

Rex tilted his head to ask, 'What?'

Not fooled for a moment, Albert looked at the table where one pile of porkpie filling was now missing, the spot where it ought to be, bearing a trace of moisture left over from the surface getting licked clean.

Albert just rolled his eyes. 'Come on, dog.'

Outside in the shop things were calmer as the two uniformed officers managed to organise the crowd. When Albert joined them with Rex Harrison at his side, the little bell above the door jingled again - two detectives were coming in.

Albert knew they were detectives just by looking at them - he didn't need to see their ID. They got them out anyway, a man and a woman. The woman - the elder and more senior – spoke loud enough for everyone to hear. 'I am Detective Sergeant Moss. This is my colleague Detective Constable Wright.' She indicated the man to her left. 'The officers will record your name and address and take a telephone number where they can contact you. After that you will be free to go.'

DS Moss looked to be in her early forties. She wore a business suit that was a little crumpled and had seen better days. It was warm out today so perhaps she chose it because it was lightweight. She was quite short, maybe five feet and two inches, Albert estimated, and retained a trim figure that suggested plenty of exercise. Her partner, a younger man in his mid-twenties and Caribbean by racial origin, was much taller at six feet four inches and carried a good deal of excess weight around his middle. He too wore a suit, but his was sharp and new by comparison.

Albert found a handy seat and used it to rest his legs. Rex placed his head on Albert's lap so he could stroke it and fuss the fur behind his ears. For Albert, it meant he had something to pretend to be focussed on while he eavesdropped on what Donna was telling DS Moss.

The two detectives were doing their job, yet in a bare-minimum way, it seemed to Albert. They were going through the steps but with little interest. It was as if they'd been assigned a case to investigate, but didn't see a crime.

'You say the meat is butchered on the premises?' DS Moss confirmed.

'That's right,' said Donna. 'We get a fresh delivery every day which is then prepared for use the next day. It is the same meat we use in the class as we use for the pies we sell.'

As the people from the class filed out of the shop, one or two at a time, a uniformed officer turned the sign around to show the world outside the shop was now closed. Donna saw him do it and sighed. It was her first full day in charge, and she felt like a failure already.

There were two women working the counter in the shop; Denise and Mandy, and two men who worked in the back called Jacob and Alan. The men prepared the meat and made the aspic. The ladies made the pastry, and all four hand-formed the pies each morning, starting at five o'clock so the pies were fresh on the shelf each day when the shop opened at nine.

DS Moss went through a dozen routine questions about whether there were other staff who worked at the shop and who else had access to the property. How many keys there were, and who had them? Who delivered the meat? Donna answered them all one at a time. Albert learned that her mother owned the shop and was in hospital recovering from emergency appendix surgery. That was how a teenager came to be in charge today.

While she talked about it, Albert watched the faces of the other staff. Denise was in her late sixties, he estimated, maybe even her early seventies. He wondered how she felt about a teenage girl running things when she must have so much more experience. Belinda made it clear she didn't accept Donna's rule, but how did the others feel? Did they see her as a child?

'Any idea how the thumb might have got into the meat?' DS Moss asked. 'If the meat is delivered the night before as whole cuts which are then hand butchered on site, how did a thumb get added to the mix?'

Donna pursed her lips as if trying to decide what to say. 'I think this is sabotage.'

Albert's head snapped around and up at her comment, surprised and intrigued by the statement.

'What makes you say that?' asked DS Moss.

Donna nodded with her head, a motion to draw their attention out of the large front window. 'The Simmons family and their staff at Simmons Perfect Pork Pie Palace across the street are always playing dirty tricks on us. We are the established provider. Our pies win all the awards, but they have a small factory out the back which produces ten times as many pies as us each day. Their quality is terrible, but they mass produce, so their prices are lower, and they keep targeting our big customers. Not everyone cares enough about taste.'

'Oh, I know,' gushed Detective Constable Wright. 'I eat your pies every week, they are just scrummy. I only ever tried a Simmons pie once.' He gave an exaggerated shudder at the memory.

Donna smiled at the compliment. 'I thought you looked familiar.'

'I come in every Saturday,' he beamed.

'Wright?' DS Moss cautioned him with a bored tone. His smile ran for cover as he folded his lips inward and stopped talking. 'Where was I?' DS Moss asked herself. 'Oh, yes; saboteurs. You think someone at a rival establishment might have placed a thumb in your meat in a bid to damage your business.' Moss said it as a statement, but made it sound ridiculous, her voice dripping with incredulity.

'Um, maybe?' replied Donna, sounding far less sure now.

'The thumb hasn't been severed from its owner for long,' said Albert standing up.

DS Moss looked his way. 'We'll get to you in a moment, sir.'

She meant to dismiss him, but Albert kept right on talking, 'It means the owner is almost certainly in hospital right now, and if not, then ought to be showing up there really soon. It wasn't severed, you see? It appeared to have been ripped off.'

Now DS Moss looked more interested. 'Ripped off? Your name, please, sir?'

'Albert Smith. I'm a retired detective superintendent from Kent. I just happened to be taking the class today.'

'He stopped Belinda from throwing it in the bin. She wanted to get on with her class,' added Donna.

DS Moss nodded and started to move toward the classroom. Her whole attitude had changed in a heartbeat. What was a duff case with a misplaced thumb might now be a crime worthy of her attention. 'I think we should see this thumb.'

Pork Pie Pandemonium: Chapter Three

REFUND

Albert decided to stick around; it wasn't as if he had anywhere else to be and the day was turning out to be more interesting than expected. His timely announcement about the thumb meant he was included now as they went back toward the classroom. They were interrupted before they could move very far by a man as he barged into the shop. On his shoulder was another man, this one wielding a camera and taking shot after shot of the surprised faces inside.

The first man held his phone in his right hand, clearly using it to record as he spoke. 'Famous pork pie shop selling pies filled with human parts, any comment?'

'What!' screeched Donna.

'Will you be renaming the shop? Sweeney Todd's Human Pie Emporium perhaps?'

Albert guessed that the man was a hack reporter, reacting quickly and trying to get the scoop on a local story, but quite willing to exaggerate to sensationalise it.

DS Moss gave him her bored face. 'Peterson, you really are a scumbag.'

Undeterred, he pushed the recording device her way. 'Police suppress truth yet again. Backhander bribes suspected as public health is put at risk.'

'You print whatever garbage headline you like, Peterson,' she snapped, jabbing her finger at the two uniforms who she felt should have been preventing entry.

Getting no joy from her, Peterson swung his device under Donna's nose. Standing in the customer part of the shop where the rest of the staff were still behind the counter, she was an easy target to pick out. The uniformed cops were hustling both him and his photographer back toward the door, but not fast enough to stop him hassling her some more.

'Will you be publishing the new recipe? Where do you get your human parts from?' then he swung it back toward DS Moss, 'Is this part of our justice system? Are the police working with Agnew's Pork Pie Emporium to get rid of local criminals by eating them?'

As his shoulder hit the doorframe, his phone got knocked from his hand to skitter across the floor. The uniformed officers had their hands out to their sides to walk him from the shop, but he tried to duck under them now to retrieve his phone.

Unfortunately for Peterson, it landed next to Rex's feet, and before Albert could consider stopping him, the dog picked it up and bit it. A very definite crunching sound came from the dog's mouth – not the sound one would wish to hear from a piece of delicate electronic equipment.

'Spit it out, Rex,' Albert instructed.

Rex was happy to do so. He thought the man had thrown it to him and perhaps it was a chew toy since it didn't smell like food. It wasn't nice in his mouth though. It didn't squeak amusingly and didn't seem like something he could chase. Into Albert's hand went the pieces of phone and a good deal of slobbery spit.

With a smile, because he wasn't a fan of reporters, Albert said, 'Here you are,' as he tipped the fragments into Peterson's disappointed hands. Then the cops backed him out of the door and closed it.

DS Moss jabbed a finger at them. 'You, stand guard outside. You, lock the door.' Now that no one else was getting in, she turned back toward the classroom door, and muttering, went inside.

The thumb was exactly where it had been, exactly where Claire had found it forty minutes ago. It sat right on top of the pile of meat as if it had been positioned there deliberately, or perhaps … fell there, Albert thought, looking up. Above the thumb was nothing but solid ceiling.

'Who places the meat out for the customers?' asked DS Moss.

'The instructor,' Donna replied. 'For this class, it would have been Belinda.'

Moss said, 'I shall need contact details for her,' but she didn't look up. She was bent over to inspect the thumb, much as Albert had been earlier.

Rex sniffed the air again. He could still smell the mix of old engine oil and gasoline. He could also detect a scent of it on the air that wasn't coming from this room. There was a mechanic's place nearby somewhere. That is where they ought to be looking. Content they would work it out sooner or later, he laid down for a rest.

'Ma'am, there's something here,' Wright said excitedly. 'One of the piles of meat has been taken. I think that might be significant.'

'My dog ate it,' admitted Albert, stopping the young detective before he could jump to a wild conclusion.

Folding his lips in again, Wright walked around to join DS Moss near the thumb. She straightened up and exhaled through her nose in a slow, deliberate manner. 'Okay. I'm calling this a crime scene.' She looked directly at Albert. 'I'm afraid I am going to have to ask you to leave. Wright will take your details but retired superintendent or otherwise, I need to shut this place off and get the crime scene guys in. Thank you for your help.'

Albert was surprised to have been allowed to stay here this long. It had been fun, a blast from the past in some ways to be at the pointy end where a case is just being started. Young Donna was looking more than a little lost, but it wasn't for him to console her. The shop would be shut down, the paper Peterson worked for would probably print something horrible, but the shop had been around long enough, and he felt sure it would reopen soon once the matter was cleared up.

He waved the girl goodbye as he left her to deal with the police and went merrily on his way.

Outside the shop, Albert paused to decide what to do with the rest of his day. He came here only to make a pork pie but didn't fancy going to the other shop. He could see people in there now - some of them from the abandoned class. He had eaten Agnew's pork pies in the past and considered them to be the gold standard. If he couldn't make one now, he could always push on to Bakewell and circle back here at the end of his trip.

'Where shall we go, Rex?' he asked the dog.

Rex swung his head around to look up at the human. He could smell the garage. 'I think we should go this way,' he said with his eyes. 'Around the corner is where that thumb was before it ended up in the tasty meat shop.'

Albert looked down at the dog. 'I swear it looks like you are trying to tell me things sometimes. Let's go for some lunch, shall we? Maybe I shall have a half pint of stout and some fish and chips. Would you like a glass of stout? Would you, boy?'

Rex wanted to roll his eyes at the easily distracted human. 'There's a crime to solve, you know?' he indicated, knowing it was hopeless to expect the human to understand. A glass of stout sounded good, though, so he started walking, the human seeming to know where he was going even though Rex knew how badly his nose worked.

Many hours after lunch, and back at his B&B, Albert was surprised to have his quiet afternoon of reading disturbed by the landlady. His timetable, having arranged his tour of Britain with the help of his daughter, Selina, and granddaughter, Apple-Blossom, was to take a train to Bakewell tomorrow. It meant he had time to kill this afternoon so had chosen to relax in the rather nice garden the landlady kept behind her house. It even had a small river babbling along beside it as a delightful countryside touch.

'You have a visitor,' Mrs Worsley announced. 'It's a young lady,' she added as if that ought to mean something.

Albert was dumbfounded, but he thanked Mrs Worsley, closed his book with a prayer that he would remember the page number even though he couldn't remember to pick up a bookmark. He shuffled out to the front door to see who it was with Rex Harrison trailing behind him. This was his first visit to Melton Mowbray which made him question who on Earth could be calling. The answer, once he got to the door, was obvious.

'Oh, hello, Donna. What brings you here?'

The teenage girl from the pork pie shop had an envelope in her right hand. 'You left so quickly, I never got to give you your refund. You were really helpful this morning so I thought I would drop it off in person.' Her apron was gone, replaced by a bright red puffy jacket that zipped up the middle to ward off the cool Autumn air. It matched the bright red Nike running shoes on her feet. Her legs were shod in tight, bleached, skinny jeans which just looked uncomfortable to wear in Albert's opinion. He felt fashion had died when people stopped wearing flared jeans.

'How did you know where to find me?' Albert asked, his forehead crinkling in confusion.

'It was on the waiver you filled in.'

'Oh, yes.' His memory really was getting spotty these days. Donna was holding the envelope up for him to take. Albert wasn't worried about the money, it seemed harsh for the firm to have to hand it all back. 'Do you think you will be closed for long?' he asked.

Donna cast her eyes down and when she looked back up, she had a tear leaking from her left eye. Albert immediately reached for his handkerchief, mumbling an apology.

'That reporter had a story about us on his paper's website within the hour. He didn't even bother to find out any facts,' Donna said as she accepted the handkerchief in exchange for the envelope. 'The health ministry will have to recertify the shop if the police forensics people find any human flesh on the premises. They are there now inspecting it all. They took away all our produce and all the meat for tomorrow's batch, not that we will be open tomorrow. There's been a rush of cancellations already, so even if we did reopen tomorrow, the classes will be half empty. It's going to take ages to undo this damage. Mum is terrified because we don't have enough cashflow to pay everyone back. If any more people cancel, we might be in real trouble.' The young woman's face was turning to a tear-filled mess which left Albert wondering what the right thing to do might be.

Rex Harrison didn't understand crying, but he recognised when a human was upset and knew that getting attention from him was wonderful enough to cheer anyone up. Sitting by his human's feet, he leaned forward to nudge the young female human's hand.

She sniffed and wiped at her tears, then reached down to ruffle his fur. 'What's his name?' she asked.

'It's Rex Harrison,' Albert told her.

She wrinkled her eyebrows. 'That's an unusual name.'

Albert explained, 'He was a police dog before he switched careers to be an assistance dog. They get hundreds of new dogs every year and struggle to come up with names, so they pick a theme. He was taken in when they were in Hollywood month.'

'There's an actor called Rex Harrison?' Donna had clearly never heard of him, but had her phone out, like all kids seem to do now. Moments later she had a list of his films and a picture of him on her screen. 'Dr Doolittle. I've heard of him.'

To change the subject, and because he was curious, he asked, 'You told the detectives earlier that you thought the chaps in the rival pork pie place might be behind it. Why is that?'

Donna patted Rex on his head again and handed back Albert's handkerchief. 'They have been quite vocal about wanting our business. Mum says there's enough customers for us to both exist without anyone feeling the pinch, but they have tried all kinds of dirty tricks. They tried to bribe our staff into giving away our recipe. They shut off our electricity and slashed the tyres on our delivery van. They came into our shop and *accidentally* dropped a bucket of dye into our pastry.'

'I see. Getting hold of a fresh thumb seems like quite an escalation,' Albert observed. 'That's not something you can just decide to do. Could it have come in with the meat?'

Donna shrugged. 'I guess I don't know where it came from, but it might shut us down regardless of its origin.'

'What if we found the owner?' Albert asked, surprising himself because he hadn't planned to volunteer his services. Too late now, the offer had been made.

Donna searched his face, staring up at him with caramel coloured eyes. 'You mean like solve the crime ourselves?' The hope in her voice almost broke Albert's heart. He couldn't change his mind now. 'I remember now. You told the police you were a retired supervisor or something.'

'Um, yes. A retired detective superintendent. It was a while ago, mind you.'

Donna's imagination was off and running already. 'We could find out how they did it. Get all the evidence and then nail those Simmons brothers to the wall. Yeah!' She punched her left fist into her right palm. 'I bet they killed someone and cut his thumb off just so they could put it in my mum's shop.' Then she gasped. 'I bet one of the customers was a plant. Maybe it was the woman who found it. She could have placed the thumb there and then screamed and pretended like it was there the whole time.'

Grab your copy...
vinci-books.com/porkpie-pandemonium

About the Author

When Steve Higgs wrote his debut novel, *Paranormal Nonsense*, he was a captain in the British Army. He would like to pretend that he had one of those careers that must be blacked out and generally denied by the government, and that he has to change his name and move constantly because he is still on the watch list in several countries. In truth, though, he started out as a mechanic - not like Jason Statham in the film by that name, sneaking around as a hitman, but more like one of those sleazy guys who charges a fortune and keeps your car for a week even though the only thing you went in for was a squeaky door hinge.

At school, he was largely disinterested in all subjects except creative writing, for which he won his first prize at the age of ten. However, calling it the first prize he won suggests that there were other prizes, which is not the case. Awards may yet come, but in the meantime, he enjoys writing mystery and thriller novels and claims to have more than a hundred books forming a restless queue in his mind because they are desperate to be written.

Now retired from the military, he lives in southeast England with a duo of lazy sausage dogs. Surrounded by rolling hills, brooding castles, and vineyards, he doubts he'll ever leave, the beer is just too good.